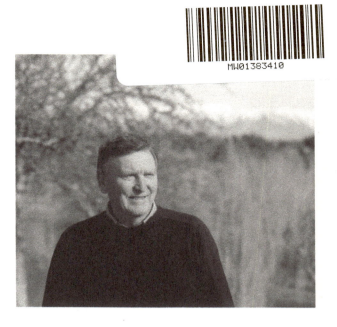

OWEN MARSHALL is an award-winning novelist, short-story writer, poet and anthologist, who has written or edited thirty books including the bestselling novel *The Larnachs*. Numerous awards for his fiction include the New Zealand Literary Fund Scholarship in Letters, fellowships at Otago and Canterbury universities, and the Katherine Mansfield Memorial Fellowship in Menton, France. In 2000 he became an Officer of the New Zealand Order of Merit (ONZM) for services to literature; in 2012 he was made a Companion of the New Zealand Order of Merit (CNZM); and in 2013 he received the Prime Minister's Award for Literary Achievement in Fiction. In 2000 his novel *Harlequin Rex* won the Montana New Zealand Book Awards Deutz Medal for Fiction. Many of his other books have been shortlisted for major awards, and his work has been extensively anthologised.

He was a school teacher for many years, having graduated with an MA (Hons) from the University of Canterbury, which in 2002 awarded him the honorary degree of Doctor of Letters and in 2005 appointed him an adjunct professor. See more at www.owenmarshall.net.nz.

Reviews of Owen Marshall's Previous Works

'New Zealand's best prose writer.'

— Vincent O'Sullivan

'I find myself exclaiming over and again with delight at the precision, the beauty, the near perfection of his writing.'

— Fiona Kidman, *The Dominion*

'I'm an admirer of Owen Marshall's literature, with my favourite stories, chapters, etc.'

— Janet Frame

'He's not just the finest short story writer we have, but the finest we have ever had.'

— Sue McCauley

'Quite simply the most able and the most successful exponent of the short story currently writing in New Zealand.'

— Michael King

'Owen Marshall . . . charts those loves and griefs and brief encounters with an eye so sane and honest that it takes your breath away.'

— Justin Paton

'Marshall is too versatile, too adept at adjusting his narrative technique, ever to be described as a formulaic writer.'

— *The Oxford Companion to New Zealand Literature*

'Owen Marshall has established himself as one of the masters of the short story.'

— *Livres Hebdo*, Paris

'Marshall is a writer who speaks with equal intensity to the unbearable loveliness and malevolence of life.'

— Carolyn Bliss, *World Literature Today*

'Marshall is held in uncommon affection by New Zealand readers — generally we admire and respect rather than love our writers.'

— Peter Simpson, *New Zealand Listener*

'"Mumsie and Zip" is the blackest and most brilliantly sinister portrait of the suburban marriage in New Zealand fiction.'

— Lydia Wevers, *New Zealand Books*

'[I]t is only when we have finished reading a given story that we understand that besides a story in the more usual sense, we have experienced an environment which has mysteriously become a kind of character in its own right. [*Supper Waltz Wilson and Other New Zealand Stories*] is as fine a book of stories as this country is likely to see . . . one that will stand close re-reading for many years to come.'

— Frank Sargeson, *Islands*

'The satisfyingly unsentimental humanity of Marshall's work [*Coming Home in the Dark*], combined with his great eye for detail and his striking similes, reassures us that we are in the firm but sensitive hands of a master craftsman. Timaru's answer to John Updike is once again in fine form.'

— Michael Morrissey

'After finishing this book [*The Best of Owen Marshall's Short Stories*], you feel as if you've read it all, know it all. As if you've just finished a comprehensive tour of the human heart, experienced every human emotion, met every type of human being. But you're not exhausted because Marshall maintains full control, always. His ability to express our paradoxical, chaotic lives so honestly but with such precision and grace — it's a paradox in itself, and it's breathtaking.'

— Sarah Quigley, *The Press*

'Owen Marshall has the gift of telling stories that take hold of you in a personal way and bring echoes of people, places and events you have known, but not paid enough attention to at the time. It is a magical heightening of the ordinary . . . [H]istory demonstrates that few things in the world are more emotionally compelling than a well-told story, and the true test is how consuming and satisfying are those in this book [*When Gravity Snaps*]. Well, I was enraptured. It is 25 years now since readers realised that among us was a remarkable talent continuing the long literary tradition of the short story that has enriched the culture of this country. From time to time I still feel exasperated that he is not better known, not more widely acknowledged.'

— Gordon McLauchlan, *Weekend Herald*

'Among active New Zealand writers only Maurice Gee writes with comparable — and equally unfashionable — moral and psychological weight. In such books as this [*When Gravity Snaps*] the New Zealand tradition of a morally concerned humanist realism is kept alive in a post-modern age.'

— Lawrence Jones

'Marshall [in his poetry] weighs his words as if regarding you with a raised ironic eyebrow. The poems employ the same bluff, resilient, yet harmonious language as Marshall's prose.'

— David Eggleton, *New Zealand Listener*

OWEN MARSHALL

LOVE AS A STRANGER

VINTAGE

The assistance of Creative New Zealand is gratefully
acknowledged by the publisher.

VINTAGE

UK | USA | Canada | Ireland | Australia
India | New Zealand | South Africa | China

Vintage is an imprint of the Penguin Random House group of companies,
whose addresses can be found at global.penguinrandomhouse.com.

First published by Penguin Random House New Zealand, 2016

1 3 5 7 9 10 8 6 4 2

Text © Owen Marshall, 2016

The moral right of the author has been asserted.

All rights reserved. Without limiting the rights under copyright
reserved above, no part of this publication may be reproduced, stored
in or introduced into a retrieval system, or transmitted, in any form or
by any means (electronic, mechanical, photocopying, recording or
otherwise), without the prior written permission of both the
copyright owner and the above publisher of this book.

Cover illustration and text design by Carla Sy © Penguin
Random House New Zealand

Author photograph by Liz March © Siobhan Harvey, 2010

Printed and bound in Australia by Griffin Press,
an Accredited ISO AS/NZS 14001 Environmental
Management Systems Printer

A catalogue record for this book is available from the
National Library of New Zealand.

ISBN 978-1-77553-857-8
eISBN 978-1-77553-873-8

penguinrandomhouse.co.nz

In memory of my mother, Jane Ella Jones (née Marshall),
who died before I was three years old.

When love is not madness, it is not love.
— Pedro Calderón de la Barca, 1600–1681

Chapter One

People in love have a longing to tell others how they met, even if the circumstances are banal, or best suppressed. It's an expression of their wonder, and gratitude for having found each other. Sarah and Hartley met in the old Symonds Street cemetery, though neither had links with any of the residents there. Summer — and the shade of the large trees was inviting, despite the dereliction of the place, and the long, disordered grass encroaching on the sloping paths. The aged headstones and statuary, some at tipsy angles, gave a Dickensian impression, yet looming above were the great concrete supports of the overpass bridge, and the noise of the unseen city traffic was loud and persistent.

Sarah had been at an afternoon high tea at the Langham hotel. Afterwards she crossed the road and went down the steps into the sloping and shadowy cemetery in search of quiet time before returning to her husband and their apartment.

Almost the first grave she came to proved a fascination. A small headstone set before a larger one:

SACRED TO THE MEMORY OF
EMILY MARY
THE BELOVED DAUGHTER OF
GEORGE & EMILY KEELING
OF ARCH HILL
WHO WAS SHOT
WHILE ON HER WAY TO
THE PRIMITIVE METHODIST CHURCH
BIBLE CLASS
ALEXANDRA STREET
APRIL 12TH 1886
AGED 17 YEARS.

The surface of Emily's grave had collapsed, as if the coffin had been spirited away and left a sunken rubble of concrete and bricks. Two stunted cabbage trees stood ineffectual guard, and the sun through the leaves made a play of harlequin patterns over it all.

Sarah had bent over the rusted iron railing to read the inscription and as she stepped back became aware of someone stopping beside her. A lean man in a quality dark suit, but wearing yellow and white sneakers that gave a touch of incongruity.

'Yes, there must be quite a tale there,' he said. 'Sad, isn't it, but I suppose a cemetery is like a library in a way. So many stories, but in tombs rather than tomes.'

It was clever enough, but also a little glib, and Sarah wondered if it was rehearsed. 'Yes, it is sad,' she said. 'I wonder who did it.'

'I've meant to Google it, but never got round to it. Auckland was such a small place then you'd think they must have found the murderer, though what could possibly be a motive for shooting a girl on her way to Sunday school?' Hartley gave a sudden, attractive smile, as if pleased that they shared an interest in such unusual history. It was the moment for one of them to move on, or for them to introduce themselves and keep talking, but Sarah made no reply, and he smiled again, gave a nod to excuse himself and walked up the path, then the steps and onto the busy street. She didn't like the colours of his shoes. His hair was greying, fluffed above his forehead, generous above his ears, softly thin over the crown so that a shaft of sunlight through the trees had shown a glimpse of scalp beneath.

I should use Google myself, Sarah thought. She had no pen in her handbag, and so repeated the name and the date on the gravestone several times. She'd forgotten both by the time she was home, and would have forgotten Hartley almost as quickly if they hadn't met again.

Robert was interested in her description of the cakes and sandwiches at the hotel's high tea. He liked food, although his appetite had dwindled. The little chocolate cups filled with raspberries sounded bloody good, he said. He asked later about the old schoolfriend whom she'd met there, Deborah, who seemed to have amassed a startling number of grandchildren, whose talents and appearance she extolled exhaustively one by one. The silence of the graveyard had been welcome after that.

'What about you?' Sarah asked her husband.

'I watched tennis,' he said. 'Slept a bit.' Since his illness, sleep had become an acknowledged activity in his day, as playing golf, work, or section chores had once been. Two years ago his prostate had been removed, but subtle cancers had since emerged that sapped his energy and took the colour from his face. She had expected illness to make him more self-absorbed, and that had happened in regard to much of what had been important to him before, but towards her Robert had become solicitous, more aware of her place and significance in his life. As the scope of his activities contracted, they spent more time together than in any other period of their marriage.

'I thought we might go down to the little place by the Aotea Centre,' he said. 'Have something light and listen to the buskers.'

'Of course. Why not.' Little of relief was happening in their own lives, and it was diversion to watch other people act out theirs. 'As long as you feel up to it,' she said. 'It's a good sign that you want to get out for a bit.'

Although his cancer dominated their lives, they rarely talked about the thing itself: the glare of it was too great to face directly. They talked about the treatment, the new people introduced to them by the disease, the necessary changes to their lifestyle, their plans for a future they pretended was assured. More than the future, though, they talked about the past. The past had been good to them, until recently.

———

SARAH AND HARTLEY MET again two days later when she went in the afternoon to a gallery not far from the apartment to see an exhibition of Samoan art: younger practitioners who had been born in New Zealand but esteemed their own culture. There were wooden forms at a calculated distance from the walls, and closer, on the floor, blue tape beyond which observers were asked not to advance. Hartley recognised her as soon as she came in — tall, smooth walking, a little overweight perhaps, but any excess carried on the breast and hip rather than the waist.

Weight was important in his assessment of people. He could eat a horse and not have to change a notch in his belt, and he was rather proud of that, although he realised it was linked to his metabolism and not some virtue in himself.

Hartley watched Sarah stroll the length of a wall and then sit before the work of her choice. She didn't fidget. She sat relaxed with one hand on the red handbag beside her and the other in her lap. Even from behind he could see enough of her face to notice her eyebrows lift, as if to ensure the best view of the paintings. He went forward and reminded her of the cemetery on the slope of Grafton Gully, and their brief meeting there. 'Do you mind?' he said, giving a small gesture towards the space beside her on the form, and after her smile he sat down.

'And I did finally Google the murdered girl's name,' he said, when they had exchanged their own.

'I suppose it's so long ago it was difficult to find anything,' Sarah said. 'Poor girl. Terrible really.'

'The opposite actually. It was huge news in the papers. It said up to ten thousand people watched the funeral procession, or were at the graveside. That must have been a good proportion of Auckland then. A scriptwriter could hardly come up with a more heart-rending tragedy, and it was all about love, of course. The murderer was besotted with her, and after shooting her he ran off and killed himself on a street corner.'

'What agony for them both, and she was so young.'

'"Love me. I am dying." Those were her last words.'

'How sad it is. How difficult young people find life sometimes,' she said. 'Did she really say that — love me, I am dying?'

'Yes.'

There was a pause in conversation, not because of any awkwardness, but rather a sense of ease in each other's presence. For him that wasn't unexpected, but Sarah was a little surprised. In the cemetery two days before, she'd been aware of no particular affinity with him. He wore the same suit, moved with the same deftness and economy, but wore quality, dark shoes instead of the yellow and white sneakers. 'No walking shoes today?' she said.

'I keep them at the office so I can slip out somewhere for a breath of air if the chance comes up. The parks mainly. In the winter the cemetery's too cold and greasy, but the summer's fine. Are you a walker?'

'I used to be, but not so much now, and we're only up here for a few months and don't know the best places.' She used the plural quite deliberately. Better for Hartley to have that information early in conversation. He made no reference to it of course.

'I've been to Manono Island,' he said. 'No vehicles are allowed there,' and because a painting of the place was directly in their view, the change of subject was a natural enough transition.

So they began a conversation about travel that flowed easily to other things. Sarah wasn't particularly concerned about his motives for wishing to talk. A married woman of fifty-nine with a career behind her, she was confident socially, and she was in a city not her own, without her established activities and friends to divert her from Robert's illness. It was a pleasant release to talk of art, other countries and the idiosyncrasies of Auckland's transport system without any of those topics bearing emotional weight, and with someone who felt no need to temper everything with commiseration. Talk with a stranger was leaving old territory and welcoming the new.

Hartley's interest was from the very first partly sexual, but without particular design: he had been attracted by the sight of her at the graveside, still, full-figured, well dressed and with her dark brown hair burnished by the glint of the sun. She had it coloured, he imagined. He now knew that she was married, but it was still a satisfaction to be seated with her, and find that she was quick and intelligent in conversation. A good thing that he'd bothered to look up the information on Emily Keeling's murder. He would go back to his office and continue work on conveyancing, family trusts and advice to a business that imported fabrics, feeling better for having met Sarah again. Hartley told her something of that occupation. 'I don't work a full week now,' he said, and although he couldn't be much older than herself, she didn't seek any explanation.

'Have you always lived here?' she asked.

'Pretty much. My parents farmed in Southland, but I came north after leaving school. I never felt I wanted to be a dairy farmer. You're supposed to talk about the country always being with you, love of the land and so on, but I've never missed it. I sometimes think there's a sort of aesthetic snobbery at work. Look, I've got spiritual affinity with the land! I like the city just fine. What about you?'

'We live in Hamilton, which is just a big town, it seems to me, rather than a city. It's got bigger without growing up somehow.'

'People knock Auckland because they realise it disregards those outside it. For us there's only Auckland — or somewhere else that doesn't matter much. I wouldn't live anywhere else but here. A city gives you choices.'

As they talked, he wondered how he could segue from any of the things they discussed to the possibility of another meeting. Almost certainly they wouldn't cross paths a third time by chance, yet what could he suggest to her that wasn't suspect? Her company was ambition enough, but how in the circumstances could any invitation be free of a possible sexual intent? He sought an answer even as they continued to talk of the advantages of city life — and its frustrations. They were both able to draw from wider personal experience: as a young man he had a year scrabbling for a living in London, and she had spent almost as long in Berlin while overseas after completing her degree. For a time he'd worked for a removal firm, carrying things in and out of people's houses and eating pies, or chips, in the cab of the truck. 'One day packing crystal in Knightsbridge supervised by the Indian housekeeper,' he told her, 'the next, lugging collapsed sofas and stained mattresses from a basement flat behind greyhound kennels, while the husband and wife swore at each other, smoked, and kicked holes in the walls to get at the landlord. It's all there in London, isn't it.'

'Every weekend in Berlin,' she said, 'I made a point of going to a different gallery, or museum, or maybe a building of special interest, and I never got round half of the places I wanted to. Just so many of them. There were a few times, though, when the snow meant I couldn't go out. It's a tough winter there. For a lot of people the culture of the place seems to be obscured by its political history, which is a pity. I like the Germans: their energy, the ability to get things done, their pride in craftsmanship.'

'I had trips to Spain and France, but I never got to Germany. Berlin sounds great.'

The noisy entrance of a school group broke their concentration, and filled the gallery with extrovert adolescent energy. One boy shambled behind the woman teacher's back in the posture of a gorilla, and the others tried to hide their delight so as not to give him away.

'Happy days,' said Hartley.

'Well, I'd better be on my way,' Sarah said, standing up, smiling.

'I'd like to talk again,' he said simply. As she considered that, she let the smile remain and met his eyes. She felt the same. She knew almost no one in Auckland, and she and Robert had weeks there before his care was complete. A friendly local might unlock the place for them as well as providing variety.

'We could all meet perhaps for a drink. My husband's not well and is having treatment, but he likes to sit and watch the world go by.'

'My wife died two years ago.'

Did it make a difference? Of course it did. Was she to return to her husband and say that she'd invited a widower, met in the cemetery, to go out with them for drinks? The security of her marriage may well have been sufficient for that, but more important was Hartley's possible interpretation of the offer.

'Oh, that's sad for you,' she said, even as she sought for appropriate phrases to follow it. 'I imagine that your work now plays a larger part in your life,' and she took up the red handbag with resolution that signalled she was leaving. 'It was nice to have a chat.'

'It was. It was,' he said. 'I hope things go well for you here.'

They parted with surprising ease, without shaking hands, or even the awkward proffering of them. They smiled, and Hartley nodded, as if in acquiescence that this was the only way it could be. Sarah was rather pleased with herself as she left the gallery. As a young woman the situation would have embarrassed her, and no doubt she would have made clumsy endeavours to explain why she couldn't sustain an invitation to meet again. It had been managed well enough. She might tell Robert how comfortably she had extricated herself from the situation.

IT WAS UNEXPECTED, HOWEVER, that she should meet Hartley for a third time, a few days later when she'd seen Robert off in a taxi to get his hair cut. It was almost a trip in itself to walk slowly with her husband from the lift, across the small, cropped square of lawn before the entrance to the apartment block, and then to the car. He didn't need support, but accepted an arm on the long, smooth steps from the main entrance in case he slipped. When he'd gone, Sarah returned to the lawn and sat in the morning sun on one of the benches by the small fountain. There were no flower beds, just one cherry tree that had been heavily pruned to keep it low, but spreading. It reminded her of her own garden and the pleasure she felt when working in it. Perhaps they should go back in the weekend and make sure everything was being looked after.

She was about to go back into the apartment building when an Asian woman with two black dogs half her own height went past the gateway, and then Hartley, who spotted Sarah immediately, turned in and came towards her.

'So this is where you live,' he said, as if surprised. He wore light blue jeans, a red jersey that caught the sun, and she noticed how lithe and active he was. He sat down beside her as a friend would, and amused her by saying that as he'd walked behind the Asian woman both dogs had done their business in sudden unison at a crossing lights pole, and she had adeptly captured the droppings by placing plastic bags over her hand, and had gone on quite unruffled, nonchalant, with the bags swinging in her free hand as if containing grapes purchased to accompany Gruyère cheese and cabernet sauvignon, to share with friends who wore sunglasses and laughed together.

'What an imagination you've got,' Sarah said. 'A whole story about dog poop.'

'No, no. It's the composure she showed that impressed

me. There were other people there and she was quite unconcerned.'

'It's one of the things with dogs in public, isn't it. I couldn't be bothered, and I don't like dogs inside the house. They smell and scratch.'

'Nor do I,' he said.

Both preferred cats, and they endorsed each other's opinions with satisfaction. 'Where are you off to anyway?' Sarah asked.

'I'm not in the office today. I've done a few chores, and now I'm going to have a coffee at Magnus on the corner just down from here.'

'We've been there sometimes. It's one of the best places within walking distance for Robert, and you can sit outside.'

'Come with me.'

'I'm not dressed to go out,' she said.

It gave her a moment to think. Why shouldn't she walk with an acquaintance to a café, talk and have a drink, watch people going by, while she waited for her husband to return? There was no reason at all except outmoded decorum, and strangely perhaps as she got older herself she cared less about that.

'Come anyway,' said Hartley. 'You look fine.'

'I can't be away long. Robert's just getting his hair cut, and hasn't got a key with him.'

'As long as you've got then. It's only down the road. The woman with the dogs might be there, and we can turn our backs on her, or complain about the smell.'

'All right,' Sarah said. She would have preferred to go back in and change her shoes, put lipstick on, but that would mean inviting him into the apartment and she wasn't ready for that. For various reasons. 'All right,' she said again, 'but I have to be back by half past eleven at the latest.'

Only when they were walking together, well matched in

step, did she realise how slow Robert had become. It was a pleasure to walk at a natural pace, to take notice of what was around her rather than just a companion, to be aware of no responsibility for another's progress. Robert in his infirmity tended to catch his feet on anything above the level of the ground.

There were no dogs at Magnus, and few seats not in use. Sarah and Hartley had to hover at the fringe watching for any departure, and then hurry to claim a small table. They moved the dishes left there to the far edge. 'Is the sun in your face?' He moved her chair to make it easier for her to sit comfortably. They seemed to her natural courtesies, rather than ploys to impress. 'Let's each guess what the other is going to order,' he said.

'What's the prize?'

'If you win, I pay. If I win, I pay and you agree to come again.' Before sitting, he took off his red jersey, not tugging at the back of the neck as Robert would, but crossing his arms to grip the bottom and peeling the garment over his head. He folded the jersey and put it on the chair back, smoothed down his fluffed, grey hair. 'I'll go first,' he said. 'I reckon you're a green tea sort of person.'

'Wrong.'

'Okay. Your turn.'

'Hot chocolate. Slim people seem to like it, and the marshmallows that come with it.'

'I do actually. Not all the time — sometimes I have a cappuccino. You've won, though. What should I order for you then?'

'Flat white,' Sarah said, and she sat watching him as he went to order. The conversation and movement around her meant she couldn't hear his words, but he was talking to the young guy behind the counter, making him laugh with some pleasantry. When he returned with the small chrome stand holding their order number, she asked more about his job, but he said they'd talked enough about him, and he wanted to know more of her. He was a good listener and his interest was flattering, but while she told him of her life and what had brought her to the city, she made her own assessments, as Hartley made his.

He was okay for his age, she decided objectively. She and Robert both tended to put on weight, but Hartley was leanly agile, and quick to smile. His eyes were dark, and his skin slightly brown as if he had worked mainly outdoors, which wasn't true. The years showed most in the lines of his face and neck, but the wrinkles were multiple and fine rather than pronounced, like those on a paper bag that has had repeated use. The arrival of their drinks caused a pause in their talk, and when the girl had gone, Sarah leant towards him to overcome the surrounding chatter and the traffic noise and said, 'How old are you?'

Well, it was that sort of unconventional friendship, wasn't it? Unlike any she'd experienced for many years. He recognised the question for the rejection of pretence and shallowness that it was, smiled, looked at her directly. 'I'm fifty-eight,' he said, 'but only for a couple of months more.' Sarah, a year older, made no mention of that, and he knew better than to ask.

'What about children?' she said.

'One son, Kevin, who has his own courier business in London. It seems to be going well. He's got three drivers now. A girlfriend, but not married — well, as far as I'm aware. What about you?'

'A daughter, and she has two daughters of her own. It's great because they're in Wellington and we get to see them often.'

'How's your husband coping with the treatment here?'

She meant her reply to be brief and brisk — who wants

the full travail of a stranger's illness heaped on them while they sit in a sunlit café with a new acquaintance — but he was attentive and she found release in talking of it. She realised that motive even as she spoke, but found satisfaction in the sharing nevertheless. 'Anyway,' she said, after it was all out, bar the most personal, 'I'm sorry to have gone on about it, and now I'd better get back so that I'm there to let Robert in to the apartment. Thanks for the coffee.'

'On Monday I'll be here at the same time. I hope you can come, even though I didn't win the bet. I'd like to meet Robert, too, if he's up to it.'

She didn't make any promise, or refusal, and when she looked back she saw him raise a hand in farewell, then take his red jersey, place it on the back of the chair she'd been using, and sit down in his own again. She liked him, she decided, felt happier and taken out of a reduced, apprehensive life for the first time in weeks. She thought idly how unusual it was that Hartley should be passing the apartments at just the time she'd returned from accompanying Robert to the taxi.

It was, of course, no coincidence. As Hartley watched Sarah walk towards her home he was glad that, after she'd left the gallery days before, he'd followed at a distance, aware of an almost cinematic element of espionage that he half indulged, yet endeavoured to suppress, until he saw her reach her apartment block. And before their present meeting he'd sat for over an hour on warm stone steps of a real-estate agency not far away, hoping to see her come outside her building. It had been worth the wait. He hadn't been so drawn to a woman for a long time, and while they had talked, seated among the crowded tables of the café, he had regarded her with admiration.

A tall woman with the frame to carry some kilos without appearing overweight, her fullness retained the attractive contours of her face, which had no deeply incised wrinkles, but rather showed the softness from many years of quality creams and moisturisers. Only at the base of her neck was there a gathering of soft, pale flesh, and on the backs of her hands the skin was thinning and the first age spots showing. She would be perhaps a little younger than him, Hartley decided. He was drawn also to the calmness of her manner, her intelligence, an absence of petty preoccupation. A woman who didn't prattle: Hartley suffered enough of that in his work. He imagined the two of them on a sofa and watching television, or just talking. The weight and warmth of her against his shoulder, and her glossy brown hair close to his face. She would come again, he thought. He had this certainty that she'd enjoyed being with him, and would come again.

Chapter Two

Sarah had intended to tell Robert about the café and Hartley, but because she hadn't mentioned the earlier meetings, it was slightly awkward to explain the later one. Easier just to leave it, and there was no reason to feel uncomfortable. She was a grandmother of fifty-nine, and some aspects of her married life had always been her own, as in most long-standing relationships: certain friends, activities and hobbies that registered only dimly for the partner of a shared life. Not hidden, but accepted as of little concern, or interest. Anyway, on Monday morning she might well have more to do than walk down to the Magnus café to have coffee with a male acquaintance.

Nothing, however, arose to prevent it, and so she asked Robert if he'd like to come the short distance and sit with her in the summer weather, observe the bustle of the city without being caught up in it. It was a sort of test of herself — proof that her intention was open to scrutiny, and if he came and

Hartley was there, she would introduce them, despite having mentioned nothing earlier.

'I don't think so, thanks. I'm going to get on to some of those emails I've neglected,' he said. 'And I might ring Donna.'

'No, wait until I'm back for that. I want to talk, too.' Their daughter and her family had become the most pleasurable focus in their lives.

'Okay. I know it's nice outside, but I just can't be bothered at the moment. There's that stuff to get off to the accountant, too.'

She admitted to herself no special preparation, but when they met, Hartley noticed the bright lipstick, the casual, gauzy scarf. A woman would have seen that they matched her shoes. He'd come early and table-hopped until he held one of the best places, quieter and with an umbrella, even if slightly tattered. He stood up, gave his pleasant, open smile. 'Great,' he said. 'I knew you'd come,' and before talking about himself, asked how things were for her.

From their first meeting by the grave of poor murdered Emily Keeling they had been open in conversation, and as familiarity grew so did the significance of what they said, and the enjoyment they took in it. Without any spoken pact, each made the decision to be honest with the other: to open their lives, share what had happened and what they hoped for. The worn fringe of the umbrella gradually moved a late-morning shadow across the table as their talk went on, yet for them time had light feet. Sarah told him of the narrowing of life since Robert's illness, her apprehension of old age as a fighting withdrawal. Hartley told her of his wife, and the consequences of her death. Nothing to belittle her, but a selection of the truth. Life is an imprecise experience, and he wasn't consciously shaping his past.

'Where did you meet?' asked Sarah. Meetings and partings

are the stuff of life. Beginnings and endings impose some order on the rush of experience. He'd met Madeleine in a café in Ponsonby Road not long after joining the legal firm of Hastings Hull. He had a place then in Clarence Street, not far away. Quite often after work he would have a coffee on his way home from the office. The impersonal congregation of the place provided transition time before he went to be alone in his flat. Madeleine had been at the next table, reading, hair half covering her face as she leant forward. She was groomed without being titivated: an accountant maybe, or a government department receptionist, he'd imagined.

Hartley would have thought no more about her, but as she closed the book he saw a thin silver bracelet fall from her arm to the cork flooring. He expected her to retrieve it, and when she didn't, and got up and walked away, he went over and picked it up. A short, fine chain hung from one end. He'd followed her and caught up as she stood at the door to put on her coat.

'Have you lost something?' he said.

'Lost something?' she repeated, bemused, yet not disconcerted.

'Yes, lost something,' and he held the bracelet up by the chain that had failed. Her gratitude was somewhat underwhelming. She thanked him fully enough, but with no excitement at having the jewellery returned, and they didn't exchange names. She slipped the bracelet into her pocket.

'Thanks again,' she said. 'It has sentimental value,' and she went into the gathering darkness outside, where the street lights turned the drizzle to drifting aurora, and the surface water hissed underneath the cars, and people hurried past with their heads bowed.

Hartley didn't tell Sarah all of this. Nothing of what was actually spoken, not the description of the fine, swaying silver chain, or the winter street, both of which were still clear to him as he talked. He did try to make it entertaining by stressing the random element people find interesting in life.

'You seem to meet women by accident,' Sarah said.

'So what about you and your husband?'

'Rather mundane, I'm afraid. We were both finalists in a provincial sports person of the year event: myself for netball and Robert for rugby. Different categories, of course, but neither of us won. We were seated together at the dinner, though, and had a good time. Got on well. The night became a bit of a fiasco later when a drunk guy set off the fire alarm.' She remembered someone shouting that they were all to go out of the building in an orderly fashion and assemble in the carpark, but most people didn't do either. Robert had taken her home, kissed her and put his hand down the front of her dress. She didn't share that recollection with Hartley. Robert had always been direct in matters of sex.

Hartley imagined her as the netball player she'd once been. Tall, rangy, with big hands and elbows, her hair tied back, her pale face with a sheen of sweat like the glint of winter light on a wet window. That young woman and the resolve she had would still be there, cloaked by the much fuller figure of an older woman and a mature manner.

'I was never much at team sports,' he said. 'Distance running I was okay at, but nothing special.' In fact he'd been no athlete at all, and city walking was now his chief physical recreation. 'You must have been pretty good,' he said.

'I went to one of those girls' schools where you had no choice. Well, except which sport you were going to play, rain or shine.' She remembered that even the plea of having her period as exemption had been regarded with suspicion by the Amazonian phys ed teacher, but said nothing of that. 'I wasn't a boarder, but all of us had compulsory sport, summer and winter. I didn't mind. You're with your friends, and that's what matters. My mother was quite sporty actually, more so than Dad. One or other would cart me around on Saturdays when it was too far to bike. It wasn't until we had to do the same for Donna that I understood the commitment. All the things you do for your kids.'

'My father never offered,' said Hartley. 'It was the farm first, second and third, yet he was mad keen on the All Blacks, of course, and liked to suggest, without being specific, that he'd been promising himself as a young guy.'

'My parents were great, and the older I get the more I realise it. I was always made to feel special.'

'I was just there,' said Hartley. 'I was just there in the family, like another chair. I don't imagine there was any sense of loss when I left home. I didn't feel any.' When his father had taken him to the bus station in Invercargill, he hadn't waited with him until departure, simply lifted the suitcases from the car boot and told him he'd be okay.

'Don't get pushed around up there,' he said. He had to get on to see the bank manager, he said. Hartley had stood by the cases as the car left, but his father didn't look back to see him, just gave a wave that was more an arc of dismissal than a farewell. It had been another of those cold, southern days, and Hartley was keen for the bus to be moving north through the frosted paddocks. 'We were all separate in our family,' he told Sarah. 'Mum would've been different perhaps in other circumstances, but basically we were together by biological chance rather than affection.' He smiled, to show he was realistic rather than bitter.

A girl with fat legs and a very short skirt came and asked Hartley the time. She was polite, but he found the silver rings in her lip and eyebrow offputting. 'Jesus,' he said when she'd gone, 'I just can't understand it. Why would you do that to your face?'

'To be different to fuddy duddies like us maybe.'

'You can't tell me you like it?'

'No.'

'I bet we'd be in agreement on almost anything you like to mention,' he said. 'We think the same — we see the world in the same way. I knew it from the first time we met.'

'We hardly said a word to each other.'

'I knew it, though. There're people who are on the same wavelength, just a few, and you get this shock of recognition, knowing that they see life in the way you do yourself. I love it when that happens. Most of the people I meet I feel no connection with, but you still have to smile, talk and maybe do business with them.'

'I would've guessed you liked being with people,' Sarah said. He had an open manner, seemed to engage with people with friendly ease, and she was surprised by his assessment of his own personality.

'But how many really matter to you?' he said. 'That's the thing.'

'Maybe that says something about you as well as them.'

'Oh, I'm as much a selfish prick as anyone. You might as well know that.' His pleasure in being with her was unforced, and Sarah was conscious of it. 'Sometimes at home when the phone goes, I don't answer it, just sit and enjoy my own company. At work you have to accommodate all comers. At least it's usually one on one. I don't know how teachers put up with a whole swarm of kids at once, and day after day. Jesus. I couldn't hack it.'

'Maybe they keep you young,' Sarah said.

'I've been young and didn't find it all that great. It's better when you grow up, and get to choose your own food and occupations. Being a kid's overrated, I reckon. The world's run by adults for their own benefit.'

He was right, Sarah thought. He was right about a lot of things, or seemed so in his obvious pleasure in her company and the moment. She experienced a minor epiphany: an awareness that she was happier than she'd been for a long time. The air was warm, even though tainted with the fumes of traffic, the sky was blue, and she felt herself the centre of his admiration and the cause of his enjoyment. The illness, responsibility and apprehension that so shadowed her life were for once forgotten. She felt she would like to touch him — reach out and put her hand on his, or run a finger down his cheek as he talked. Just touch him, to get the feel of him. Not a sexual urge at all, but a sign of compatibility and pleasure.

They had come round somehow to speaking of the fallibility of memory when Sarah realised with a start that they had been together for almost two hours.

'Would you like me to walk back with you?' Hartley said.

'No, thanks.' Her apartment faced the street, and from the large window of the living room, and the balcony, the people and traffic passing were clear, and drew attention.

'Well, give me your number and I'll text you so that we can arrange to talk again, maybe have a walk.' They stood together so that he could programme the number into his phone, and when that was done, he gave her a quick, friendly kiss on the cheek. He was her own height, she realised then, and that was what she remembered of the kiss; no particular frisson, but his face briefly level with her own. To kiss Robert, her face needed to be upturned, unless they were lying together.

'What a good thing we met,' said Hartley cheerfully. 'I think so anyway.' He wore an unusual sleeveless grey jacket, almost like a tunic, that she didn't fancy as much as the red jersey. 'You look after yourself,' he said. 'I'll be in touch.'

'I could be quite busy going with Robert to hospital,' Sarah said. 'It's always the priority. Everything revolves around that and how he responds.'

'Of course.'

He waited until she was on her way before leaving himself. She didn't look back and so neither did he when he walked away. He didn't know if anything much more than a friendship would happen between them. He hoped it would, but even what they already shared made him feel better than he had for years. For a long time there had been only him, and other people as a block at considerable emotional remove, and now there was an individual already special to him. 'Yes,' he said loudly to himself as he walked. He felt he was in a good place at a good time. Colours and sounds were sharper somehow around him. 'Yes,' he said again emphatically, oblivious to those who glanced at him in passing. Chance had favoured him and its touch was pleasing.

Robert was on the phone when Sarah got back. She could tell immediately by his tone of voice that it wasn't their daughter. She took off her shoes, then went into the kitchen and began preparing lunch. Their meals were usually light. Long gone were routine family dinners with full settings and meat every day. Their age, their comparative inactivity, their waistlines, Robert's illness, all disposed her to calculated moderation and ease of preparation when she considered meals.

Sarah made tomato and cheese sandwiches for them both, spread margarine on halved apricot muffins and took from the fridge what pasta remained from the evening before. 'You'd like that?' she asked her husband, pointing to it when he came in. 'Do you want it in the microwave?' He shook his head, picked up the bowl and wandered back into the living room.

'That was Margaret, wondering how things were going,' he said as he went. 'They may be up in week or so. Hugh's thinking of going in with his partners to buy a place on Waiheke Island, and they want to have a look at it.'

Sarah came with her plate and sat beside him on the sofa, looking down on the busy street. She was happy to talk with Robert about the things they always talked about, because she'd been for a time free of them. The interlude with Hartley had been a stimulating change that she needed, and the awareness that he found her attractive was flattering. He was a different sort of man to her husband, engaging aspects of her nature to which Robert rarely appealed. The contrast wasn't consciously made, and wasn't judgemental, it was just that she'd enjoyed the new companionship. Nothing was threatened, or denied.

'You were a fair while this morning,' said Robert later. 'I was half pie waiting so that I could ring Donna.'

'I went on to the shops for a bit.' It came readily, as if produced for her by another self before she could provide an alternative. It was the first lie.

Chapter Three

Hartley would text, and Sarah would reply, agreeing to a meeting when that was possible. Robert's hospital treatments were not opportunities, because he liked her to come with him, and she would never have felt comfortable choosing to be with someone else while Robert faced the trial on his own. There were times, though, when he just wanted to rest up at the apartment, and gaps between visits when the doctors wished him to have a chance to bounce back a bit from the necessary assault of drugs and radiation therapy.

Usually she and Hartley met at Magnus, and most times they stayed there, but not always. Once they went to a film, they had several walks and gallery visits, and listened to a free concert by a quintet in the Ramsay Hall. Mainly they sat and talked. Sarah was never away more than two hours, and that became so much the accustomed span that their conversations evolved to have a natural conclusion then, without the need to refer to their watches. They would have their brief kiss and part. They never ran out of things to share, each gradually unfolding a life before the other without conscious deceit. Because their time was short and opportunities were difficult to predict, the meetings possessed a heightened quality, and a concentration on each other lacking in the extended and routine companionship of marriage, when interaction and attention are sometimes stretched thin to cover all the time spent together.

Because Hartley lived alone, the interludes with Sarah became central emotional experiences: more important than neighbours, or long-standing professional acquaintances, more immediate than the occasional calls to his son in London. He found himself intently observing oddities of event and personality in everyday life not just for his own comprehension, but to pass on to Sarah when they talked. He became more conscientious in his housekeeping, vacuuming the spare rooms, lifting the door mats to sweep dust away, aligning rows of spice and herb jars that had a faint yellow tinge to the glass, and had been rarely touched since Madeleine's death. He never asked himself if it was logical to think that Sarah would ever visit him, or if she did that a spare bedroom would be entered, or a coir mat lifted for inspection.

A house with street appeal near Titirangi isn't cheap. In many people's estimation Hartley would be considered well off, and that wasn't so much his doing, or even his wife's, but the unintended generosity of her parents. Madeleine's father had been a successful manufacturer of battery plates. He was dead before Hartley could know him, but his wife, Irene, had initially taken a shine to Hartley, mistakenly thinking he was then already a qualified solicitor.

The three of them had met on the Devonport ferry. He was on his way back from delivering significant documents to the naval base. Madeleine had been close to him on the moving deck, the silver bracelet on her left wrist. 'I'm pleased to see you have the bangle on,' Hartley had said, and was a little surprised that she recognised him, although only days had passed since their meeting in the café.

'Thanks to you I'm still able to wear it,' she said, lifting her bare arm with the bracelet, and in a friendly way she corrected his reference to it. Bangles don't open, she told him. Irene's presence may well have been the reason she felt comfortable about being approached. Her mother kept the conversation going by listing the features that made Devonport unique, and then the superiority of her own part of Auckland. It was an early indication of the sort of woman she was — preoccupied with the instruction of others and the emphasis on her own significance. Because of that inattention to anything apart from herself, she formed the impression that he was a lawyer and so someone to be encouraged. Without her to prolong their talk, Hartley might never have asked them if they would like a coffee after the ferry ride, or later had the opportunity to arrange to see Madeleine again.

He and Irene never became close, but learnt to accept each other's company for Madeleine's sake. Irene held him responsible for her initial misunderstanding concerning his status within the legal profession. No doubt she had hopes of a more charismatic and successful husband for her daughter, and was dead before he qualified, later than most, and so saved from the need to revise her opinion.

Irene's main interest in life appeared to be the correction of other people — their dress, their taste, their political and spiritual views, even their speech. On one occasion when Hartley was visiting, he heard her admonish an electrician who had come to fix her water cylinder.

'I rung up the workshop guy for the part,' he said.

'No you didn't,' said Irene.

'What?' he said.

'You didn't rung him up, you rang him up. Now you have rung him up.'

'Whatever,' said the man, who had no idea what she was on about, but realised he was being ridiculed. Hartley had rather hoped that the cylinder's subsequent persistent malfunction was the electrician's revenge.

Another time, when the three of them were at a concert, she had leant forward and told the man in front she wanted him to shift. 'I can't see,' she'd said. 'Your head's too big.'

'There's no other seat,' the man said.

'Slump down then,' said Irene. 'For goodness' sake, I can hardly see a thing.'

Once, when she'd been drinking, she told Hartley he didn't smell like a winner. He was surprised she'd ever been close enough to make the distinction. Irene was thin and always well dressed, but age ravaged her, and although she kept out of the sun her skin darkened and loosened until it seemed as if she wore stockings over her limbs. Towards the end there was so little of her that she appeared in the process of mummification, with only her dark, jewelled eyes glinting from the wrappings.

She had a heart attack while watering the flower pots on her deck, was found soaked and speechless, and died in hospital within a few hours, without being able to give any farewell to her daughter, or any reprimand to Hartley. He felt no unease afterwards whenever he sat on the wooden boards where she'd collapsed. He could never quite decide which was the more crucial in bringing Madeleine and him together — the silver bracelet, or Irene. The rather fine, architecturally designed home was left to Madeleine, and they were able to sell their own and move there, amid the kauri and ferns and with a view back to the central city.

It wasn't the ghost of the battery plate manufacturer that Hartley imagined in the house now, not his resolutely pained and alienated mother-in-law, not even the presence of his dead wife. He liked to think of Sarah sitting by the large living-room window as they talked; maybe walking with him into one of the more intimate rooms.

That may never have happened if she hadn't gone to Titirangi, ostensibly to be part of a class in flower arrangement. She knew what it meant as soon as Hartley suggested it. It was the next level, as they say, a cover, an assignation quite different from the café, the walks, even the cinema.

'You mean come to your home,' she had said.

'Yes, if you could. I'd love that. I'd love you to see the place.'

'And then?' she said, with a slight smile that banished pretence.

'Whatever,' Hartley said. 'Whatever you're comfortable with. We're not kids, are we? Mainly I want to be with you for a while in my own place and be able to show it to you.'

It took two days for Sarah to decide. What attracted her wasn't the possibility of sex, and what deterred her most wasn't guilt regarding her husband. She hadn't made love in the fullest sense since Robert's prostate operation, but felt no urgent deprivation. Copulation had been a customary and regular thing during many years of marriage, and no longer had mysterious allure. As to guilt, she knew of two affairs that Robert had enjoyed with nurses at his dental surgery, and the marriage had survived them. As husband and wife they had become reconciled to deficiencies in each other that were outweighed by proven, admirable qualities.

No, the reason she decided to enrol for the floristry course, with the knowledge she would meet Hartley in Titirangi, was that when she was with him she felt she was at the surface of life again, with fresh experience and possibility, with the sense she was in some way courted. A woman is never too old to appreciate that. She was surprised by the effect his open admiration and desire had on her: the power of it caused a quickening. She began to understand why some ugly men were nevertheless such successful lovers. There is a fascination for a woman in seeing herself magnified and exalted in a man's fierce adulation.

On Saturday she left Robert with lunch prepared, and took a taxi to the War Memorial Hall in Titirangi. Hartley was waiting there in his car, but she just waved and went on in to see the organisers. The tutor hadn't arrived. A woman of about her own age was placing buckets of long-stalked flowers and greenery on the trestle tables, a few early arrivals for the class were making themselves known to one another, and a young guy in jeans and a T-shirt announcing 'ART MATTERS' was at a desk by the door. Sarah gave him her name, said that family sickness meant she couldn't spend a whole day away, but that she had come to explain and pay. He was embarrassed to accept the money, but didn't have the authority to waive the fee.

When she came out, Hartley was standing by the passenger side of his car, ready to open the door for her. 'Everything okay?'

'All set. They have some lovely blooms, even orchids. I'm sorry to miss it,' she said.

'But a day, nearly a whole day together. Fantastic.'

'Yes,' she said. She would make the most of it and not do anything silly. No sex. She would relax and for a brief time be somebody other than her regular self. For just a day she would put herself ahead of any responsibility for Robert. For just a day she would see herself as Hartley saw her.

'You know what, you're looking great.'

'Thanks,' she said. As a young woman she had often worn shorts, or jeans, but now she considered that her legs had become too thick. Once, as he stroked them, Robert had told her that she had thighs like a wild mare. She supposed he intended it as a compliment.

She admired the house, the conscious design, the abundant light without sacrificing privacy, the real wood and the quality of the curtains and furnishings, the deck that extended into foliage like a ship's prow above a green sea. She did notice that Hartley was more fastidious about tidiness than cleanliness. Nothing gross, just that the Venetian blinds needed wiping, and the glass of the oven door was speckled. For a guy, he was doing well enough. She would have been surprised to know how carefully he'd prepared for her visit, how often he'd envisaged it.

They sat on the large, dark leather sofa looking out over native bush towards the city, just as Hartley had imagined they would. They could see the Sky Tower in the distance, somewhat obscured by the shimmer of summer. He explained how he had come into possession of the house; about Irene and Madeleine. He embellished Irene's faults and peculiarities for effect, but made no criticism of his dead wife. They agreed it was odd how things worked out sometimes — Irene and her husband building a home that meant so much to them, and it ended up the possession of a man one of them never met, and the other disliked.

'I don't know if Kevin and his girlfriend will ever come back,' Hartley said. 'I like to think the place will stay in the family, and he's got more right to it than me. When you're young, though, you're more interested in moving on than coming back. I certainly was. I couldn't wait to get out of Southland and come up here.'

'But you don't regret it.'

'No, not at all. I was always cold there: that's my first memory,' and he told her of the damp, grey/green cold of the Southland farm, of standing shivering in gumboots and a hand-me-down Fair Isle jersey while his parents worked in the milking shed. He was so cold, even when in bed with the blankets to his chin, that his nose was like putty to the touch. All those boots on the back-door sack, and they were cold, too. The winter mist reluctantly revealing immediate landscape as he walked, and rapidly closing everything to obscurity again behind.

The only consistent warmth he recalled, emotional or physical, was from the living-room fire that the family sat around during winter nights, he cross-legged on the worn carpet close to the hearth, with a board on his knees for his homework books. He'd found the fire almost mesmerising, and spent hours gazing into its red, coal-fuelled heart, watching the creation, and then collapse, of miniature fiery kingdoms, and the occasional wonderful scatter of firefly lights in the soot of the chimney-back.

He remembered hardly anything before he was five, and was amazed and sceptical when people talked about their lives as small children. There was rivalry and disputation with his brothers, but their father was handy with the stick and they kept most battles out of sight and earshot. As the youngest, he became accustomed to the stark, offhand realities of power. As the youngest, too, maybe he took less interest in farm tasks; there were always others more competent to hand. The air between the pressing cloud and the receiving wet grass was odorous with shit, cow breath, sweat, moist hides and the fragrance of wild flowers. The half-eaten swedes in their soil sockets had the skeletal paleness of worn back teeth. Seagulls rode the high, bucking winds, and hawks patrolled for road kill. The willows had a sodden droop and the primary school football was always too heavy to kick over the bar. There were summers as well, but they were brief surely in reality, and even shorter in memory.

All of that remained quite clear to Hartley, but could be

only baldly represented in his description to Sarah. 'When I left school I headed straight to Auckland for the warmth and city living, and I've been here ever since, apart from the year or so overseas and a few trips later. The family hardly noticed I'd gone. I'm not trying to suggest that I was ill treated, or neglected, more that it was a busy place and if you weren't interested in the farm, then the farm wasn't interested in you. My brothers run the place now, and there's no reason I should say any more about it.'

'I've gone the other way, but not so far,' said Sarah. 'I grew up in Wellington and I've ended in Hamilton: from little city to big town. A few years ago we talked of going to somewhere like Wanaka, or the Coromandel, when we retired, but Robert was keen to carry on working, and then he got sick. As you get older you have to think about how close you are to facilities. It pays to be practical then.'

'Today I'd rather be romantic,' Hartley said. He leant deliberately towards her, giving her time to forestall his kiss if she wished, but she didn't turn her face away, or speak. At first they kissed with a sense of friendship sealed, even curiosity at the first press of mouth on mouth after all the talk that had gone on between them, the brief pecks on her cheek. He was surprised by the softness of her face, and she by the harshness of his breathing. He'd told himself that he should at first kiss and talk, put an arm around her shoulders, and not touch her elsewhere, but he couldn't resist placing his free hand on her breast, allowing his fingers to follow the full shape, squeezing slightly.

Sarah hadn't been as urgently close to any man apart from her husband for years, and what she felt initially wasn't arousal so much as novelty. For a moment she was reminded of those fierce, passing sexual encounters when she was single — back-seat contesting, skirts rucked up, insistent male bodies, premature ejaculations hastily sponged from her clothes, carpet burns, the heady awareness of desirability. But all that was over surely and didn't the blood cool in maturity? Robert had been an almost relentless sexual partner for much of their marriage and she'd never felt the need for satisfaction elsewhere, accepting that his vigorous, self-focused and mute performance was how sex was meant to be. And she'd become reconciled to the end of it with his operation and illness.

It was nice, though, with Hartley, kissing, talking, pressing closer so that she could feel the warmth of his body. 'Have you been alone since your wife died?' she asked him.

'Yes.' He bent down and surprised her by taking off her shoes.

'Nobody at all?'

'No one that I cared about half as much as I care for you. No one that I fucked, if that's what you mean.' He gave the word no emphasis, but it passed with a small charge between them.

'I didn't. I just thought it must have been very lonely for you, coming back to an empty house day after day.'

'I'm in a share club, and a U3A, and an art film society. The sort of things you do to fill up your life. It's not so bad.' They kissed some more and she was relieved that he didn't put his tongue deep into her mouth. She never liked that. He ran his fingers up her thigh, relishing the warmth, the smoothness, the expanse.

'Aren't we a bit old for this?' she said. He took her hand and placed it on his crotch, pressed slightly.

'What do you think?' he said.

'Not here, and not at all unless you've got a condom. Maybe we should wait, not do anything silly. It's just nice to be together, isn't it?'

'I'm tired of waiting.' He stood up, took her hands separately in his own and pulled gently to encourage her to rise. 'Come into the bedroom,' he said.

Why not go with him, please him? He was so easy to please, and it seemed wholly natural. The bedroom was warm, sun from the window laid a rich light over the cream bed cover, and the heat encouraged Sarah to undress quite deliberately, following his example, and they concentrated on that without talking. Then they stood clasped together full skin on skin for the first time, not kissing, but with heads side by side and their hands on each other's back. She could see an angle of his shoulder blade beneath the slightly olive skin and feel his cock on her thigh; he was aware of her breasts and stomach against him, could see her large, pale bum. 'Come on then,' she said and they lay down, face to face but no longer clasped. She watched him take a condom from beneath the pillow, gave a slight smile as recognition of his planning. He wasn't an accomplished lover, however, and was clumsy in putting on the sheath.

'Bloody thing,' he said in exasperation.

He didn't keep going as long as she would have liked, but she enjoyed it, climaxed strongly and was glad to welcome back the sheer physicality of the act. The lifting arc of involuntary sensation, the tensing and the release, the spiral descent back to self.

Most of all she loved the tenderness Hartley showed afterwards, the caresses and the gratitude expressed in words and touch, the closeness maintained and valued when the atavistic drive was satisfied. Robert had never been one for communing in a post-coital glow.

She lay naked on the bed with Hartley, so close that she was aware of the gradual slowing of his pulse, and of her own.

'Bloody marvellous,' he said quietly and let his arm lie across her waist, while she gently brushed his grey hair back from his forehead almost as a mother would for a child. A fern swayed slightly outside the window, fracturing the light that played over the bed. He turned his head from the flickering in case it triggered a migraine.

What time was it? In the Titirangi hall the flower class members might be comparing their morning bouquets with politely suppressed rivalry. In the apartment Robert might be eating his cold lunch, the bean salad, coleslaw and sliced ham, and watching television as was his habit.

'We'd better get dressed,' she said.

'Not yet. You don't regret anything, do you?'

'Not yet,' she repeated. Not yet, but although the situation was new to her, she feared somehow that regret would come, the realistic corollary to the pleasure.

'I love you,' Hartley said. 'Do you know that? I love you so much.'

She got up first, went to the bathroom with her under-clothes and then returned to dress, but he was quicker to finish and went off towards the kitchen. 'I've made lunch,' he said cheerfully as he went. 'It's all done.' The crumpled condom lay on the bed, opaque against the cream cover. It had been a signal precaution against disease rather than conception, more a gesture of responsibility than either. It looked forlorn, and she found that thought strangely inappropriate.

In the living room Sarah saw her shoes still lying casually by the sofa, as if nothing of importance had happened since she left. She and Hartley sat there again, with a tray on the bow-legged wooden occasional table, and globed wine glasses. He'd made egg sandwiches, and tomato ones: he had bought a small, circular quiche and dark chocolate biscuits. She knew they were all signs of the value he placed on her visit. He came back from the kitchen a second time with a bottle of wine in each hand. Without a word he held out first the merlot and then the chardonnay and she pointed to the white. They didn't talk in detail about their lovemaking, not because of embarrassment, or guilt, but because it had been complete pleasure in itself, and any discussion was inadequate. Words added nothing to the fullness of the experience. They sat close, felt the intimacy that comes only after bodies have joined, and which then imbues all the other forms of contact. It occurred to Hartley that no matter how rich a friendship is between a man and woman, it's never complete until they have been to bed together.

'We've still got more than a couple of hours before you have to go,' he said. 'I'll run you home.'

'No. I need to arrive in a taxi. Robert could be watching from the window.'

'I'll take you close, and then you can get a taxi from there.'

'No.' It was very definite, more so than she intended, but she didn't want to talk about the subterfuge that was increasingly part of their friendship, an element best suppressed. 'Tell me how you came to be a lawyer,' she said. 'How on earth you ended up in a suit and black leather shoes after starting in gumboots.'

'You don't want to hear all my boring life story.' But she did, and he, naturally, was flattered. Most of us like to talk about ourselves. It's the most natural topic in the world. And having claimed each other's bodies it was natural to assume free range of each other's lives.

He had a job in retail when he first came to the city, assisting with stock records and replacement at a plumbing and bathroom warehouse in Grey Lynn, and retained a fondness for the gleam of new chrome and pristine whiteware. While there he did a secretarial and management polytech course that was largely extramural, and having completed that he joined the office staff of Central Legal, moved within three years to Butland, Reeve and Purvis, and finally to Hastings Hull Law, where he was a legal secretary and ran an office of five people, mainly women, while also doing law papers at the university.

How quickly much of that had melted away, even in memory, most days as indistinguishable as the routine conveyancing documents he photocopied year after year, so that decades were reduced to a few cameos that captured spikes of humour or tension, or were conscious turning points. These Hartley tried to make revealing for Sarah. The file loss disasters immediately after the office went fully over to computers, the earthquake that shook down the bookcase, Mrs Vallance dying on the loo after being told her savings had been lost in the collapse of a finance company, Michael Leen, a junior partner, punching Barry McIntosh in the face because the latter was preferred by the best-looking woman the firm ever employed. After-hours they would occasionally go into the records room together. Renee Cooby she was then, Renee Simm later, and an absolute stunner. Guys would hand-deliver letters just to get a look at her.

Hartley knew that, gloss them as best he could, his anecdotes were a dull reflection of his experience, and blatantly self-referential. 'I've rabbited on long enough,' he said.

'No. It's interesting, really. I want to know all about you.'

'What haven't I told you?'

'Tell me the worst thing that's happened to you, and the best.'

'Madeleine died so suddenly. No warning, justification, or farewell. No chance to say stuff. The best thing has been meeting you. Absolutely. Again something right out of the blue. What about you?'

'I suppose the worst of all was watching my mother die and not be able to say a proper goodbye because she no longer knew us. The best was having Donna. Nothing beats having a child and having her grow up well and happy.' She wondered if he'd hoped she might have ranked meeting him as equally important.

'I've never understood people who don't want kids,' he said.

'Unless you're especially religious, it's the only way you have a sense of continuity.'

'It's the busiest time of your life and then suddenly they're off.'

'But you never stop loving, or worrying,' said Sarah.

'You do get more time again for your own life, though. Important stuff.' Like this, he thought. Like being close to Sarah on the sofa after making love on a sunlit bed. Like finding someone to share everything with after being alone for too long. Always maybe — until now. 'What's your favourite colour?' he said. He was eager to know everything about her.

'Blue,' she replied without hesitation. 'Powder blue, like the blue of a clear winter sky after frost. What's yours?'

'The same. Exactly the same.' The choice was made in that instant, but he felt it sincere.

The time soon came, however, when she had to go back to her husband and a life firmly established in the past. Once a taxi was called, they began the slight distancing that was essential to move from being lovers in private, to appearing before others as merely friends. Her careful scrutiny of herself in the bathroom mirror, the check that nothing had been left in the house she didn't live in, a change in the tone of voice they used, an awareness of how they touched each other, an assumed brightness that disguised the small, real pain of necessary separation. There was her token resistance to his insistence she accept fare money, the look between them when they parted that was more meaningful than the conventional words of farewell in the presence of the taxi driver.

Robert was at the table with his laptop when she came back, and in the moment that he was turning to welcome her, she had a sudden jolt of fear that what she'd done would somehow be undeniable: that written on her face, or manifest as an overpowering scent, was the glaring evidence that another man had been inside her. But Robert's brief, friendly glance was the same as always. 'How did it go?' he asked, and before she could reply, 'I've just had a call from Mr Goosen and he thinks I'm okay for the next treatment.' And so apprehension left her as swiftly as it had come, and she asked him more about Mr Goosen the specialist, and then what he felt like for their meal. Nothing was false in that. Having given and received pleasure, she wanted Robert to be well and happy, too. Only moralistic convention insists that love for one person excludes love for another.

'Did you eat everything I left for your lunch?'

'Yes.' He had been a big man, tall, solid, resisting stoutness, but illness had stripped muscle from his limbs and added weight to his torso, his features seemed to protrude from his face and his shoulders to slump. He tended to sit for long periods in the first posture assumed, rather than making adjustments as fit people do. Sarah knew he mourned the loss of the man he once was, but neither ever talked of it.

'No flowers?' he said, wanting to show his interest in her day.

'I didn't make anything worth bringing home,' she said. 'I learnt heaps, though.'

'It's good for you to get out like that. Were they a pleasant lot?'

'They were,' she said. 'As a group they were.'

In the evening they watched a documentary on the Nepalese people, and Robert commented on their teeth. As a dentist that was the first thing he noticed, whereas Sarah, who had majored in geography, was always drawn to landscape, even if it featured only as a backdrop. Your occupation becomes the lens through which you see the world. As they sat together, watched mountains and yaks, talked over the commentary occasionally, as was their way, Sarah felt comfortably distanced from what had happened in Titirangi. It was later in the shower that the lovemaking with Hartley returned most strongly, perhaps prompted by nakedness and the touching of her own body. She was slightly tender from the unaccustomed penetration. The recollection was pleasure, but while lying in bed soon after, with Robert's heavy and irregular breathing as familiar background, she decided she wouldn't go all the way with Hartley again. It was a burst of sensual experience best sequestered from the rest of life, and with no future in it. No, she thought, they could carry on as friends, but the sex was over.

Hartley hoped it was only just beginning. He lay on his bed, his face close to the slight indentation their bodies had made. He thought he could smell the perfume she wore, and something of himself, too. He relived the peak of sexual pleasure and the languid aftermath of shared disclosure that was almost as significant. She must be nearly his own age, he thought, but remembered the full breasts rather than the faint arc of crease lines low on her belly, or the loose flesh at her hips. He loved it that her body was large, strong and well contoured, that she showed little shyness concerning the use of it. He remembered the involuntary, high-pitched noises as she pulled with both hands on his bum to urge him in. He remembered her knickers on the bedroom floor, the light material still collapsed on itself just as she had stepped out of them.

He didn't wish to make comparisons with Madeleine, but they came nevertheless. His wife had been apprehensive and reluctant in bed, as she had been in life generally, one of those people fearful to strike out in their existence in case the fates are aroused to take revenge. She would make love only in darkness and anxiety. They had been happy enough in a subdued way that offered no means of comparison, but with a sense of necessary accommodation to each other's natures that was unspoken disappointment.

Hartley lay still dressed, the room warm, the window open and the moon giving a pale lustre to the bush. The city lights pulsated in the distance. He'd found someone to love, he told himself: and someone who loved him. He lay content, conscious of a complete relaxation he hadn't experienced for a long time — perhaps never. He felt a strange and elevating sense of arrival, although the destination was still not clear to him.

Chapter Four

He sent several texts over the next days, but Sarah was busy accompanying Robert to hospital for his treatment and looking after him when it was over. There was nothing of avoidance in that, but it made a statement of priority that Hartley, alone and in love, found difficult to accept.

After six days — Hartley had counted down each one — they met at Magnus again. A cool, grey drizzle in which nothing looked at its best, and people moved impatiently with heads down, yet both Sarah and Hartley felt a catch in breath when they met. Had Sarah not turned her head slightly at the last moment, he would have kissed her on the lips instead of the cheek. They took up their mutual concentration as before, oblivious of those drinking and talking close to them, the cars swishing by on the wet street outside, the amateur watercolours for sale on the wall. The intensity of awareness they had for each other sucked colour and definition from all that surrounded them. They were larger, brighter, centre-stage and more favoured in the world, as people in love feel themselves to be.

They talked at first about the last thing they should have talked about as lovers — Robert's health, his response to the treatment, his stoicism, the growing recognition of his dependence. Hartley was sympathetic because he understood Sarah's need to share with someone, and because her choice of him as a confidant gave him a sense of advantage over her husband. He knew intimate things of the partnership, while Robert was not even aware of his existence. It wasn't at first an assumed sympathy, for what most concerned Sarah was of importance to Hartley too, and he understood the ties of marriage. Later they talked of the time together at Hartley's place, but not about the lovemaking itself. Instead they spoke of the view, his skills as a lunch-maker, further minor revelation of their lives. More and more they were filling in a picture of each other, both chronological and emotional, so that in every new conversation less had to be explained and much could be conveyed by a smile, a pause, a passing reference to things already held in common. In each of them the emotional space occupied by the other grew so rapidly that it seemed they had been close for years.

To others they could pass as husband and wife, except perhaps to the more insightful observer of the close attention they paid each other. A tall, slightly heavy woman in what might tactfully be termed late middle age, well and casually dressed, the colour of her thick brown hair salon reinforced. A slim man, no taller, with darker skin, fine lines on his face, soft greying hair and quick gestures and movement in contrast to her calmness. An unexceptional, older couple with little outward sign that much was happening in their lives, as was the case with most of those around them.

Only one person drew attention to himself. A thin, elderly

man in gaberdine trousers who was reading a hardcover book when approached by the proprietor and told politely that the tables were for customers, not passers-by seeking a dry place to sit down. It seemed just the intervention that the reader had been hoping for, and he created a scene as he left, holding aloft the heavy, dark book, declaiming against the restriction of personal freedoms, walking off with an odd jerky action and the knowledge that he had, briefly at least, imposed himself on the attention of others.

Hartley enjoyed the incident, especially as he wasn't alone himself. 'You know what often occurs to me,' he said. 'Peculiar people walk in a peculiar way. I reckon it could be a test in psychiatric diagnosis.'

'But you only noticed the way he walked after he'd kicked up a fuss. If he'd just gone past us you wouldn't have said anything.'

'It's more than that. There must be some close connection between the motor centre in the brain and the behavioural one. I visited the Acute Mental Health Unit once with a client, and every inmate there walked in a strange way, often a sort of clockwork awkwardness.'

'Just your expectation of peculiarity I'd say.'

'Not at all. I bet there's medical literature about it.'

They amused themselves by commenting on people passing hurriedly in the drizzle outside, and then their own manner of walking. Hartley possessed an unusual sharpness of observation that Sarah enjoyed. She'd decided that they wouldn't have sex again, but his pleasure in their being together again was so sincere, and her own so much greater than she expected, that she went with him the short distance to a motel in a somewhat incongruous Spanish stucco style. She stood out of sight, and uncomfortable with that need, while Hartley made arrangements, telling the proprietor that he had a friend arrived from an international flight who would need to freshen up before they went on their way.

They made love in a studio unit with prints of Basque fishing boats on the walls. When they were young their expectation would have been two, even three, energetic climaxes, but now both were content with one long bout with more time spent on foreplay, and gentle, restful caresses when they were side by side again. Neither made any further demands, regretted the reduction, or mentioned it. Hartley felt a certain pride that he was capable of one good stand without recourse to any pills. He wished that they could lie beneath a single sheet and talk and touch and laugh for much longer. He noticed again the flush that lovemaking brought in patches to Sarah's pale, soft body, and even as he watched her dressing he wished that she was again taking off her clothes.

'Don't put anything on for a bit. You look great. You've got the tits of a thirty-year-old. Jesus, I just love to feel you.'

'I'm getting fat,' she said, but she paused in unconscious response to his flattery so that her boobs were bared for a moment longer before she scooped them into her bra. 'I don't eat as much, but I still seem to put it on. I never used to. I suppose it's not getting the same exercise, and I guess your metabolism changes as well.'

'You're beautiful. Absolutely.'

'You don't have to say that.'

'I could do it all over again.' It was said in admiration and bravado, for his cock was a soft droop when he too got up to put his clothes on. Given more time, though . . .

'There's no time,' she said, abetting his false pride. When she was a young woman, when she and Robert used to have what they called their 'sessions' before Donna was born, she had often remained naked for hours at a time and enjoyed the provocation of it, the confidence of her own physical allure, even of those parts of her body not visible to her. It was different now, whoever she was with.

'I feel great,' he said. His chest was flat, the symmetry of bones clear, a small patch of grey hair between his nipples, and rather more at his crotch. She noticed again the colour of his skin, liked it, and wondered if far back there were some Spanish or Italian blood to account for it. 'After we make love, time seems to slow down. Don't you think?' he said. And following her laugh, 'It's true. There's all this flurry and then a sort of drifting suspension.'

'And I've got to be drifting home,' said Sarah, speeding up her preparation.

They walked together some of the way back to the apartment. He would have gone farther if she'd wished. 'We must look different,' he said.

'What do you mean?'

'After a fuck as good as that I bet we look different to all these ordinary people. It must show, surely? We must be lit up like Christmas trees.'

But Sarah was in the process of bringing herself back to the everyday reality of being a fifty-nine-year-old woman with a sick husband and a settled life. And fuck was a coarse word, even though she had to allow that it was an apt one for what they had experienced.

'It doesn't change anything though,' she said. 'We shouldn't get silly. Being friends is the most important thing and we're entitled to that.'

'I love being friends and I love being lovers.' Hartley put his hand briefly low at her back just for the pleasure of touching her.

'I do, too,' she said.

They felt that sense of privileged exclusion that lovers feel when among people of less entitlement. They parted with a quick kiss; the faint, moving drizzle brushing with their lips. Who was there among all those passing who would recognise them, or care?

So a new pattern was set. Hartley's numerous invitations by text, her acceptance when circumstances allowed, and sometimes their rendezvous in the same motel — the small, clean and stark room that was a cell for happiness, but ruled by the clock. Both of them would have preferred to meet in his home, but the travelling time was better spent otherwise. There was, however, a furtiveness about their coming and going that Sarah in particular disliked, and could never quite banish. It was there like the slightest of odours as she approached the unit, was there when she left until she regained the street. Once they were together behind the closed door, though, nothing of their other lives mattered much at all, and what they did there was of no concern to anybody else.

Her time with Hartley, his attention and affection, his gratitude, his openness concerning his feelings, all gave a balance to the unnatural life she had with Robert since his illness. Rather than growing impatience, she felt better able to support him, more resilient. Sarah didn't think guilt was involved, but if it were, the consequence was to her husband's benefit. She was of an age to be realistic, she told herself. Surely if she had happiness in her own life then it would spread to all those for whom she cared. There was nothing to Robert's detriment in friendship, even love, had elsewhere. Her trysts with Hartley were not a response to grievance in her marriage.

Robert had always approached his life with confidence that was in the main justified. He had succeeded in his profession, in his recreations and in his family; not in spectacular ways, but sufficiently to feel satisfaction. The prostate problem, the consequent operation and then the more sinister complications didn't cower him. Sarah admired his fortitude, and he seldom sought sympathy, despite realising what he faced. He knew his stag days were over, and liked to talk of the trips they had shared, the home in Hamilton they had created together, their daughter, son-in-law and granddaughters who seemed to prosper, and even more important, seemed happy together. His own parents had been selfish, preoccupied with their own lives, and Robert had grown up ambitious and self-sufficient, but also with something of the detachment that marked his mother and father.

Increasingly he'd come to value his marriage, even as his ability to contribute to it was eroded. No partnership is ideal, and if there are no passing disagreements, or tensions, within it then the likelihood is that one person is subjugated to the other. Robert had, in the way of his upbringing, often put himself first, but he had learnt from mistakes. The sexual advantage he took of his dental assistants still came as arousing memories, but the liaisons had stopped years before when he saw the greater value of what was threatened by them. And in more subtle growth he came to experience the pleasure of contributing to the happiness of others, without expecting reward. But what was done was done, and part of the mesh of admiration, loyalty, reliance, disappointment and acceptance that is a marriage in continual transition.

'When I'm better, we'll go overseas again,' he promised her, after one of the more difficult and unsettling treatments. Sarah had just returned from the supermarket, and, although she had taken a taxi, she was wet from a sudden squall that caught her as she reached the apartment building, and that still pelted on the glass of the window and French doors, and bounced on the surface of the small balcony beyond. She pressed her hair with a towel.

'It seemed to blow in from nowhere,' she said. She looked at her hands, which had red marks on the palms from the weight of the shopping bags.

'Where would you most like to go?' He was trying to

summon up the energy to get out of his chair and take the bags into the kitchen, but Sarah, with a touch of impatience, had it done before he moved. 'Where's your favourite place?' he said.

'Germany, I suppose,' she replied from the kitchen.

'Where?'

'Germany,' she said more loudly, and came back to be closer to him. The noise of the rain was still in opposition, but she knew he was making an effort to interest her, and that it was a form of gratitude. She sat on the sofa, ignoring the slight dampness of her clothes. 'Bavaria,' she said. 'I'd like to do some of the less well-known walking trails. The weather's better in the south. I remember a fun couple of days in Füssen, close to the Austrian border. The food's good, too.'

'We'll go then,' Robert said. 'We'll have a decent European trip and not stint on anything. Not only Germany, but all over, eh?' It was a promise to her for all that she was putting up with, also a challenge to his illness. If his plans were unequivocal enough, surely they must come true? 'And we could have one of those long cruises where you stop off at great places and come back to the ship at night. There wouldn't be a hell of a lot of walking, would there?'

'I guess not,' she said, but it was Hartley whom she could imagine accompanying her. Hartley energetically in step with her on excursions off the beaten track; Hartley with his quick conversation, always attuned to her own interests, and his undisguised pleasure in her company. She admitted to herself the unaccustomed thrill of getting to know a new man in an intimate way.

Robert was waiting for an answer, smiling, teeth seeming enlarged. He was in the slumped, head-forward posture that had become typical. Most of his hair was gone, and what remained was dry and lifeless. She remembered the dark, glossy hair he had had when younger. When he was handsome and unaffected by it; when he was resolute and made a bow wave in his progress through life. Sarah felt suddenly that she could cry for him quite easily, but resisted doing so because it would dismay him. 'A trip would be fantastic,' she said. 'When you're over all this, we'll treat ourselves to something really special.'

'We will,' he said, still smiling. 'We bloody well will, Sarah.'

'If it ever stops raining,' she said lightly. And that was happening: the squall cloud moving away, the rain no longer driving on the windows, even shafts of sunlight glittering, flashing, on the wet and busy street.

'I love to travel, even though things change so quickly,' Robert said. 'So much goes by before you get the chance to understand it.'

'Sensory overload, I suppose, though that's certainly not a problem for you here. Maybe we should try a holiday not too far away at first. Perhaps Aussie for a few days. One of those wine and river tours. Anyway, I'd better put this stuff away.' She went back to the kitchen.

Sarah's mention of Australia brought Robert sudden recollections of Gareth, the guy originally from Penryn in Cornwall and then Liverpool, who for almost a week had been his constant day and night companion and then left his life for ever.

Robert had crossed the Tasman after the end of his second university year, hoping to combine a change of scene with earning money. He got a job with a renovation firm in Mildura and was sent with Gareth to paint shearers' quarters far out of town. They drove there in a VW Kombi loaded with gear, and lived in the building they were working on, the smell of paint with them constantly. They used sleeping bags on the uncomfortable box-frame beds, and cooked mostly on a barbecue so as to be in the fresh air. In all the time he was there, Hartley never saw one kangaroo, or wallaby. There were, however, flocks of parrots so brilliant they could have flown out of a kids' colouring book, and with harsh, jarring voices as the trade-off for their beauty.

Robert and Gareth had contact with the owners only when one of them went up to the farmhouse to get vegetables and meat. A tall, purposeful, rather watchful woman of few words and formidable elbows, who always stood on the verandah, or behind the fly-screen door, after Robert's visit to ensure he drove away. Her husband was in hospital for heart surgery.

Gareth was in his forties, a British ex-soldier who had served in Northern Ireland. Robert had thought that military men didn't like to talk about their experiences, but Gareth talked about little else. In his reminiscence he made no distinction between Catholic and Protestant, hating the Irish indiscriminately, and the officers of his own unit almost as much. He went on about house searches, protest marches, brutality and reprisals, the inaccessibility of young Irish women. After a day or two, Robert ceased to pay much attention, deciding that he was a bull-shitter of the first order. He was slap-happy as a painter, too, and even Robert, who lacked any trade experience, knew they were making a poor job. Gareth did the minimum of preparation. 'Paint over it,' he'd say. 'We'll be well away before any fooken bastard twigs.'

They soon drank what beer they'd brought from Mildura, the woman at the farmhouse didn't offer more and Gareth became increasingly in need of alcohol. The nearest pub was almost an hour's drive away, but after five days Gareth decided to take the van in the evening and have a session. Robert stayed back: he would've liked a drink, but the money saved was more important to him, even though Gareth thought him a wimp.

Gareth didn't come back that night, or the next morning, but just before midday a police car came with the news that he'd crashed into a creekbed on the way back and been killed. Robert had returned to Mildura with the policeman, even though the painting of the shearing quarters wasn't completed. He never went back. The firm was unable to contact any of Gareth's relatives, and there were only seven people at the funeral. Robert, assumed to be the mate Gareth knew best, received the commiserations of the others. He was asked to speak, and said that Gareth had served his country in the army, and was a good sort. In truth, Robert felt no connection, and no sorrow, except for the random futility of such events in general. He hadn't even liked the guy.

Now Robert sat looking over the busy street and offices, the resurrected sun in his face, then abruptly blocked by cloud, then bright again. Even Gareth's appearance was difficult for Robert to recall, and he best remembered the uncultivated voice — going on and on about the fooken Irish, and the fooken military. Robert hadn't taken any photographs while working in Australia, and he regretted that. Somehow, now that it was under threat, he felt an increasing need to document his life. Since being in Auckland he'd started sorting family photographs. There were hundreds more at home, though, and more on their computers. He would get them, sort them, that's what he'd do: a useful occupation while he had so much time. He would strengthen himself by better understanding and valuing the life he had.

Chapter Five

With welcome unexpectedness an opportunity came for Sarah and Hartley to have a full day together. Robert decided to take up an invitation to attend a reunion of professional contemporaries in Christchurch, and although Sarah offered to go with him, he said he was fine to go alone. His former partner, Bill, now living in Auckland, was keen to fly with him, he said, and would make sure he didn't drink too much. 'I'll be out of your hair for a couple of nights. It's good to go while I'm feeling okay and before Mr Goosen needs me in again.'

'What will you do there?' Sarah enquired.

'Talk about everything except dentistry.'

'Are you sure you're up to it?'

'Bill knows I need to take it easy,' said Robert. 'He'll do all the legwork. Why don't you go down to Donna and the girls in Wellington?'

'There's plenty of things I need to do here. My glasses

need checking. I might even get my hair done.' Until meeting Hartley, she couldn't imagine anything keeping her alone in the apartment when she could spend time with her daughter and grandchildren.

When she told Hartley, he was full of plans for spending the time together, and wanted her to come to Titirangi for both nights that Robert would be away, but she said someone might ring, or call round, or people at the apartments would notice her absence. They could have the whole Thursday, though, she said, and Hartley put off his work at Hastings Hull. He made plans for the day, and wouldn't tell her anything of them except that they would probably involve swimming. 'I need to know what else to wear,' she protested.

'Nothing flash,' he said. 'The more time we can have alone together the better. Maybe a hat, too. Yes, bring a hat.' She had swimming things and a sunhat, but she had a fair idea there would be sex, so she bought a tube of KY jelly, and put it behind the medicines in the small cabinet beneath the bathroom basin until the day came.

Bill came for Robert at three o'clock on Wednesday afternoon. A talkative man with high colour, who didn't seem to understand that Robert wasn't as fit as he pretended, and left him to carry down his own suitcase from the apartment until Sarah intervened. At the car, Sarah managed to get a word with him out of her husband's hearing. 'You won't let him overdo it, will you?' she asked. 'He won't say, but he gets tired very easily. He's been looking forward to it, so he's making an effort, but he can run out of energy so quickly.'

'I'll keep an eye on him,' said Bill. 'We're all old buggers there, and things won't be riotous. He's allowed booze, isn't he?'

'A glass or two, no more, and he won't want to eat a great deal. His stomach is so easily upset, but it's mainly just getting enough rest. You never know how he'll be from day to day.'

'Leave it to me,' said Bill airily, but Sarah wasn't prepared to do that until she was sure he realised how things were.

'Look,' she said. 'He's full of cancer. He's had treatment for months and it's ongoing. He's really sick, although he's between visits at the moment. This trip's great for him, but he's not the fit guy you remember. I really appreciate you looking after him, but that's what it is, okay?'

Bill was taken aback by the directness, slightly affronted even, but he recovered and was adamant he'd make sure Robert was fine. As a sign of this he went around to Robert's side of the car and checked the door, and when seated himself leant across to make sure that Robert's seatbelt was fastened. When they drove off, Bill tooted, Robert lifted a hand and gave his toothy smile. A few years before he would have privately scoffed at such a reunion, but in his present life it was a welcome adventure.

Sarah had barely got back to the apartment when Hartley rang. 'He's gone?' he asked. 'I could come round. I'm at the office and I could scoot round straight away.'

'No.'

'Why not?'

'We've got all of tomorrow, and you never know who's watching here. I'll walk down to Magnus at half eight in the morning, as we said. I'm looking forward to it.'

'So am I,' he said. 'I haven't thought of much else for days. It'll be the longest time we've had together.'

'We might have a row,' she said. 'A bust-up because we're not really used to each other.' She said it for the pleasure of the denial she knew he'd make.

'Never. I can't get enough of you. You know that. I don't think we'd ever quarrel.'

In fact, although she was looking forward to time with him, she also found delight in being alone in the apartment. That, too, was a rare experience. When Robert was there, she always suppressed the inclination to tidy up what she called 'his end' of the dining table, on which were scattered the photographs that he was sorting, along with a shifting array of computer, cell phone, letters, newspaper, his glasses, junk mail that he thought might contain bargains, the packet of Jaffas that was a familiar indulgence. She had a good straighten-up, cleaned the big window and French doors, vacuumed the curtains and carpets, pushing the furniture about with her knees.

Afterwards she opened a small tin of salmon and ate the pink flesh on biscuits. It was good for once to have an evening meal without the television on, and she sat with her food and a glass of sav blanc, and watched the busy street three storeys down with the shadows stretched in the slanting sun. Soon, she told herself, she would sort out what to wear the next day, and she must remember to take the KY jelly from the back of the bathroom cabinet and put it in her bag. And she would sit close to the mirror and use her slender, pink electric shaver to remove hair from her legs, and the tops of her inner thighs, and cream away, too, the fine hair on her lower face that had become more noticeable in the past few years.

Robert would be in Christchurch with Bill and the other dentists. She hoped he would be happy remembering good times. She worried about him: maybe he would overdo things and have a fall, or get sick. Sarah had little faith in Bill's care.

Hartley would be alone in his home among the trees, thinking of her and the next day. She was sure of that. She knew also that he'd given much thought to the secret location, but she rather wished he'd been more forthcoming. Maybe she should wear trousers, not a skirt. She would be informal. The one clue he'd given was the need for swimming costumes, so surely they were going to a beach. In a reassuring, but illogical, way she felt that the accomplishment of household tasks entitled her to spend time with Hartley. The certainty of his anticipation added to her own.

Hartley was early to the Magnus café. To leave a woman alone in a public place was discourteous. Such considerations were outmoded, and not the residual observances from his upbringing. A rough and ready equality had been the practice on the southern farm. Push in, keep up, or miss out. It was in the law firms that he had been instructed, sometimes primly, in the niceties that are expected to compensate for excessive fees. 'Awareness and solicitude,' old Mr Soper had often advised him. 'Awareness and solicitude when dealing with our clients.' For years Mr Soper had so successfully glossed his avarice with impeccable manners that he possessed a Queenstown apartment and a young Australian woman to go with it. Hartley's courtesy was less cynical.

The day was fine and still, dispelling his fears that the weather might spoil his plans. He stood by the café entrance, facing the way that he knew Sarah would come so he would see her even before they met, and when she was visible, walking easily despite a carry bag, and with a smile as she recognised him, he felt a strange pride and gratefulness that she was coming to him. Coming to him willingly despite being married to someone else; coming to him because she preferred that to any other purpose for the day. Coming to him when she knew he expected that they would make love.

'So where are we going?' she asked when they had kissed, squeezed hands and were walking on to his car.

'We're heading north.'

'But where?'

'You'll have to wait and see. How well do you know places past Auckland?'

'I've been to Whangarei several times. I had an aunt who lived there, but she's been gone for years now. And Robert and I went up to Cape Reinga one holiday just to say we'd been there. The same reason we went one year to Stewart Island, though that was a lot more interesting. We went back, and stayed longer the next time.'

'We're not going as far as Whangarei,' said Hartley.

Did it matter where they were going as long as they were together? A day, a whole day was a luxury. They talked and laughed, taking little notice of anything they passed, and even the few silences between them were full of easy understanding and the sense of their close presence. Together and in love. Nothing else mattered.

They turned off the main road at Warkworth and drove to Matakana village. Sarah liked it, as Hartley knew she would. The owner-operated shops and businesses, the open space and easy pace, the pub built from a single kauri. They had coffee at a pottery and wandered through the showrooms enjoying the bright glazes on the platters, bowls and planters.

'Let me buy you something,' he said.

'There's no need,' she said. 'I'll remember it all.'

'I'm going to,' he said firmly. 'Either you make a choice, or I'll do it for you.' So she chose a small blue jug that wouldn't draw Robert's attention when he came home.

Omaha Bay was their destination: a long, pale beach, and behind it the expensive holiday homes of the Auckland élite. Hartley had a client who had offered him the use of one of these; not the most grand, but impressive nevertheless, with a double garage and a balcony opening from the upper bedroom, and lines of juvenile buxus in the recently landscaped garden.

'Omaha?' said Sarah. 'How on earth is that a connection here?'

'My guess is it's after Omaha Beach in the Normandy landings where all those Yanks went ashore.' Sarah didn't see that was relevant to where they were, but she let the topic drop.

Hartley was briefly interested in the number of rooms, the view, a quick calculation of the overall value, but Sarah had a woman's more intimate response. She noticed the matched washing machine and tumble dryer in the laundry with the stickers for economical use of electricity still showroom new, the pristine carpets showing no wear even in the doorways. She opened the kitchen cupboards to reveal the stacked and matched sets of cutlery and crockery. Everything new and in the same impressive price range. What would it be like, she wondered, to go into the shops and in a day or two outfit a new home?

Yet there was a sterility in the cupboards and drawers that gave no clues as to the personalities of the people who came there. Nothing was chipped, or worn, among the utensils there were no old favourites handed down from Gran, no scatter of corks, plastic ties and cheap souvenir spoons, no jar lids, broken sellotape dispensers, or the screw tops of rubber hot-water bottles. No sense of life's accumulation that gives individuality to a place. 'It's rather like a huge dolls' house,' she told Hartley.

'Yes,' he said, without understanding, but willing to give affirmation. 'I don't suppose they come here more than a few times a year, and they don't rent it out. Let's go down to the beach and have a walk after being in the car. There's plenty of time. I'll just bring in all the stuff.'

'You didn't need to arrange a house,' she said. 'We could've just been on the beach.'

'Yeah, but I wasn't sure about the weather.' There was another reason, but he didn't mention that. You couldn't expect a woman like Sarah to lie down among trees or dunes to make love, have her clothes rubbed into the earth, or sand, and her hair roughed by the ground.

He brought packages and a chilly bin from the car, put things in the fridge, refused any help from her.

'What have you got in there?' she said, knowing the care and time he would have taken over every choice, each purchase, and aware all of it was because of her.

'Never you mind. All in good time,' he said. 'Anyway, get your togs on and we'll be off to the beach. I've been before. It's not far.' It was a long time since she had heard anyone use the word 'togs'. It carried associations of school baths and family picnics.

Omaha wasn't a collection of seaside baches, but more like a town suburb: sealed roads with kerbs, pricey homes with double garages, fenced gardens and television dishes. The beach of pale sand was natural, however, and not crowded. Hartley and Sarah sat on their towels, wore their hats low to avoid the glare of the sun, talked with an almost dreamy freedom, as if most days were spent together and in a similar way. They talked of likes and dislikes, expectations and realities, things funny peculiar and things funny ha ha. They didn't talk of Robert, or of Madeleine. With their talk they drew a perimeter around themselves as if to keep time from moving on.

'I wonder what was the closest we came to each other before that day at the murdered girl's grave,' he said.

'What do you mean?'

'There must have been times since you've been up here that we were quite close, maybe even passed each other in the street, or in a shop, and didn't know we loved each other.'

'Well, of course we couldn't.'

'But everything was waiting for that connection, wasn't it? The important things are set up, I reckon, and the opportunity comes round.'

'I'm not much of a believer in fate,' said Sarah. 'It seems to me you make decisions and live by the results. There's chance, but self-determination as well.'

'Well, anyway, we met and we're here. Bloody marvellous.'

His openness, his vulnerability, was almost boyish, and surprised her. How easily he would be hurt.

'What was the murdered girl's name again?'

'Emily Keeling.'

'What did she say at the end about loving and dying?' asked Sarah idly.

'She said, "Love me, I am dying", according to the newspaper report.' Each knew the other was thinking of the contrast between past tragedy and their present happiness, and neither felt the need to allude to it. To be alive, together and in love set them on a special height too fragile to be questioned.

Afterwards they swam with others, drawing in breath and stomach at the first encounter with the cool, swelling sea, and then relaxing, lolling almost in it as they became accustomed to the temperature. The one-piece costume caused small bulges of white flesh at Sarah's armpits and cut into her thighs, but Hartley thought how beautiful she was. They went far enough beyond the small waves to be in unbroken water, and swam rather clumsily and happily there together. She didn't want to get her hair wet, but he ducked himself completely under the surface several times, and came up laughing, his soft, grey hair plastered like seaweed to his face. Because of that his features seemed more marked, his ears standing out, his eyes larger, darker.

'This is the way to work up an appetite,' he said.

'What?'

'We'll have an appetite for lunch,' he said loudly.

First, though, they left the water, sat a while on the towels again to let their bodies dry. The sand on their legs, dark and damp initially, was soon grey-white and loose, falling away with just a brush of the hand. There were other people, some lying passively in the heat, some loud with companions, some wandering at the water line, but not a crowd, and none close enough to intrude.

'I haven't been to a beach for ages,' said Sarah.

'There's always that same smell, isn't there? That smell of the ocean and the land at the same time.'

'Ozone, they say.'

'Yes, but what is ozone? I think it's more about old shells, dead fish and kelp — salt and stuff,' he said.

There were three small yachts not far from shore. Clones except for the variety of colours, they passed briskly at exactly the same speed and direction, as if drawn by one piece of string. Sarah and Hartley watched for a time without needing to refer to them. Hartley had a strange sense that he and Sarah were coming closer and closer together, even though there was no movement. Their warm, bare arms and legs would touch as the yachts retreated across their field of vision.

He was about to say how happy he was, when he noticed a large white dog running with purpose along the beach, right to left. No owner was obvious, and the dog passed by and went on for a hundred metres or more before turning and running back with equal resolution. It came directly to Sarah and Hartley, and stopped at hand's reach. Despite the dash, its mouth was closed and there was no panting. A large, slim dog, with hair rather curly and very white, and a bright red collar in contrast. It stood quite still for a moment, as if expecting a greeting from them, and when that didn't come it squeezed carefully between them, lying down with head extended on its paws.

Such amiable familiarity was infectious, and Sarah and Hartley remained seated and relaxed. 'Good dog, good dog,' she said, and ran a hand along the warm, rough hair of its coat. Hartley patted its head and the dog closed its eyes in pleasure.

'It likes you,' he said.

'He likes us both.'

'He understands our closeness,' Hartley said, accepting the gender without substantiation. 'Dogs have a sense of such things.'

'He even smells good.' She bent down, put her face close to his back. 'A woodsmoke smell, with a bit of old sacks in it as well.'

'I don't usually like dogs, but this fellow's a bit different, isn't he?'

For a couple of minutes the white dog lay between them, then got up, looked at each in turn and bounded off again, taking no notice of anyone else on the beach. It ran with the same sense of purpose that had marked its arrival. It diminished in the distance, swerved inland and was lost to view among the dunes.

'Not sure what that was all about,' said Hartley.

'A welcome, that's what it was. He's a member of the local beach committee.'

They both felt a minor privilege in being singled out, though other people had paid little attention, and the oddity of it gave them a talking point as they gathered up their things. They walked back to the house, having put on just their shoes and hats, and carrying their towels. Through the fabric of his floppy hat, Hartley could feel the sun's heat on his head, and it smote his bare back as he walked. It was after one o'clock.

'I'm hungry now,' he said.

Casually, but with a certain pride, Hartley assembled their lunch on the glass-topped table of the kitchen. Boutique cheeses, fresh salads and bread that he had bought on his way in that morning from Titirangi, finely sliced ham, lemon cake in a plastic dome, and a bottle of Pol Roger enclosed in a shaped chilly bag.

'I didn't bring anything,' she said apologetically. 'I thought we'd be having lunch in a restaurant.'

'You brought yourself. You came,' Hartley said. It was turning out just as he had imagined it, and that was unusual — for once to have experience match expectation.

'You've done all this, and I've just taken everything for granted.'

'But you've got all sorts of difficult stuff to deal with. Come on, come on, let's enjoy ourselves. Let's get through as much food as we can. I don't want to take bits and pieces back.'

'I haven't had real champagne for ages,' she said. What reason would there have been for it?

'I gambled on this place having decent glasses, and they have.'

He sprang the cork with a satisfying explosion, and they sat in their swimming costumes in the new kitchen of glass, stainless steel and chrome, and drank champagne, feeling the last of the sand grains beneath their feet. Hartley could have almost wept for joy, and they hadn't even begun to fuck.

That was done in the main upstairs bedroom. Although the room wasn't overlooked and they could see no one in other houses, they drew the net curtains over the open doorway to the balcony. The light sea breeze moved the curtains so that they whispered and rustled on the wooden floor like the hem of a full dress, and the sun remained strong behind them. Sarah had a shower to rid herself of the last of the sand and salt of the sea, and Hartley came and stepped into the shower box with her, and they stood silently, breast to breast in the water and steam, ran their hands over each other's backs. They dried themselves without hurry and when Hartley went back into the bedroom, she used the jelly.

'We'd better take off the cover,' she said when she joined him. It was white cotton with satin edging and embroidered wild flowers, and they folded it and left it on the floor. They lay on a plain, green blanket, and at first he stroked just her arms and shoulders, and kissed her.

They engaged in the most intimate of physical acts in the pristine house of complete strangers, and yet she felt more relaxed, more at home, than in the faux Spanish motel of the city.

Afterwards they lay side by side, facing the same way, but not pressed together because it was too hot for that. They were not exposed to each other, and so comfortable in nakedness. The hems of the pale curtains whispered on the floor, and the blaze of the sun was dissipated in the folds as falls of colour.

'On the DVD remotes they have that pause button, don't they,' he said after a while.

'So?'

'You push it and the scene stays as a tableau on the screen. That's what I'd like now. A pause button and we'd just lie here together for ever.'

'Romantic, but not realistic. Actually, I feel the need to go have a pee, and after that I'm going to have another shower,' she said, and he laughed. 'And I didn't notice any pause button in your repertoire a while ago.'

'If we were together I wonder whether every day would be like this?' he said.

'I've just remembered that our clothes are still downstairs. Damn.' Practicality was a defence against emotion in which she might make declarations that were impossible to sustain.

'I'll get them,' Hartley said. He stood up, took the swimming costumes from the floor of the ensuite, and went downstairs. She noticed again his lack of height, the slimness and finely lined face. There was something boyish about him, despite his age. His cock had become small, retreated into a nest of greying pubic hair. What was she doing, taking pleasure and relief in this way when she was a grandmother and still loved her husband? She got up and went in to the shower, refusing, or unable, to give an answer. What harm could there be in love and friendship when no pain was intended? She couldn't help comparing the gratitude and solicitude shown by Hartley after sex, with the common-place sense of entitlement and release she remembered as Robert's response.

When dressed they made coffee, and spread what remained of their lunch on the kitchen table again. As one hunger had been assuaged, another had returned. There was even some champagne left. They talked of trips and holidays, and whether they would have a home like this if they had the choice. They talked of those decisions and happenings in their lives the crucial nature of which had been hidden at the time. They talked of their day, the white dog on the beach, the champagne, and Hartley reached his hand to hers on the table.

The time still came, however, when they had to leave. Sarah became an assiduous cleaner, determined that the unknown woman of the house would find nothing to object to, nothing smeared, crumpled or stained, nothing even of the sand they had cheerfully carried in on their bodies. She bagged up the detritus of their food to take with them, rather than leaving it in the lined and empty bin beneath the sweep of the stainless steel bench. Unconsciously, perhaps, she wished to erase the actuality of her day, so nothing remained that deserved accusation, and all the pleasure was a blameless exercise of the imagination and could be carried away with them.

So back they drove, the places of the morning still there, but reversed in order and in an altered angle of the sun: Matakana with its vivid pottery, Warkworth, Puhoi, Orewa and Silverdale.

Hartley's mood was precarious, buoyed by the success of the day, and simultaneously dragged down by its approaching end. 'Come home with me and stay the night,' he said. 'Robert's not back until late morning. I'll run you in early. What do you say?'

'I can't,' she said.

'Why not?'

'What happens if he rings?'

'Well, you're out, that's what happens. You've gone out to a film, or something. Jesus, surely you're able to go out of the apartment when he's away?'

'It's not like that,' she said. 'You know that.' They drove for a while without talking. Then, 'Let's not spoil it,' she said quietly. 'Thank you for a wonderful, wonderful day. Everything about it. You know I'd love to come back with you, but it's just not possible. We can have other times. There'll be other times.' A grey ute overtook them, a Maori youth sitting in the back with his long hair flowing in the slip-stream, and one arm around a sheep dog. He raised a thumb and smiled.

'I don't think you've ever called me "darling",' Hartley said, drawing back from the brink of any disagreement, wishing to keep the mood of the day intact. 'Don't people in love call each other "darling"?'

'Well, I don't think you've ever called me "darling" either.'

'All the time when you're not there,' he said.

'Doesn't count and can't be proved.'

'Let's do it now then,' and he leant towards her as he drove. 'Darr — ling,' he drawled extravagantly.

'Why yes, darr — ling,' she said. They didn't kiss; they laughed. That's how they returned to the city, amusing each other in flippancy as if they were young again, and yet holding to the present while they were able. The low sun was strong and gave the landscape a chequerboard quality of sharp features and shadowed concavities.

Hartley felt down after he'd taken Sarah home and returned to Titrangi. He knew it was reaction to the emotional high of the day, but understanding didn't lessen the effect. The Pol Roger bottle he didn't throw out with the other rubbish, but placed on the bench as a sign of the outing's success. What would it be like, he wondered, to have a string of such days — on and on until they become an accustomed life? What would Sarah be doing, alone in the apartment? He hoped she would be just as convinced of the worth of a future together.

All he saw began to shiver and fragment as twilight deepened, not because the light was failing, but as a harbinger of a migraine. He wasn't surprised. Everything had to be paid for. He took the tablets straight away, changed and lay on the bed. If he were lucky it would be only the headache, and not the retching until even a thin bile was exhausted. He shrugged his shoulders to relax his neck muscles. He endeavoured to concentrate on the day: the rich glazes of the pottery at Matakana, the muscular movement of the ocean's swell, the high bedroom in his client's new house, the white dog that chose to come and lie with them on the warm sand of the beach.

Chapter Six

Every meeting was the more special because of the difficulty in achieving it. On several occasions there was bitter disappointment when something came up for Sarah at the last moment and she couldn't make the time and place. Because such care, preparation and subterfuge were needed for each assignation, it startled them both when once they met by accident.

Sarah had been to the optometrist for a check, and been advised to buy new glasses, just as Robert had cynically predicted. He understood how the professions prospered. She had afterwards gone on the brief distance to Queen Street, and as she turned away from looking into the window of a dress shop, she noticed Hartley in the café next door. He was wearing a lighter suit that she hadn't seen before, and a pale blue shirt and darker blue tie. It was unusual for her to observe him objectively, for almost always they were swept up with each other when they met, eyes locking with all the signals that lovers have. Even when she was alone and thinking of him, she imagined them together, and now she saw him in his separate life, focused on someone else.

He was angled forward in his typical intensity, his longish, grey hair slightly unruly. He was talking, and moving his right hand palm uppermost in small jerks as if bouncing an invisible balloon. In a film the plot would dictate that Hartley's companion was an attractive, younger woman leaning in with reciprocal close attention, but in reality the person opposite was a man of similar age to Hartley, and similar occupation judging by his suit and dark shoes, but quite distinct in appearance, his balding head seeming to sit directly on his shoulders, and his face full.

Sarah could have walked on, content with the glimpse of Hartley in his workday world, but she was in love and needed the frisson of his attention. Because the meeting was authentically a coincidence, she felt somehow, illogically, free of any guilt. She went into the café and up to the counter as if she hadn't seen him, and he noticed her immediately, as she knew he would. He stopped talking, excused himself and came over.

'What are you doing here?' he said, his voice infused with unexpected pleasure.

'I had to have an eye test,' she said. 'I'm going to have to get new reading glasses. More expense.'

'It's so great to see you. You should have said and I'd have popped out to meet you. Well, anyway, come over and meet Simon.'

'I don't want to interrupt. It's one of your business days, I know.'

'Not at all. It's such a bonus to run into each other. Come on, really. He'll be going back in a minute anyway.'

Simon Drummond worked with Hartley at Hastings Hull, and they had been to the university to listen to a visiting academic talk on the law of contracts. Sarah was introduced as a family friend and found Hartley's colleague to be both affable and courteous, but he soon apologised and left to return to the office.

'You should go, too,' she told Hartley.

'No way. We meet little enough, and this is great. Serendipity, or something like that. How long have we got?'

'You don't need to stay.'

'Nonsense. How long have you got?'

'Well, I suppose as long as I'm back by five or so. A couple of hours anyway.'

'We'll go to a hotel, or motel.'

'No,' she said. Making love was joyous, and affirming, but this meeting was different to the others and she wished it to play out in a different way. Not everything was about sex. She had thought the day had no other point than the remedy of her increasing long-sightedness — presbyopia the eye woman had called it — but now she was with a man who loved her and she felt lifted, favoured, because of it. 'Let's walk somewhere together,' she said. 'We could go to your office. I've never been there. I could be an influential client with a big business deal to discuss.'

'Why not? I'm happy to take you.' And he was. He would be proud to take her anywhere.

But she was joking. Really she wanted them to walk together in the sun and talk, enjoy the time with each other that had come so naturally as a gift of chance. So they turned up the slope from the main street heading towards Albert Park. Hartley took her hand, and Sarah responded by giving his a squeeze.

Hartley paused at the window of a jeweller's and looked closely at the display. 'I'd like to buy you something. Something special that you really like, something lasting, and I don't care what it costs.'

'Don't be silly,' she said.

'I've got no one to spend money on.'

'You've got a son. You'll have grandchildren.'

'That diamond solitaire,' he said. 'There on the second pad, or that sapphire one in platinum.' The diamond was over nine thousand dollars, the sapphire more.

'Come on,' she said, tugging at his arm slightly.

'I absolutely mean it.'

'You know I couldn't take it, and I couldn't wear it anyway. There's no way I could explain something as valuable as that.' She knew that he was serious, that if she agreed he would go right in and buy it then and there. Such a demonstration of his love, and her own ability to create it, gave her a brief and almost giddy charge.

'I'm not letting you go home until I've bought you something.'

'Okay, you can buy me something flippant then — something that I'd buy myself, and ordinary enough not to be noticed.'

'Flippant?' said Hartley delightedly. 'What sort of a description is that?'

'You know what I mean.'

'Lingerie. I'll buy you French undies.'

'Like hell you will.' They were close to a shoe shop. 'You can buy me slippers. I need a pair. All grandmothers do.'

That's what happened. They went in and had fun trying on far more pairs than were necessary for her to make a decision. Hartley took over the duties of the slightly dour woman shop assistant, sitting down with Sarah and putting her foot on his knee, making extravagant commentary on each slipper he tried.

'Stop being so silly,' she said. 'It's embarrassing.'

'Flippant you said, so I'm giving you flippant. Right? And anyway we're going to buy blue ones. You know that.'

Blue velveteen they were, with leather piping. Rather silly slippers really, but that was their mood, and they loved the mood, the slippers and each other, and Sarah knew she could have had a diamond or sapphire ring worth thousands if she'd wished. That's what a pair of blue slippers represented, she thought, and she smiled to herself as Hartley took up the wrapped cardboard box. She thanked the quiet shop woman, aware that she had stood by and witnessed the little play of affection, and despite herself Sarah felt pleasure in that, too, for there is almost always an element of vanity in love.

It was too hot to walk far, and when they reached the park they sat on a bench shaded by the trees and talked. A group of young Chinese women came happily past, dark and pretty, chatting in English, but not with a Kiwi accent. Although Sarah had been in Auckland for many weeks, she still found it unusual that she shared it with so many Asian people. She hadn't mentioned it to anyone except Robert before, in case it was thought that she resented their presence, but she was safe with Hartley. 'I'm still not used to it,' she told him. 'The malls especially. You're outnumbered, aren't you?'

'Well, it's like that in the world at large. We've been so isolated, so focused on British heritage, that we think the world's white.'

'When you go south, though, it's different. Even Wellington hasn't attracted anywhere near as many.'

'They come from big cities and they like big cities. So do I. And they work their arses off to succeed at school and afterwards. Most of the rest of us are slack by comparison. Just look at the cars coming past. Toyota, Nissan, Kia, Mazda, even Great Wall. When I was a kid it was mainly Austin, Morris and Ford. I suppose they come from places where it's work, succeed or starve.'

Sarah wasn't sure quite what he meant, so moved on. 'Tell

me about the lecture,' she said. 'About the law of contracts. Was it good value?'

'The law of contracts in relation to electronic commerce isn't exactly sexy stuff. It'll send you to sleep.'

'Okay, but just an expert summary, Mr Lawyer.'

'Well, he was talking about the rapid growth and change in electronically made agreements, whether they're enforceable in the courts, and the significance of recent judicial decisions affecting such business dealings. Actually he was quite good.'

Hartley and Sarah sat in the warm shade surrounded by garden plots, lawns and paths and he talked about his profession, patting the top of the shoe box from time to time for emphasis, but for both of them what they were experiencing had nothing to do with the law of contracts. The bustle and noise of the city was not far away, but they sat with flowers and grass close, and even butterflies that dipped and fluttered as if on puppet strings. Neither of them wished to be anywhere else, or with any other companion.

Hartley was still talking about the lecture, and its application to his own work, when a woman and child approached. The woman was elderly, wore black tights beneath her summer skirt, and a knitted top, but she and the clothes were clean. The little girl, three or four years old, had a pony-tail and green plastic sandals. They came steadily closer, the woman gently urging the girl in front, hands on her shoulders, until awareness of their close proximity made Hartley stop speaking. There was a pause during which he and Sarah waited expectantly, the child watched the butterflies and the old woman grinned. Then she said, 'No one cares about this one here. I'm no relation whatsoever, but I've taken her in, haven't I. Fostered her because no one cares about her. There's all this talk about people desperate to adopt, but plenty of kids like this one pushed from pillar to post.'

'You're doing a good job then,' said Hartley tolerantly, yet unsure of what was expected of him. The little girl was fair, with a pear-shaped face and small blue eyes. Her toenails had been painted a variety of colours and showed clearly through the straps of her sandals.

'And what's your name?' Sarah asked her.

'It's not right for them to go into one of them homes,' the woman said.

'I suppose not,' said Sarah.

'It's not personal, you see. Kids need one on one, because that's the natural way of it. Bonding is so important for little ones. It's not as if any of it's their fault. You wouldn't believe what kids like this one have seen. You wouldn't wish it on a dumb animal I always say.'

'What's your name, sweetheart?' Sarah asked again, and the child slowly opened her mouth, but was forestalled by her foster mother.

'Trauma,' she said. They call it trauma, don't they, the horrors that kids like this one have been through. I've twice been to talks on it by high-ups at the agency, and you wouldn't believe what the kids themselves tell you. Shocking, shocking stuff. Really nasty things.'

'It's a credit to foster parents,' said Sarah. 'It can't be easy.'

'The one before this one was scalded all down her legs. Looked like a road map in white and pink it did, even when it healed up. Mind you, others have their scars as well, but not on the outside. Kids and elephants never forget, that's what I always say.'

The woman stood there, slightly formally, with the girl still loosely held before her, and for the benefit of Hartley and Sarah she explained the exigencies of foster children and her own role. Hartley, wanting to be alone with Sarah again, misunderstood the reason she'd approached them, and offered some money. The woman was affronted.

'I thought you'd be interested in the cause. The work being done for little ones in peril. People need to understand, I reckon.' She took the girl's hand and began moving away.

'Goodbye,' Sarah said.

The woman didn't reply, but the child half turned, smiled and said 'Shit,' with a strangely adult emphasis.

'Now, now,' said her foster mother without alarm, and kept going without looking back.

'What was that all about?' said Hartley. 'Why come up to us if she didn't want something?'

'She did want something. She wanted to share: to talk about the work she does. I suppose no one much ever bothers to listen to her. I admire her. We just shut our eyes to so much that's going on.'

'I thought for a moment the kid's name was Trauma. Did she really say "shit"?'

They laughed, but without voicing it, both were aware of a panorama of restricted, difficult lives beyond the comfort and security of their own. Hartley leant over and kissed Sarah on the mouth, squeezed her thigh quickly. 'Thank God for the optometrist,' he said. 'It's made my day.' Even the thought of child misery and need couldn't shake his enjoyment of the afternoon. You took happiness where you were lucky enough to find it, and you held onto it for as long as you could.

They left the park and walked together into the city to find a taxi stand, and Hartley relinquished the shoe box, watched as Sarah was driven away. He had work to catch up at the office, but he gave in to a sudden quirky inclination, went back to the park and sat down exactly where they had been before. The sun was still bright, the air warm even in the shade, the flowers abundant. He was alone, but his senses were so heightened by the time with Sarah that he was able to prolong the pleasure of being with her in just that place, and he sat at ease and smiled, and regarded with goodwill all who came walking on the paths not far away. He took up a handful of gravel and flicked the stones away with his thumb one by one.

Rather to his surprise, he also thought of the woman and the foster child: how the woman had approached them out of the blue to explain her calling, how the little girl had stood watching the butterflies and then sworn as she went away. For a moment their lives had intersected, and then spun on again with no effect from the meeting. In other circumstances he may have found sadness in that, but instead he remembered Sarah's laughter.

LATER, IN THE APARTMENT, Sarah put on the blue slippers, but they possessed no magic in that setting. She mentioned them to Robert as part of the recital concerning her eye test and shopping, and he made dutiful comment, before going on to say he wanted to talk to her about the possible purchase of a holiday home at Manaia in the Coromandel. A Hamilton friend was thinking of selling. 'It's nothing flash, but if we liked it, everything could be done directly with Greg and we'd cut out agents and limit the legal fees. He said there's no bother letting it out on a casual basis if we wanted income from it.'

'Why do Greg and Cath want to sell, then?'

'All their children are overseas now except Andrew, and he flies helicopters in Antarctica.'

'Have you ever seen it?' Sarah asked. She was thinking of the park, the warmth, the foster mother with the child with painted toenails, Hartley close beside her. She was thinking of the brilliant, unblinking colours of the rings in the jeweller's window.

'No, I haven't. He often talks about it, though. They've had it for ages. Anyway, maybe we could go over and take a look. I just thought it worth mentioning.' Robert's latest test results were encouraging, and he took that as incentive to plan positively for the future. He wouldn't do any more fill-in work at the surgery when he was cured; he had money, and he'd decided that he would spend it on easy and happy times for them both.

'Well, we can think about it,' said Sarah. 'It is lovely on the Coromandel, isn't it.'

She felt dispossessed. Which of her lives was real? She was talking to her husband, but thinking of her time with Hartley. She would've liked to tell Robert about the little blonde girl — how she said 'shit' so decisively as she went away. Robert would have enjoyed that, but it was part of an increasing store of experience that she was unable to share with him.

When she was with Hartley it felt quite natural, and she was happy. When she was back with Robert and living the old life, with so much that was indispensable, she could scarcely believe all that she was doing outside it, and how much risk that entailed. But what was life without some daring in it, some reach and peril of feeling, some promise and some giving?

Chapter Seven

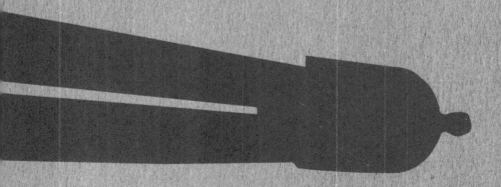

Hartley had no one to return to after his trysts with Sarah: no other life of significance to distract him from love, no personal obligations, no guilt or special ambition, to lessen his conviction that he had found the woman he needed in his life.

However, for a time after he began making love to Sarah, memories, almost visions, of Madeleine came strongly when he was alone. Almost as if she were attempting to hold his allegiance from the grave. Their early days were the more vivid, when both of them knew each other less well and had high expectations of their marriage.

Madeleine had not been beautiful, but she'd been attractive. She was short, thin, inclined to breathe through her mouth, always neatly dressed and well groomed. Her skin needed no disguise, her fair hair was lustrous, and she tended to smile as she listened to people, whatever the quality of the conversation. How was Hartley to judge the success of his marriage when he had no intimate knowledge of another to compare with it? It was placid enough, there was little dramatic unhappiness, but her subdued apprehension of life was constraining. After Kevin's birth her interest in sex, which had never amounted to enthusiasm, dwindled further, until his own satisfaction seemed almost an imposition.

Increasingly, her ever nervous energy had been spent on her work. Madeleine was accomplished, despite her trepidations, and became a policy manager at Auckland airport. Her salary was greater than his for most of their marriage, though that was never an issue. She died in her fifty-fourth year, as formal records like to phrase it, from hypertrophic cardiomyopathy. A rapid death, as had been her mother's, but even quicker. She was giving a PowerPoint presentation to staff, and in mid-sentence fell unconscious against the glass door of the meeting room. Hartley went to her office once after her death, to collect her things, but never again. The airport became a sad place for him, no matter what the reason for coming or going.

He could recall their final conversation. 'I don't feel great,' she'd said, sitting for a moment before leaving the car at the airport.

'You don't eat enough, don't have a decent breakfast, that's the trouble.'

'I feel something's going wrong somehow.'

'You always do, but then the day turns out okay.' There had been a strong wind that blew a cardboard pottle against the car — blat — and made her flinch. 'You'll be fine once you're in there with your friends.'

'I hate the wind,' she said. 'It pushes stuff out of place.' He had watched her hurry away, clutching her coat close to her, always wishing to be somewhere safe.

He wondered if perhaps she'd never felt completely well, and that had led to her constant anxiety. There had been something that prevented her from being fulfilled, prevented her from facing life full on, and neither of them had been able to work out what it was. Maybe it was him. There was a time in their marriage, after Kevin left home, that she cried a lot, for no reason that she could explain, or Hartley discern. It could happen at the table, in the car, or in the middle of the night. 'Nothing. It's nothing really, I'm just a bit down,' she'd say.

Once she started crying when they were in the showroom at Neenall Furnishings looking at carpets. She wept right in front of the salesman, and Hartley felt such a fool. 'It's nothing. I'm sorry,' she had said. Not long after that they went to see Rory Menzies, the counsellor. He seemed more interested in Hartley than Madeleine, and had asked a lot about Hartley's indifference towards his own family. Madeleine recalled the time one of his brothers had arrived without warning, and Hartley had gone into the bedroom and told her to tell his brother he was away. She said only Hartley's mother had come up for their wedding.

Rory, as he liked to be called, had encouraged them to be forthright in their comments, but Hartley couldn't help but find disloyalty in his wife's mild, truthful revelations. Maybe the sessions worked, because Madeleine stopped crying so much. Maybe that would have happened anyway, without Madeleine telling Menzies things about her husband. 'He never got on with his father,' she said, 'never keeps in touch with any of them.' Hartley had said it was just that he was self-sufficient, but she was right: he didn't get on with any of them. Madeleine found relief in talking to the counsellor, but Hartley would have preferred not to have been drawn into it.

Hartley admitted to himself that he had needed to do more, but was unable to say, during the marriage, or since, just what it was that required augmentation. Selfishness must have been his failing. How often he read in books and articles, and saw in films, that women accused men of selfishness. He hadn't cheated on her, beaten her or ridiculed her, so it must have been his selfishness, and Madeleine's conviction that life was hostile, that prevented greater happiness. And she was right: something terrible did happen to her. If you wait long enough it always does. At least for her it was sudden.

Life with Sarah would be different. Already Hartley was sure of that; when he was with her he wanted nothing else, and when he wasn't, she remained in his thoughts. He felt their love was so natural that the random meeting that had led to it assumed special significance for him. How she should happen to be standing by the Grafton Gully grave of Emily Keeling and he come walking by. It was surely meant to be, he told himself. Make the most of it whether it was fate, or chance.

Every morning and every afternoon he sent at least one text, often in the evenings also, as a sign he was thinking of her, and also, unconsciously, to prompt evidence that she was aware of him no matter where she was, or what she did. Sarah responded when she could, but increasingly his messages occasioned anxiety rather than giving pleasure. What if Robert became aware of the numerous chirpings? How would she explain them? Most of the time she left her cell phone turned off to minimise the risk, and that meant delays in reply that Hartley interpreted as unconcern on her part. It was the cause of their first argument, during a coffee meeting, when they sat at a table without shade, and next to them two women talked of bridge hands.

Maybe the disagreement wouldn't have happened if there had been time for them to go to the motel as Hartley hoped, but Sarah and Robert were expecting visitors from Hamilton who had notified them only hours before. She knew it wasn't an ideal time to mention the texts, but she'd promised herself she would. 'You know I like to keep in touch,' she said. 'I always do, it's just that often Robert's there, and if he hears he might ask about it. A few times doesn't matter, but you send so many and it could get difficult. That's why I sometimes turn the phone off, and it takes a while for me to get back to you.'

'Tell him then,' said Hartley. 'Why not? Tell him you've made a friend that you need to spend time with. Someone who's important to you. Tell him the truth.' For days he'd been looking forward to being with her on the bed in the sparsely furnished motel room, and now they would have just an hour in the café, and then she would go back to a semi-invalid and a fat-arsed couple from Hamilton.

'I can't always do what I want. You know that. I can't just live as if I'm not married, as if I'm not a mother and grand-mother.'

'You could, though. You could if it meant enough to you. We haven't got years and years, you know, and if we're going to be together then the sooner we make it happen the better.'

'I never promised I'd leave him.' She had never said it, rarely permitted herself to think of the possibility, for there was too much to lose. Hartley's face was intent as he leant across the table, as if to somehow compel her acquiescence.

'Call the director, that's what I say. I never hesitate to call the director if there's any argy bargy whatsoever.' It came from the table close at hand, but Sarah and Hartley didn't glance towards it, their own presence all that mattered. Even a sparrow, cheeky enough to perch a moment on the table, was no distraction.

'So this is all we're going to have, then,' he said in a voice both low and urgent. 'This is the lot. Chats and coffee, walks, a few motel shags, and then it's all over when Robert and you go back home. Thanks very much.' The sun was behind her, and he turned a little from the glare, dropping his eyes at last. It was the end of the first careless bloom of their affair, the beginning of its scrutiny for a future, the confrontation of diverging needs and expectations.

'How can we know what to do after only weeks? At our age you don't ditch everything all of a sudden. We've got lives, with a lot of other people involved.'

'Everyone's got lives.'

'You know what I mean.' She paused to let the bridge players pass close to the table, noticing automatically that one of them had a bag of soft Italian leather, just like those she'd seen in Florence and Sienna. 'We've got families, that's what I'm saying, other people we've committed to for all sorts of reasons.'

'Well, you have. I've got bugger all except a son on the other side of the world.'

'And a lovely home, and you're still working. And you've got colleagues.' She needed to go, but didn't want to mention this when it would so obviously reinforce his grievance. 'It's made all the difference recently,' she said, 'having time with you, having a part of life that's nothing to do with illness. It gets all so complicated, doesn't it? So you can't go back, or forward. Anyway, maybe we need to make more time for ourselves. I'm sorry about these people coming today. I'd much rather be with you. If I'd known earlier I would've said.'

'There's stuff we need to sort out,' he said.

'I know there is, and we will. We'll find our way through it.'

'Anything's worth it to be together, isn't it?'

'Yes, yes it is,' she said, not sure whether she believed it, or should say it, but wishing the present parting at least to go well, and they kissed quickly as they stood up. She caught the slight saltiness on his skin caused by the bright sun, and Hartley had the smell of her clean hair and the perfume she wore. It reminded him of the motel room where they were always close, and which wouldn't be visited that day.

———

AS SHE MADE PLUNGER coffee in the apartment later in the afternoon and spoke loudly enough to carry on a conversation with the Hamilton friends in the living room, she checked her phone: 'Sorry 2 grump luv u c u soon H.' Even as she came through to join the others, even as she took pleasure in seeing how Robert was animated by the presence of visitors, she imagined leaving them all, taking a taxi to Titirangi and arriving unexpectedly at Hartley's home. How the smile would come to his narrow face, how he would hug her as soon as the door was closed, how he would set himself to entertain and beguile her before leading her to the bedroom. She knew he loved her, and that gave a sort of fullness to everything she did, an odd significance to the most ordinary of tasks and routines, an awareness, even as she enjoyed time with her husband and friends, that elsewhere another man was thinking of her, waiting for her, jealous of all others who might be with her. Love is a spotlight in the mundane progress of the world, and those caught in its bright circle are always aware of it, always turning to it.

And he was thinking of her. In his high living room, amid the fine leather chairs and inlaid tables, the Cappadocian rugs and hand-blown Nelson glass, gathered by dead Irene and dead Madeleine, he was alone, with the television on mute, but flickering colours at the periphery of his vision in an uncomfortable resemblance to the drifting hachures of a migraine. I'll turn it off, he thought, but stayed put, just turning his head away. He imagined Sarah with Robert, and the friends whose visit had prevented his own time with her. Hartley had seen Robert twice: once when he'd been going to get his hair cut, a second time when Robert and Sarah had been on the lawn seat at the front of the apartments, and Hartley had been spying from his parked car. A big, ungainly man, he'd decided, who had spent a professional life scraping and probing in people's mouths. Maybe he'd been a bit of a sports star when younger, but he didn't look it now. Just how bad was the cancer? It was difficult to tell from what Sarah said, for her accounts were sometimes optimistic and sometimes not. Perhaps that was a reflection of the varying medical reports, but he wouldn't be in Auckland having such drastic treatment if it weren't touch and go. He might die quite soon, surely, and although Hartley didn't make a conscious wish for that, no incantations, no scattered runes, he thought how much easier a future would be for Sarah and himself if it happened. What would be a socially acceptable time before Sarah could remarry? A year? And even during that time he could find ways to be with her.

And if Robert didn't die soon? Then if she couldn't bring herself to leave him, at least she must put her husband to the side of her life. It wasn't easy, but love made it all worthwhile, Hartley was sure of that. You got one chance at the sort of perfect fit they made, and if you let that pass then what was left of life would always be in its shadow.

The next day was one of his work days at Hastings Hull: there were papers in his study that needed attention, but he stayed on the leather sofa, remembering the afternoon when Sarah had been there with him. So clear the recollection that she was almost a holograph figure, despite the mellow afternoon sun above the bush of the Waitakeres. Hartley turned off the television, and with no distraction went back to the sofa. What pleasure it had been to talk with her of their families and their differing histories, to prepare a meal for her and share it, to make an inconsequential choice of wine that was less so because they were together. And then to join her on the sunlit bed, and on later days on the smaller, more sequestered bed in the Spanish motel. Her head would fall back during their lovemaking, eyelids aflutter; her breasts would slide and tremble in the grapple. And afterwards ease and tenderness and talk again, and the understanding that things of greatest value are freely given in love.

Nothing must be allowed to stand in the way of such togetherness. He was nearly sixty and had at last an opportunity to live in a fashion so much richer than anything he'd known before. Most people weren't happy, but didn't admit it to themselves, or anybody else: just kept up a pretence which finally became so accustomed that challenge was not possible.

Chronologically, most of his life was over, and an account of the times during which he had experienced any transcendence, anything close to exultation, wouldn't even fill a kid's notebook.

Madeleine had a notebook. It was among her most personal things in the small drawer of her dressing table. Because of the suddenness of her death she'd been unable to tidy her life, no opportunity to shape, to hide, instruct, burnish or destroy. That drawer had been the saddest to go through: the jewellery in a soft pouch, the scatter of foreign coins and small batteries, a hair dryer guarantee, a mini-torch, cheque book, spare car key, lip salve, her father's watch, pills for ailments long forgotten, the instructions for use typed on the faded labels, crumpled tissues — some with lipstick smears, some perhaps once damp with tears. And the compact notebook, a freebie from their accountant.

It contained no dramatic revelation. Even in communication with herself, Madeleine was constrained. The entries were mainly a record of Kevin's juvenile progress — first steps, first words, oddities of affectionate behaviour. A muted expression of grief for her mother and father, some apprehensions concerning her health, and criticism concerning her workplace and her colleagues. A record of expenditure and a few lines of unattributed poetry about flowers, birds and spiritual release. References to exotic places, Lake Titicaca, Moldavia and Kashmir, to which she could voyage in imagination, perhaps, without the dangers of actuality. Little of the writing seemed to relate to recent years.

Hartley had been able to read it all in less than half an hour, sitting on the bed. Only twice in his wife's jottings was there any reference to him — both inconsequential and in passing.

Chapter Eight

They met in the same motel only two days later. The timing wasn't easy for Sarah, but she wished to show Hartley that seeing each other was important to her also, especially after his disappointment and the tension between them at Magnus. She gave Robert no elaborate excuse for going out. 'I need some time to myself,' she told him. 'I feel cooped up in here when the weather's good. Maybe I'll walk to one of the parks, even down to the wharves. I could be a fair while.'

'Go for it,' he said. 'I'd like to come, but I don't feel up to it.'

'You'll be okay?'

'Absolutely fine.' Actually he was having a bad day, but wasn't going to admit that. He disliked people who whined, or were clingy, and was dismayed to recognise those tendencies within himself since his health had packed up. 'I thought I'd give Donna a ring. Remember it's this weekend she's going up to check on our place. I'll ask her if there's any mail still going there. Since we had it redirected I reckon some stuff hasn't come. And I'll ask her to send up the rest of the family photographs and albums. I'm sure there's more in the sunroom cupboards. I'm going to have a real sort-out: something that should have been done ages ago.'

'So what hasn't been sent on?'

'Nothing from the share group, for example. Nothing from the practice lately either.'

'Right. Anyway, tell her I'll ring sometime when they're in Hamilton. I really miss the kids.'

'Maybe we should get a rental and drive down then?'

'Let's talk about it when I get back,' she said. Her mind was on other things: the chance to talk with Hartley, to lie with him hand in hand, or with her head on his chest, each of them concentrating on the other and keeping everything else away.

And later that's how it was. They shared everything, bounced from the deepest to the most superficial of concerns, spent time in indulgent and trivial disagreement as to the number of times they had been together. Sarah had a passing sense that the small, plain room was a stage set, that she could view them both from a high angle, lying on the bed together and talking the nonsense that lovers talk. Were they the one couple that came regularly there? Did others come and lie and talk and feel themselves the only people in the world, use the small ensuite and the folded towels — white, always white — smile at the Bible set square in the otherwise empty top bedside drawer, watch through the high window the dreamy passage of occasional clouds. 'Maybe the proprietors keep tabs on us,' she told Hartley. 'Maybe they have names for every couple, and fully understand their purposes.'

'They're jealous, if anything. The woman's always chewing,

and grips the credit card like an assassin. I've never seen thicker ankles. Other times it's the guy who's there and he always asks me how long I want the unit for, even though he knows the answer. And he wears tartan slippers.'

'They probably call us the geriatric couple,' Sarah said. She couldn't imagine any of her woman friends doing what she was, and so people would surely never think it of her. When she was with Hartley she never felt inhibited by her age. They were who they were, and that's all that mattered.

'Would you like to walk afterwards?' she asked. 'Go down to Aotea Square perhaps?'

'Afterwards,' he said. 'Afterwards we will. Anywhere you like — afterwards. I want to tell you about the dream I had. We were together on a sort of cruise ship. No, not that so much, ahhh, it was big sometimes and other times quite small. There seemed to be just passengers and no captain or crew. Everyone milled around without purpose and we couldn't find our cabin. You kept giving me room numbers, but when we'd go there the door wouldn't open, or the people inside would be pissed off with us. Someone we couldn't see kept shouting "Man the lifeboats!", but there weren't any, and no one was bothered about that. Everyone except us was young, and for some reason I had no shoes on, but was carrying a naked mannequin. Well, it started off naked and then later I noticed it had a sort of jester's costume.'

'Ah, the symbolism's pretty easy there, even for an amateur psychologist. The boat is life, and all the rest is evidence of lack of purpose, direction, or security.'

'You're probably right, but you don't analyse a dream when you're actually in it, do you? You just feel bewildered and a kind of anger that things don't make sense. I wanted to dump the jester, but people kept making a fuss of it.'

'I haven't got an explanation for the jester. Maybe your alter ego.'

'You must have strange dreams at times, too. Tell me one,' he said.

'Not very often, and they're just all nonsense, aren't they?'

'Come on, tell me one.'

There was one that had been with her sporadically for years, a dream that morphed in unpredictable ways, but had an essential core. And she told Hartley of it, the only person she'd shared it with apart from Robert. About the strumming noise and sense of desolation that were always the prelude, and the parade of outlandish animals across a barren, plague-coloured landscape. Troops of sullen creatures in some forced migration, at times reptilian and with Jurassic dimension, other times lemming-like hordes pushing inexorably on, yet with futility somehow apparent. Mostly she was just a disquieted onlooker; once or twice there was malice in a rush towards her and she woke calling out and twisting in distress.

'Weird,' said Hartley. 'I've read about recurring dreams. They must tap into some pretty basic fears and insecurities.'

'There are good dreams, though,' Sarah said, and although he didn't reply he squeezed her hand. Both knew they shared the idea that what they had was a dream. You woke from dreams, though, Sarah thought, but she didn't want to start on that.

Instead they made love, and from the outside the white building looked just the same: the large, dark number seventeen above the door, the empty, golden-lipped earthenware pot beside it, the thin aluminium rims of the windows, Hartley's red car between marked lines and shimmering slightly in the sun. Only twice in their meetings had that unit been unavailable, and they had felt a sense of grievance, even though the alternative was much the same. Surely number seventeen was theirs, always quiet and empty in their absence, waiting until they came to take possession.

'It's only with you that anything I talk about matters,' Hartley said. He lay on his back and aimed a finger idly at the smoke alarm on the ceiling above the bed.

'What do you mean?'

'I mean everything else is just practical, or window dressing, or passing time. Discussion with clients, neighbours, the woman handling vehicle registrations, or the guy coming to fix the security light. Every time I walk past Gillian at our reception desk I ask her how she is, how things are going, and pay no attention to her answer. We know nothing essential about each other, nothing at all. It's different with you and me. We say what we feel, don't we? We mean what we say.'

'Well, that's because we trust each other. Why would you bother telling the truth about your feelings to someone who didn't care about you?'

'I've always been lonely.' It was only when he said it that Hartley acknowledged it to himself. Yes, he'd been lonely amid the noise and activity of his Southland family, lonely when he came north, still lonely in his marriage and even after his son was born. He'd been lonely all his life and never got used to it, never understood that it was the reason for enduring dissatisfaction, until meeting Sarah.

'I suppose being misunderstood is a form of loneliness,' she said. But she didn't want him to start talking about Madeleine, who was vulnerable to criticism because she was dead. 'Anyway, no loneliness now,' she said, and put a hand to his cheek. 'Tell me more about what you've been doing at work. Tell me about the world of wicked lawyers. I guess it isn't really as unscrupulous as on television.'

'It's just as mercenary, but not as much fun.'

'My father always said keep away from lawyers at all costs.'

'Someone has to be charged for every minute of the working day,' said Hartley. 'Lawyers feel uneasy when on their own time: it's not a natural environment for them unless fees are accruing.'

'So you must be like that, too?'

'I'm a late-comer,' he said. 'I'm corrupted, but still able to recognise evil.' Hartley lay happily, began entertaining her with small parodies of his profession.

———

AND IN THE APARTMENT only walking distance away, Robert talked with Donna, cheerfully evading questions about his health and asking her, when in Hamilton, to ensure the lawn and garden man was doing all he claimed. He told her he wanted to complete the photographs and albums now that he was just sitting around most of the time. He told her yet again that he wanted to write names, dates and locations on the backs, otherwise in time the photos wouldn't mean much to younger members of the family, and Donna patiently accepted the repetition while adding to her grocery list. As Robert felt himself fading in the present, the urge increased to ensure he was established in the past. All of that he shared with his daughter except the last, which was not a conscious acknowledgement even to himself.

'But how are you in yourself, Dad?' Donna asked him.

'As good as can be expected,' he said. 'It's going okay. Mr Goosen's pleased with the way I bounce back after each round of treatment and he's optimistic, I think, about things long term. I've got to know them all there pretty well. We have a few laughs. There's a nurse who comes from Hamilton.' That an oncology nurse came from the same city as himself increased his chances of survival not a jot, but it was the sort of trivial connection that somehow humanised the situation in which he found himself, as did talking with Mr Goosen sometimes about dentistry. No one wants to be reduced to a mere walking ailment.

'Your mother's gone for one of her long walks,' he told Donna. 'It's boring for her here in the apartment. I'm going to suggest we go to the movies: there's some festival of French films on, and we've seen some good ones in the past.' He liked French films, not because of any sexual explicitness, but because they dealt realistically with life, and the actors looked like people you could stand beside in a shopping queue, rather than superstars. And you soon forgot that you were reading sub-titles.

'She'd enjoy that,' said Donna.

―――――

SARAH WAS HAVING A WALK; well, she and Hartley had just reached Aotea Square and were sitting in the sun, near the grass. A man in a beanie and faded gabardine coat, despite the heat, lay asleep on one of the wooden benches. An unwashed shimmer seemed to radiate from him. Closer, a young couple lay together on the dry ground, quiet and relaxed with their arms around each other. Hartley wasn't jealous, since he and Sarah had not long before been in much the same posture and mood. He remembered that in their foreplay she had laughed. Madeleine had never laughed during sex, nor had any of the few other women to whom he'd made love. It had intrigued and delighted him as a sign of her pleasure and his ability to create it, but he made no mention of that, instead talking of the variety of people that surrounded them. Despite some months in Auckland, Sarah was still surprised by the eccentricities on display, and the equanimity with which they were usually regarded.

'You should be in Queen Street late at night,' said Hartley knowledgeably, though he hardly ever was himself. 'There's some real weirdos around then. Street people drift into these night camps in the parks and under flyovers, sleep in cartons and toilets, light fires in the rubbish bins. There's a guy who runs along the railway platforms late at night dressed as a chicken, and an old Polish woman who attacks the park flower gardens and sings to the statues. There used to be a man who preached at midnight outside the Maritime Museum, going on about the apocalypse and pointing to angels in the sky, but he got beaten up and died.'

'It must be so sad. They've started out like everybody else, full of dreams and confidence, and find themselves with nothing.'

'Most are alcoholics, or druggies. Maybe both. A few seem mad, or deliberately act that way. It's a way to draw attention to themselves when they can't distinguish themselves in any other way.'

'They all seem to crowd around here — hang around the square and malls,' Sarah said.

'There's nothing enjoyable or worthwhile in their own lives so they want to come into ours.'

'I feel sorry for them.'

'I saw three guys kicking a taxi driver one time.'

'What happened?'

'They ran off, but I helped the taxi driver a bit. He called it in and the police came. Too late, of course, to catch them. They looked as if they were still schoolkids, and kept laughing and shouting all the time. They kept shouting — go home, fuck off home — because he was Malaysian, or Indonesian, I forget now.'

'You realise how lucky you are, don't you, when you see

things like that — the lives some people have.'

'I know how lucky I am,' Hartley said. 'I can hardly believe how lucky I am.' He held a hand up, fingers spread, not for a high five, but so she could match it with her own hand in a slow press, entwine her fingers with his.

'What else have you seen?'

'Here?'

'Other odd things, anywhere,' she said. She liked to be entertained, and he was quite good at it, enjoying her attention. Neither of them demanded absolute truth, and to tell each other stories delayed discussion of those issues that might entail disagreement, or force decisions.

'I saw this road rage incident last year in the carpark of the New Lynn supermarket,' began Hartley. 'A van clipped the wing of an Audi when it was backing out. He didn't do much damage, but he wasn't going to stop and the Audi owner came running across, wrenched open the door and grabbed him. The van guy tried to push him off and kept driving so that the car owner ended up being dragged along, but he wouldn't let go. I could see his suit trousers and the soles of his shoes. It all seemed to be in slow motion: the van didn't accelerate and neither of them said anything. After a few seconds he did let go, and the van roared away then, leaving him on his bum on the asphalt. I went over to see if he were okay, but he didn't say anything when I asked. He just got up, went to his car and drove away. There were three bags of groceries he'd dropped not far off, but he didn't do anything about them. Some kids, or some drifter, had a lucky find later, I suppose.'

'He could've been run over,' said Sarah.

'He was just highly pissed off, I think, and didn't trust himself to stick around afterwards.'

'A lot of things happen in carparks. Think how often they're mentioned in the papers for fights, bag snatches or burnouts. Places to keep away from, after dark especially.'

'I usually park in a far corner,' Hartley said. 'Less likelihood of a ding. People are maniacs with the trolleys.'

They were quiet for a time, the silence between them comfortable, watching the variety of people and activities around them — buskers, lovers, mothers, businessmen, tourists and the homeless, all citizens of the public space. The lawns with immature trees and raised kerbs: the brown, tiled central area with seagulls, some standing on just one red leg, and pigeons seeking handouts. A tall man with a green and white striped shirt and his suit jacket on his knee, sat leaning back with his eyes closed. A professional taking brief reprieve from the office, Sarah decided. Below the balustrade of the Box Café and Bar an older man with short, bare legs and a long nose, twisted balloons to resemble animals and offered them for sale, and rather closer a young Asian woman read poetry in a high, declaratory voice, hoping to attract custom for the books piled neatly at her feet. An Indian family, all with identical red shiny jackets, went up the broad concrete steps to the Aotea Centre, and an Island girl with a beautiful smooth, high forehead came down them. There were lots of young people, some in school uniforms, some of much the same age in mufti.

'Why aren't they at school?' Sarah asked.

'It's well after three,' he said. 'Mind you, schoolkids seem to be on the streets whatever the time these days. The teachers are probably desperate and send them out to do surveys or something. Anything to see the back of them.'

'God yes, look at the time. I hadn't realised. I have to get back.'

'Okay.' He stood up, ready to walk back most of the way with her; looking forward to it.

'I'll have to get a taxi,' she said. 'The time just flies, doesn't it.'

The taxi stand was close, and she was soon gone, without a kiss, but allowing her fingers to trail over his wrist and hand as he held the door. 'Bye then' was all she said. He watched the car until it turned out of sight. He tried to hold onto the mood they had enjoyed, but the place lost its gloss when she was gone. Solitary once more, and so placed at familiar disadvantage among his fellows, he walked back to his car at the motel without a word, drove home and saw to his own needs. He was accustomed to returning home to find it as he had left it, and he was sick of it. Nothing altered, nothing fresh, no welcome and no surprises, no questions about his day, or sympathetic placation of grievances perceived. No one to give him value in the life in which he found himself. He knew that most of the world's population would change places with him if they had the chance, but he found no satisfaction in that.

It wasn't quite true that nothing awaited him, for on the answerphone was a message from his doctor's receptionist, saying that before they supplied a further repeat prescription for his pills he needed to come in for a consultation. It had been some time since his last check-up, she said. Hartley thought it just a means of ensuring the practice received another payment: his own firm had policies with much the same motive. He disliked going in not so much for that reason however, as for the routine enquiry it entailed regarding any repetition of the incident that had led to the need for medication.

He hadn't said anything of that experience to Sarah, despite being open about almost everything in his life. The incident was quite clear and beyond denial, yet he was unable to own it. It was like an infection picked up while travelling, and attributable to a foreign country. He couldn't remember the motive, but had no difficulty in recalling the actions themselves. It was after a long and rather difficult day at work, and he'd gone to a café not far from the Hastings Hull office for a coffee. Other people had felt the same need and there was a queue. While he waited, Hartley had observed a man in a white Mercedes steal a parking space from another motorist, and sit smirking when he'd achieved it. Hartley had taken the metal sugar container from one of the café tables, walked into the street and hammered the bowl on the windows and bonnet of the car.

The matter never reached the courts, partly because of the efforts of his colleagues at Hastings Hull, partly because the driver had got out of his car and punched Hartley to the ground and then kicked him, so creating possible legal jeopardy for himself. The driver had acted in accordance with his nature, but Hartley's part was quite out of character. So there had been the assessment, the medication and certain reservations expressed concerning his well-being since Madeleine's death.

It had been unfortunate and unintended, yet Hartley had felt a heady release, an almost primal joy in giving way to his feelings for once and acting on impulse. The solid impact of the sugar bowl — crump, crump — on the painted metal, the astonished fury of the driver's face. Even the assault he suffered as a consequence hadn't diminished the satisfaction.

But he didn't want to spend time thinking about that. He watched television news that included a sad account of a girl murdered by a former boyfriend, and was reminded of poor Emily Keeling, beside whose grave he and Sarah had first met. 'Love me, I am dying.' Hartley decided to find out more. He was strangely drawn to the tragedy himself, but more importantly because Sarah had been intrigued, and he found pleasure in bringing such things for them to share. He left the television and went to his office and the computer. Information wasn't hard to find, and this time Hartley concentrated on the killer rather than Emily herself. Edward Fuller, a twenty-one-year-old brickyard labourer described as a 'young man who has hitherto borne excellent character'. After his death the police found a suicide note in his pocket, written in red ink.

'I love Emily Keeling as no one ever loved before,' he'd written, and 'I shall speak to her tonight and ask her whether she will have me without her father's consent. If she objects we will both die together.' And they did. He shot her twice in the chest with a British Bulldog 45-calibre pistol, then ran off and killed himself a few houses away. How painful and isolating love can be when it is frustrated. Hartley was fascinated by the all-consuming nature of it, aware of the positive form in his own happiness. He imagined young Edward, driven beyond rational behaviour into a brief place of declaration and terrible decision. It played out in his mind as a scene from an early black-and-white movie: Edward in a passion firing at Emily, then running in grief and panic past the wooden colonial houses until he couldn't bear what he'd done any longer, and turned the pistol on himself.

The tale was gothic, yet given banal authenticity by the careful, plodding detail of the reports, even of the clothes, the name of a passing boy, the shop sofa on which Emily was laid, the British Bulldog 45. Only the site of Edward's grave was unknown, unlike that of the girl he murdered. He lay grassed over somewhere, undeserving of any marker, yet refusing oblivion.

Poor bugger, thought Hartley, with some complacency, and he imagined how readily and sympathetically Sarah would respond to the further information. Tragedy at such remove is to be savoured.

Chapter Nine

Hartley was in the office at Hastings Hull, talking with a retired, unmarried school principal about an endowment to her former school, when the thought occurred that he had no photograph of Sarah; not one picture to remind him of the times they had been together and all those to come. Why the hell hadn't he taken some shots at Omaha Beach?

It wasn't unusual for him to be thinking of Sarah when engaged in other things — she was his default setting. He became slightly more animated, rocked a little and smiled as he talked to his client because he was thinking of having photographs of Sarah in his house. Some showing them together, some certainly only of her. Maybe one of her at a table at Magnus.

The teacher thought his increased enthusiasm was in response to the amount she mentioned for the endowment, and the magnanimity of her offer. She was neither prim nor authoritarian, but short, friendly and at ease. She warmed to Hartley. She liked his slim body and quick movement, the slight genetic tan of his skin and his unruly hair. He was masculine without being overwhelmingly male. She found big men offputting rather than imposing, although she was not without experience of them through both work and pleasure. Big men didn't age well.

'I have no children of my own,' said the ex-principal, 'so I'd like the money to benefit the young women of my school. I shouldn't say "my", but that's how I always think of it. One becomes identified with the institution after so many years. I have an open invitation to be on the stage at the end of year prize givings, but I don't go, of course.'

'I'm sure you'd be welcome. And would you prefer a stipulation that the endowment bear your name?'

'If you think that appropriate,' she said, pleased that he'd saved her from the need to make the suggestion and so reveal vanity. In a hundred years her name might still be heard, as a recipient came forward to receive the Jacqueline Huntly Dawe prize for head girl. She smiled at the thought of it, and Hartley smiled back, thinking of satisfaction less remote, and so they parted on good terms. The teacher imagined that she'd made quite an impression on Hartley. It was a misinterpretation of his warmth, but made her day. He was enamoured, she thought. He might contact her again perhaps on some pretext concerning the endowment.

Hartley wasn't a natural with a camera. The people in his photographs seemed so much farther away than they had appeared when he took the shot. He would do better for Sarah, though, he thought, and the following morning when he met her at the café the first thing he did, after their kiss of greeting, was bring out his phone and state his intention. He was surprised by her reaction to his enthusiasm. 'Why would we take photos, for God's sake?' she said.

'I'd like one at home. Something to remind me of you when we can't meet up.'

'Dangerous for me, though. Doesn't that occur to you?'

'Who'd know? Who would recognise you anyway? No one who came to my place.'

'Just one then, and by myself. Promise?' she said. He was right, and she too apprehensive. 'I probably look a fright anyway. You should've said.'

'You're fine as you are.'

So he took one with her sitting under the umbrella with her slight double chin showing because of the angle of her head, and one hand on the table by her cup and saucer. She did look fine, and despite the limit she'd set, he quickly took a couple more, but the first turned out to be the best, even though her smile wasn't completely relaxed. He wondered again if she coloured her hair, for the dark brown showed no traces of grey. 'No more now,' she said. He had no one to whom he was accountable, and could display what photographs he wished, but she found it hard not to assume he was subject to increasing guilt and apprehension concerning their meetings, just as she was herself.

'I should take some at the motel,' Hartley said.

'Oh, stop it,' she said.

'Let's walk a bit. The park maybe?'

'No, I can't. I've got to get back. Some people are coming soon.'

'I hate people coming,' he said. 'Other people don't deserve you.' He put a hand over hers on the table. 'Bugger other people,' he said with a smile.

'I know, I know, but there it is.'

'When do they go?'

'They're having lunch. Who knows after that.'

'I could stay in town, maybe catch up on stuff at the office, and see you when they've gone.'

'Too much hassle,' she said, 'and I'll have to get some dinner on once they've left.' They knew they were talking of the Spanish motel.

They kissed and parted, and Sarah was aware of a new emotion. When she sought to identify the feeling she realised with a small shock that it was relief. For the first time she was conscious of feeling better leaving him than coming to him. She loved him, but that affection was counter to all the other vital currents of her life. She walked faster, with greater determination, as if that in itself would provide an answer. Sarah was in the predicament so common in general that it was usually regarded with dismissive humour, but she felt an ache of growing anxiety. She could deal with it, she told herself. She could pull back to the safe ground of friendship and nobody would be hurt. There was still time to achieve that. She had gone just a little too far in companionship, as thousands of people did every day. With common sense and understanding it could be managed, as others had coped with the same situation.

Hartley drove back to the western hills and put the shots he'd taken of Sarah onto his computer. He decided that he would have copies of the first one framed and placed in the study, the living room and the main bedroom. That way, when he was at home, Sarah would be in sight for almost all the time he spent there. He could be looking at her photograph when he sent her a text, come back after being with her and feel he wasn't eating alone, glance at her face before he switched off the bedside light. And when at last she came to live with him, she would see the images of herself that had been his consolation as precursors.

He'd expected to dream of her, but rarely did. Dreams cannot be summoned, and perhaps his mind at night was eager to step from the traces of his fixation and roam at will, or maybe those dreams in which he and Sarah were united were in such core sleep and so deeply personal that he had no recollection. Only once or twice he woke in bed thinking she lay with him, and with a swiftly fading experience of eroticism.

How little fulfilment he had experienced in his life. He was almost sixty, but felt he had only recently begun to live with the richness and depth that was possible for the fortunate. Some people's lives seemed filled with variety and excitement that his own had lacked. He'd spent years in the drab repetition of commonplace travails and banal achievement that were entirely without note. Even the disappointments of his marriage were surely the lacklustre experience of so many other unexceptional people. Where was the joy and sustenance of affection? His father too selfish and uncaring, his mother too busy and partial to an only daughter, his wife too fearful of the world, his son too far away. Was there anything that stood out from the mundane and predictable?

There was Ruth maybe, the Picton woman — an odd incident abundantly clear, but as if it had happened to someone else.

It had been a few months after Madeleine's death and he'd travelled south for distraction. He took the ferry from Wellington and arrived at Picton on a blustery, afternoon feeling a little queasy after the voyage. A Maori taxi driver gave him advice regarding accommodation and drove him to a holiday park out of sight of the sea, 'Get a chalet if you've got the money,' said the driver. 'Some of the old cabins are a bit grotty, eh. You have a fair walk to toilets and stuff. I had one for a few weeks when I came here, before I got sorted. Yeah, a chalet's the thing.' Hartley had been impressed by his concern and helpfulness, and gave him five dollars in addition to the fare.

He did get a chalet, which despite its title was just a bigger cabin with its own plumbing and a small wooden verandah. On the table were three home-made dolls — small wooden figures without arms or legs, but with painted faces and knitted woollen dresses in assorted bright colours. A note said they cost six dollars each and were made by Amelia Talbot aged eleven. At the office Hartley had seen a line of similar dolls propped on the window ledge, and assumed Amelia was the proprietor's daughter, showing entrepreneurial promise despite an incomplete knowledge of anatomy.

He had left his bag in the chalet and taken a walk in the grounds in defiance of the weather, just to feel solid earth beneath him. The wind was getting worse and blew his hair back in such an unaccustomed way that it caused discomfort. He would walk down by the line of conifers and then go inside, he decided, but the wind noise in the pines was harsh, and bits and pieces from the branches were scattering down, so he turned towards several of the old cabins at the far end of the holiday park. They were army huts, no chimneys, like those he remembered on farms in Southland used for casual workers, or storage. The putty was cracked and lifting around their small end windows, some lower boards were missing, and each had a faded stencilled number above the wooden door frame. Number five wasn't a sleeper, for as he passed he glimpsed through the dull window a jumble of palliasses.

When he came from behind it, however, he almost stumbled into a man and woman fighting. The wind must have swept the noise of it away from him, because they were shouting at each other, pushing and slapping. The woman was thin and holding her own, verbally and physically, against a taller but equally thin guy with tattoos on his white, upper arms. 'Fuck you then,' she shouted.

'Fuck you, bitch,' he shouted back. Then they said something at the same time, emphatically but rendering both unintelligible, and the woman kicked his knee.

Hartley was too startled to intervene, but the man had become aware of him, and after a brief stare as a challenge, he limped away.

'Yeah, fuck off,' said the woman triumphantly.

'Are you okay?' Hartley said.

'Yeah,' and she sat on the single wooden doorstep of number seven, with an overflowing rubbish tin beside her from which the wind flicked and tumbled tissues like injured doves. She seemed not at all surprised, or curious, at Hartley's appearance. 'The bastard spent the last of our money on booze and weed.' She fingered beneath her left eye where redness showed the effect of a blow. 'Just when I thought we were getting ahead a bit, too.'

'Do you need to go up to the office? Call the police, or anything?'

'They don't want to know about domestics, and anyway it's all happened before and blown over. He's not so bad most of the time, until one of his silly-bugger mates gets shit for him.' She wore dark jeans, and no shoes. Her socks were yellow and grubby, barely reaching to her ankles. She put her arms around her knees and rocked a little on the step. 'Worse things have happened,' she said, mainly to herself, and because of the sound of the high wind in the trees, Hartley couldn't hear clearly.

'Sorry?'

'Nothing,' she said.

What had occurred had nothing to do with Hartley, but having been a witness to it seemed somehow to create an obligation, and he found it awkward to disengage and walk away. 'Well, if you need someone to back up your story . . .' He let the offer hang there.

'What's your name?' she said.

'Hartley.'

'What's your number?'

'Number?'

'Yeah, the number of your cabin,' she said. He took his key from his pocket and read out the number on the oval tag. 'One of the chalets,' she said. 'If he comes back, I might have to come up and get the police. They might want to talk to you. I'm Ruth, by the way.'

'Sure, okay then,' said Hartley, and he felt able then to go, leaving her sitting on the worn step of the shed with her inadequate yellow socks and pale shins below the legs of her jeans. 'I hope things work out,' he said.

She did come, later, but when there was still the last of the sun, and the wind had almost given up rocking the world. She stood on the chalet verandah, not much more than an extended step, and knocked on the door.

'Has he come back?' asked Hartley with some apprehension, and he looked over the rough lawns and shingle paths for her partner.

'Nah,' she said. He noticed that the bruise had come out below her eye and that she was wearing shoes. If there was no threat, why was she at the door?

'Well, that's good.'

'Can I come in?'

'Sure,' he said and stood aside. 'I've just had a bite to eat,' he said in needless explanation of the KFC boxes on the table.

Ruth picked up one of the wooden dolls still on the table. 'Jesus,' she said, 'that kid must have these coming out her ears. She gets her friends to help, you know. It's juvenile mass production. What do you think of the place?'

'It's just somewhere for the night, isn't it.'

'I clean a lot of these,' she said. That's what she did, she explained. She cleaned chalets and cabins when she was needed, and had one of the grotty ones to live in for very low rent, and had fallen behind even in that because the useless guy, Dylan, spent everything on booze and shit. 'I used to work in a garden nursery in Nelson,' she said. 'I liked that. I was good at it, but Dylan had aggro with the cops and we had to disappear pronto.' She looked about the room, and then voiced her conclusion. 'You're here by yourself.'

'Yes, just the one night, I think, and then heading on south.'

Ruth looked directly into his face and smiled. 'The thing is I'm absolutely bloody skint just now. Dylan's taken all I had, the bastard, and the Talbots here are kicking up about the back rent, though really I shouldn't be paying anything for that shitshack. I'm at my wit's end really.'

Hartley's reading was that she was offering him a shag, but he wasn't sure if he was right, or if he was, whether the offer interested him.

'I'm not rich,' he said. 'I'd like to help, but I'm not rich.'

'Two hundred bucks would get them off my back. I could keep you company for a while seeing you're here by yourself. I'd rather not be in my own place anyway just now.'

'I'd like to help,' he said. This was how it was done, he thought. Advantage taken of circumstance for mutual benefit and with a verbal indirection that avoided embarrassment. She came to him unhesitatingly, and gave him a quick hug. He wasn't tall, but she was noticeably shorter.

'Two hundred makes such a difference,' she said, stepping back, and then standing expectantly. He took his wallet from the table, and she watched with interest as he took out the notes. She folded them in half and placed the small wad deep in the pocket of her jeans. 'Thanks,' she said. She stood close to him, quite relaxed. The next move was up to him.

Whenever he thought about the whole thing afterwards, it was almost as if he'd taken the opportunity and made love to her on the hard chalet bed: the active sinuosity of her thin, almost breastless body, the short yellow socks, the bruise on her cheek bone, the brief exultation of both possession and release. He knew how it would have been.

It hadn't happened, though. She was desirable enough in her way: the way that willingness arouses lust. He wasn't even bothered by not having a condom, or the chance that Dylan might somehow turn up. What deterred him was a strangely powerful sense of random impermanence, that there was no future in it, nothing of consequence after achievement of ejaculation and her sense of obligation fulfilled.

They had sat down and had coffee together, Ruth talking cheerfully and profanely of her life when she realised nothing more was expected of her. She ate some of the cold chips from the KFC carton, but didn't touch the leftover chicken. She could tell a good story against herself, and even better ones against Dylan. She could've married an orchardist in Nelson, she said, but he was too old. He was well over sixty and told her he'd never had a woman before. He had three hectares of apples and nectarines, and a three-bedroomed brick house, but he was a bit odd and too old. He'd cried when Ruth decided not to live with him, but hadn't asked to be given back the nine-carat gold chain he'd bought for her during a weekend in Christchurch. 'I've still got it,' she said. 'I hung onto it even when I was really skint. I had a soft spot for the old bugger.'

Hartley thought at one point that she was working around to asking for more money, but she didn't. When she left, it was black outside. The holiday camp had no lights outside the buildings. He had offered to walk with her, but she said she knew the place backwards. She'd vanished quickly, without turning, or saying any more.

Ruth wasn't a name he thought would have suited her, but it did. She would probably still be there in the shed at the Picton holiday park, contesting with Dylan the loser and his silly-bugger mates as the wind buffeted the conifers, getting by as best she could, and laughing rather than shedding any tears. Hartley was pleased he'd given her money, even though she would have forgotten him long ago. So that he wouldn't do the same in regard to her, he wrote 'Picton Ruth' on a piece of notepaper and left it on the bench. Sarah would enjoy being told about Ruth, and he would make the most of it.

Hartley glanced at his watch. Sarah would be hostess now, at the apartment table with Robert and their visitors: acting out a life in which he had no part whatsoever. He was determined to change that, and was sure she felt the same. Sarah wasn't going to be like Ruth: someone flitting into his life by happenstance and then spinning away again. Someone driven by expediency into his company. She wasn't going to be like Madeleine either: someone he'd lived with, but never really known; someone physically contiguous, without becoming emotionally familiar.

The photo was great, though. He brought it up again on the computer and there was Sarah at the café table, smiling at him. At him. That was all he needed for the future.

Chapter
Ten

Almost all her life Sarah had been a good sleeper, reading a few pages of undemanding fiction, or magazine articles equally distanced from fact, and then switching out the light and rarely waking again until morning, but after her visitors had gone, her quiet routine with Robert re-established, and she was in bed with him asleep beside her, she felt an almost choking anxiety. It had little to do with the evening, except perhaps that the visit of their friends reminded her of the settled life that she and Robert had built with industry and care. It was different to the fearful apprehension that had come when Robert was first diagnosed with cancer. She'd thought nothing could be more harrowing than that, but now guilt had been added to fear. She was beginning to realise that the joy and pleasure she had with Hartley, had a counterweight of anxiety and confusion. Love had trapped her, and every way out demanded pain to herself and others. To continue the affair without intention to leave Robert was sluttish, and bound to end badly. To finish with Hartley was to break his heart and risk an irrational response. To leave her sick husband and go with Hartley was something affection, sense and obligation all absolutely rejected, despite its attraction.

She should never have gone to Hartley's place at Titirangi, or the Spanish motel. She should never have allowed the easy profit of their friendship to become the insistence of love. Yet how natural it had seemed, and how irrevocable it had become. She should have known that sharing love is not the same as understanding it in the same way, or seeking the same conclusion.

So Sarah lay in the darkened room, her mind a treadmill on which she pursued brief, phantom solutions, suffered over and over the pulsing apprehensions and angry bewilderment that she should find herself in such a predicament. She had to resist the urge to get up and wander through the apartment as some physical release at least. She squeezed her eyes closed and moved her hands on the cover, but there was no change in the rhythm of Robert's heavy breathing, except for a single cough now and again. What to do, what to do, what to do? Fuck. What to do? She was in some deep pit, and the light from the surface far above seemed to be dimming. She slept fitfully, and woke often to the problem worrying at her again with almost physical insistence.

The morning was some relief. The light, the routine activity, the presence of other people, provided some distraction. It was better during the day, and in typical human inconsistency she could even look forward to having time with Hartley. That's how it is with love and life. Tidal swings of confidence and insecurity. Things would work out, she told herself, as the alarms of the night subsided. All those involved were sensible adults with no wish to cause harm. Things would work out. Life could be lived on more than one level.

Sarah felt a special consideration for her husband, as if she'd already told him everything and been reassured by his understanding and forgiveness. She made scrambled eggs for his breakfast, and suggested that in the afternoon they go and choose some DVDs. Robert liked historical dramas and films based on real events. He had no interest in aliens, the undead or young Americans in dance academies and frat societies. Sarah was concerned that his cough had returned. It seemed to follow the chemo treatments, although Mr Goosen didn't think there was any connection. Just keep an eye on it, he'd said.

For the moment, however, Robert was more interested in his own memories than in DVDs or his oncologist's advice. Donna had couriered up the rest of the photographs, and Sarah was surprised by the intensity of his enthusiasm. He had increased his section of the table permanently for the sorting of them, and liked her to be involved as well. He wished to identify each of them, but often couldn't recall where or when they were taken, or who the people were. Sarah's memory was better, but even she found some photographs meant nothing, and could have been palmed into the folders by a complete stranger. This was especially true of the images taken on their overseas trips: vistas, classical ruins and quaint cobbled streets that evoked no more personal feelings than picture postcards, or the illustrations in a travel magazine. For Robert, those he did recognise conveyed a sense of transience, almost of loss, as he saw their earlier, more robust selves, smiling at him from the past. Some of the people had since died, some captured in the background of the photographs were utter strangers, as in the shot taken at Delphi that had in the left corner by a colonnade a fat man with walk socks, glancing their way with a self-deprecating smile. For that moment he was on the periphery of their lives, but transfixed there by the camera as a sign that he too had existed. His physical appearance was detailed, even to the sweat patches on his shirt, but his life a mystery.

Some of the most familiar pictures acted like swipe cards to open up whole rooms of memory. Robert found one of long-time friends Phil and Harriet standing together outside their house in Dunedin, and it brought back to him an oddity of experience that kept him silent at the table while a sun shower drifted across the city, and Sarah tried to convince herself that things were okay by the repetition of trivial and customary domestic tasks.

Phil and Harriet had recently moved to Invercargill and their Dunedin house was empty. Robert was to attend a conference at the dental school, and his friend invited him to stay at their former place. He could have gone to a motel. It wasn't the money, though in those days that was a consideration: Phil seemed keen to help, and sometimes it's a strengthening thing in a friendship to accept a kindness. 'The people aren't moving in until the weekend,' Phil had said. 'The power's still connected, and the phone.'

'Thanks, but I'll get a motel. It's only for the night,' Robert had said.

'Just take a sleeping bag and turn the water on. We did a deal and some of the furniture's still there. The key's on the nail under the garage window.'

So after the meeting in the afternoon Robert drove to St Kilda, let himself in and turned on the water heating. The house was rather forlorn, as if it realised that the family it had protected for many years had callously abandoned it. Robert and Sarah had visited often, and its hollow silence seemed strange to him. The house was vulnerable, like a woman caught still in her dressing gown and with hair undone. Most of the living room furniture was gone, leaving small indentations in the carpet and a red wine stain that had been hidden by the sofa. Harriet had cleaned the kitchen drawers and left them to dry, stacked on the bench. On the sills of the sunniest windows were a few dead flies, like currants against the white surface.

He could have spread his sleeping bag on what he knew had been the marriage bed, but instead chose one of the other rooms. He walked to the Thai restaurant and brought back a takeaway that he ate in the kitchen where the table and six chairs still stood. Normally he took milk, but he just used one of the tea bags from his case and sat with the mug at the table, looked over the agenda points for the next morning, and then rang Sarah, aware of the unusual taste of the tea as they talked.

'So how's the place looking?' she asked.

'A bit sad and empty, though the kitchen's still got table and chairs, and they must have sold the beds and mattresses to the new people as well.'

'Yes, Harriet told me. Good on her. Not all the old stuff seems to fit a new place. When you're back make sure you ring and thank them. It would be great if they could come up some time. Invercargill's such a long way away.'

'How's Donna?'

'She misses you. After school Sharon came over and they vanished into her room as usual, just coming out to ask for something to eat.' An easy pause. 'I miss you, too,' Sarah said.

In the southern summer the twilight is long, and after the call he'd sat and watched the shadows gather in the garden. There is a special and passing moment at dusk when, although the external light is fading, the colours of the flowers seem softly illuminated from within to form an aura. Sometimes the two families had come together for a barbecue in the garden, and although Robert tired of Harriet going on about her kids, they were good times and good friends. Sarah was right. It would be great to see them again.

He'd decided to have a shower, but the water had barely

warmed and he ducked in and out, not shampooing his hair. Even before he'd dried himself there was a hammering at the front door, and Robert tied the towel around his waist and went down the hall towards the uncouth and moving shapes he could see behind the stippled glass. He didn't open the door fully, and kept his body protected. Four people crowded towards him: a middle-aged couple in front and a younger pair behind.

'May I bloody well ask who you are?' It was the older man who spoke, short, thin and with a ploughshare of a nose. The woman beside him was taller, heavier and her neck trembled with the tension of the moment. Robert explained as best he could, and as he talked the edging pressure of the foursome forced him back until the door was open and all of them in the hall. 'I come to our new home,' said the man in theatrical astonishment despite Robert's story. 'I come to our new home to find the key gone and a naked guy inside. Jesus.'

'The Snowdens said it was arranged you'd take possession in the weekend. It was all okay by them for the night.'

'The house is ours, signed and sealed. We come to it and find a naked guy living here.'

'Well, I'm not actually naked, am I. I was just coming from a quick shower so I grabbed a towel. I can get dressed and buzz off in no time if that's what you want.'

But having taken possession of the moral high ground and established that Robert had at least a connection to the previous owner, the small man was no longer confrontational. 'Now you're here you might as well stay on,' he said with conscious largesse. 'Too late to go off finding somewhere now.' He introduced himself, Terence, his wife, Mary, his son, as something that sounded like Binge, and Binge's girlfriend, Amber. Binge was as short and spare as his father, but his nose was still growing so his features were in pleasant enough transitional balance. Amber was a head taller and a cheek wider at the arse of her jeans. She would end up a fat woman, but in the present could pass as voluptuous in a slightly ungainly way. Amber had a shy, low voice and a lovely smile as women with plump faces often do.

Robert knew no one called Terence: surely no people alive had the name. While Robert put his clothes on, the others carried in blankets, a couple of suitcases and a chilly bin. They took the six kitchen chairs into the empty living room. When he came back in, Robert wondered if another family member was expected. Terence and Mary put their blankets in the main bedroom and Binge his and Amber's in the room next to Robert's. They were going to spend a couple of days, Terence explained. A sort of tester of the new place, he said.

It was awkward at first: the five of them sitting on kitchen chairs and with nowhere to rest their arms, not even a table. Robert was the odd man out, but in the circumstances he couldn't go to bed without a minimum of social interaction. He enquired as to Terence's job, was introduced to the workings of the drainage board, and he asked a question that included the word reticulation. Good man, he congratulated himself. He didn't forget Binge. 'And what about you? What's your line, Binge?' He fudged the last word because he wasn't sure if he had the name right, but Binge made no correction. Turned out he was a helicopter pilot, and had been all over the place, even Colombia. Turned out he'd met Amber only three weeks before when she'd taken a scenic flight from Queenstown. Amber was from Adelaide and taking a break from her media studies at a polytech there. She and Binge were more interesting than Terence and Mary. Mary didn't do anything at all as far as Robert could make out, though she did have a rare condition that meant her toenails had fallen out, and more than once.

Binge said he was tired, and he and Amber went off before

ten o'clock. Robert thought that was his opportunity, but Terence made it clear that he had something of import to say. 'You'll want to hear this,' said Mary, and even straightened somewhat in the kitchen chair.

'Terence Berne, Terence Berne,' he said slowly and with an intent look at Robert. 'It doesn't ring any bells?' He leant towards Robert as if proximity would encourage recall, as if his face should strike recognition.

'I don't think so, no.' Terence's nose was more like a muzzle really, but his teeth were sound for a man of his age, and he had a good head of hair.

'The child in the stormwater drain at Tainui?' said Terence significantly.

'No, sorry.'

'It was news all over the country,' insisted Terence. 'On TV and everything.'

'He was interviewed,' said Mary. 'He would've got a bravery medal except several had already been nominated that year. Any other year he would've got an award, the superintendent said.'

'It burns into your soul, it does, something like that. You never forget it,' said Terence.

'Being a child makes it that much worse, doesn't it,' added Mary.

'Seven years old,' said Terence, and he was off on the story that was the defining moment of his life. All about the callout, and the manhole cover off, and the girl's body face-down with the parting in her hair between the braids bone white in the dimness. As he listened, Robert thought he remembered the tragedy, although it was years ago.

'He had two weeks' special leave because of it,' said Mary. 'We went up to my sister in Nelson, who's passed on now. She was always closest to me in the family, though not nearest in age.'

'You carry it always,' said Terence with a tinge of heroic dignity. He was disappointed that Robert didn't recognise him, and consequently thought less of him as a companion for conversation. Robert was able to say goodnight.

'I'll be out of your hair early tomorrow,' he said.

He didn't sleep well, being awoken at two and again at five by tempestuous lovemaking in the next room. It's never comforting for a man to lie alone at night and hear the physical pleasures of others. Amber worked up to a sort of pulsating moan that was synchronised with the loud workings of the bed. Her noise was almost unbearably sexual and quite involuntary, brimming with ecstasy and submission at the same time. Robert couldn't get to sleep again after the second time, even when the house was quiet. Binge might have been a helicopter pilot, but he was surely never closer to heaven than when clasped to Amber.

By seven, Robert was dressed and packed, hoping to slip away without disturbing the family, but although Amber and Binge were no doubt in deep, sated slumber, Terence and Mary were in the living room eating marmalade on toast, and in muted dispute over a colour scheme for the kitchen. Their single point of agreement was that the existing yellow walls were intolerable. 'You've got to be practical in a kitchen,' said Terence. His nose seemed slightly enlarged, though he may well have been telling the truth.

'The kitchen's not the place to get all house and garden,' said Mary. 'Yellow's for a sun room, or a conservatory.'

'Practicality, see,' emphasised Terence, 'cause there's all that plumbing, and work stations and storage. Yellow's not a colour for any of those, you'd have to say, wouldn't you?'

'I have to be on my way,' said Robert. 'Thanks again for putting up with me. Much appreciated. Phil must have got muddled about when you were going to take possession.'

'No harm done,' said Terence. 'These mix-ups happen.'

Terence and Mary had even come to the door to watch him walk to his rental car. The same door that showed clearly behind Phil and Harriet in the photograph Robert now held. He had to make a mental effort to break from memory and return to the present.

'We never see Phil and Harriet now,' he said to Sarah.

'What made you think of them?' She was testing the seal on the home-made chutney that was a gift from the previous day's visitors.

'This photograph,' he said, holding it up. Sarah came to his shoulder, put on her glasses and took the photograph. Robert was about to start talking about Terence and family, but his wife had no connection with them and he couldn't be bothered establishing their invisible presence in the picture. 'I stayed a night there once after they'd moved out' was all he said, referring to their friends.

'When you're feeling better,' she said, 'we'll take a trip and catch up with them and others as well. They still send cards, you know.' She gave the photo back. Maybe when she and Robert were back in Hamilton everything would be okay, everything as it had been. She would be home again and able to work things out. All that had happened in Auckland would be distanced and manageable. Please God.

Robert looked again at the house with its glass-panelled front door and the Snowdens smiling as they stood before it. He half-expected Terence to appear behind them, nosing forward, eager to recount again his experience of tragedy.

Chapter Eleven

Robert held up well after the next round of chemo, and Mr Goosen saw no harm in Sarah taking him home to Hamilton for a few days, provided he got the rest periods he needed and didn't get carried away with trying to do the little maintenance jobs that tend to arise during absence. The Goosens had a holiday home at Snells Beach, and he said there was always something needing attention. He took a little time to tell Robert of a minor plumbing job that he'd attempted to do himself, but which became rather tricky and necessitated a tradesman. As is the case with many high-achievers, Mr Goosen was impatient when others took his professional time with personal asides, but not averse to such musings himself. Robert wondered without rancour how many present cancer sufferers had been made aware of details concerning a defective toilet they would never visit at Snells Beach. Maybe the specialist's account of ballcocks and reflux was a deliberate attempt to humanise his image.

Robert and Sarah were glad to have the opportunity to be in their own home, and Donna brought the girls up for the weekend. For Sarah it was also an opportunity for space between herself and Hartley: time in which she could make decisions with some objectivity. Before she went she had the idea that she might confide in her daughter, but as soon as she was with Donna she realised that was impossible. Impossible because daughters confide in their mothers, and not the other way around. Donna sought counsel about weight gain, urinary tract infections and her husband's unwelcome enthusiasm for investment in a Queenstown property scheme, and she was oblivious to her mother's subdued mood, or accepting of it as a consequence of Robert's illness. What possible concern could her mother have other than her family's welfare?

'Dad's so lucky to have you,' Donna said. 'Imagine going through something like this all by yourself, and he was always so healthy until the prostate. Always the fit guy.' They were watching the two girls using playing cards to build houses on the carpet. Sarah wondered how she could ever have explained to them why she and Robert were no longer together, if that had happened.

'He's resilient. He's always been strong-willed,' she said.

'Oh, he'll be fine,' said Donna. 'It's amazing what they can do. The reports have been pretty good, and I think he's realising now that there's more to life than just success with the practice. I know he's got plans to take you overseas.'

'Yes, he's pretty keen. It's nice to have an aim beyond everything that's going on at the moment, and he needs something to keep his mind busy.'

'What does he do all the time?'

'He watches a lot of television,' said Sarah. 'We do try to get out, of course, but it's all centred around the treatment. And he's got really keen on cataloguing the photos. You know what he's like.'

'What do you do?' asked Donna.

As she answered with half-truths and evasions, Sarah watched her granddaughters playing and contrasted their innocence with her own duplicity. There she was lying to her daughter, as she lied to her husband. She'd never before sustained deceit for so long and its effect was painfully corrosive. Returned to her home and the pattern of accustomed life, she found it difficult to understand how she had become Hartley's lover. When she wasn't with him, the whole affair seemed something oddly imposed on her by external agency. She loved him in a way that was distanced from the rest of life, and was dismayed when that division couldn't be maintained. She blamed him only for his unwillingness to see they must let each other go. How clear the need for that was, when she was home and with her family. How incongruous the affair with everything else important in her existence.

She found Hamilton and the old life no real escape from her predicament, and every day there was something to remind her of it, in addition to Hartley's texts. Each television programme seemed to centre on infidelity, and every magazine article to include it. Her friends Katherine and Gay came for coffee, and took a voyeuristic satisfaction in sharing the news that their mutual acquaintance, Philippa, had been discovered shagging the local golf professional in the clubhouse toilets. Sarah forced herself to join in the laughter.

'Maybe her home life's been very unhappy,' she said. 'I've never quite known what to make of her husband, what little I've seen of him.'

'Oh, come on,' said Katherine. 'She's just being a slut.'

'Why would she do that, for Christ's sake?' exclaimed Gay, delighted that Philippa had provided such gossip. 'And what's he got going for him, apart from a big driver.'

That night Sarah had a dream that she was in the Spanish motel room making love with Hartley, when she saw through the window Katherine and Gay coming towards them, and with Robert, Donna and her granddaughters close behind. Further back there was a glimpse of her mother, and Janine, her hairdresser, even Mr Goosen, smiling and at the same time smoothing back his hair, moving in the unhurried way that the most successful have. In reality there was no window by the motel bed, but the dream had its own complete conviction. She had attempted to push Hartley off her, scrabbled for the sheet to pull over herself, but he'd continued to pump ecstatically, raising himself up on his arms for better leverage, his eyes closed and lips drawn back in fierce concentration. Her family and friends crowded through the door with laughter and exclamations as if arrived for a surprise party, and grouped around the bed joyfully. 'Slut, slut, slut,' cried Katherine, and the others laughed and clapped, except for the two girls, who stood wide-eyed. Sarah had tried to turn away from them, and woke herself in the desperate effort, flinging an arm across the bed and striking Robert, who woke with a gasp. When he'd turned back to sleep, Sarah lay with her mouth open, trying to slow her breathing, sweat on her upper lip, as the dream images faded, but the reason for their grotesque posturing tightened its grip.

During the time at home she spent many hours in her garden, the physical effort providing some release for the growing tension. When she was alone she felt less afflicted with guilt and worry than when with those she was deceiving. The plants were neutral and incapable of judgement. The roses were as voluptuous as ever and grateful for her care. She spent most of one afternoon sitting by the cherry tree, repainting the outdoor seat.

At times she was able briefly to forget her predicament,

but the return always came, and with an emotional thud. She knew that the opposing elements in her life could not much longer be kept apart and that the clash would be fearful when it came.

———

WHILE SARAH WAS AWAY, Hartley tried to occupy himself with work, with walks, gardening, his share group and television. He rang his son in London and was pleased to learn that the courier business was doing okay, if not exactly booming. But nothing put Sarah from his mind for long. His love for her was a sort of noose that brought him back always to their relationship. Was she thinking of him? Was she wishing to be with him rather than wherever she found herself? Was she lying with her husband in accustomed and tender embrace? Sarah never talked of sex with Robert, and although Hartley was eager to know if they fucked, and on whose instigation, he was never crass enough to ask. She spoke quite freely of her husband's illness and treatment, however, and Hartley assumed Robert hadn't been up to sex for a long time. Yet thoughts of them together were painful, images in which a fully recovered Robert claimed his wife in every way.

Hartley was aware that she became exasperated if he sent texts too often, but couldn't stop himself when she was away, became unsettled when she didn't reply. Surely she too thought that whenever they were apart life lacked the full spectrum of emotional colour. He masturbated in view of Sarah's photograph, but felt sadness as a consequence rather than pleasure, or even relief. Love became a lingering unhappiness that put all else of life at a distance.

A dispossession in which he couldn't be fully content, or at ease, except when he was with her.

Oddly, however, even within this preoccupation there came the decision to visit Madeleine's grave. He'd rarely been, and not at all since meeting Sarah. It wasn't that he didn't care, more that he believed death to be absolute, and nothing to be gained by moping beside buried bones. Maybe the visit was a subconscious wish to prove to himself that his love for Sarah deserved no reproach. Madeleine had been dead for over two years, after all. They'd made the best fist of things they could, given their natures.

Sunday morning seemed an appropriate time, and he took with him not flowers, although the garden possessed many, but the greenery that Madeleine had loved to have within the house. Arum leaves, sheaves of angelica, even the furred and partly furled koru of the ferns beneath the kauri and beech trees. Although it wasn't a work day, the traffic was heavy and it took him half an hour to reach the lawn cemetery. Dark glasses and internal climate control were some insulation from the heat and hassle, but it was still a relief for Hartley to turn off from the lines of Sunday recreation-seekers, and enter the peaceful domain of the dead.

He parked with only a few companion vehicles, and carried his foliage with him in a supermarket bag. He thought he knew the location of Madeleine's plot, but his confidence was misplaced. There were regulations regarding the nature and height of the gravestones in the new part of the cemetery, and the uniformity of low memorials, and their increased number since he'd last visited, confused him. Eventually he found Madeleine. The granite plaque had lost its sheen, and like so many others had been shat on by birds, with no intention of desecration. He should have brought a cloth and bucket of water, and he had no vase. Two rows away a hose was running, its rotating spray making a pulsating hiss, its snakish length bright green in the dry grass. Hartley followed the hose to the source, but that was a junction in a metal box set below ground level and with no provision for visitors to fill containers. Not far beyond the range of the spray a thin woman in light blue jeans and a white T-shirt sat cross-legged by a grave. He walked back and asked her if she knew where there was a water point. 'There should be a place to get water for flowers, shouldn't there?' he said.

She stood up, tears glinting in the sun, and walked quickly away. 'I'm sorry,' said Hartley to her retreating figure, and she flicked a hand up behind her back, though whether in accusation, or absolution, he couldn't tell. From a long way away came a sound like someone chopping wood, and for a short time the woman's steps were synchronised with that and then fell out of time. He watched her diminishing among the graves. 'I'm sorry,' he repeated, but softly, knowing she wouldn't hear. She walked past his car and the few others, and went on through the headstones up the slope towards the more haphazard and varied shapes of the old part of the cemetery. 'Be like that then,' he said, his voice even more subdued. What had he done except ask a simple question.

Hartley stood at the edge of the water spray and held his handkerchief out as far as he could to receive a little on each rotation. His trousers and shoes caught a bit as well, but the handkerchief became sufficiently wet for him to go back and clean Madeleine's memorial. And without compunction he took a metal container from a grave three or four along and used it for the foliage from their home. Without water it would soon wither, but for the moment the leaves were upright and glossy. He felt no overwhelming sense of loss as he stood at his wife's grave, but there was sadness that they had lived together for so many years without either being able to provide what the other needed. They had remained separate even in the bond of marriage. They hadn't been slothful, cruel or unfaithful, just inwardly disappointed that life was no better together than it had been alone. Kevin, though: without the marriage he would have no child, and he loved his son. During his childhood Kevin had provided a shared focus for Madeleine and Hartley, so it wasn't true the marriage was a failure. 'He's doing fine,' he told the grave. 'He's in London with a nice girl and a business. He seems happy. We keep in touch. We did all right with Kevin — we can say that.'

As Hartley walked back to his car, the wood chopping over, the noise of the water jets diminishing to a whisper at his back, it was Sarah who was in his thoughts. With her the life he had always hoped for was surely possible. They were a fit for each other in every way. At the car, Hartley stood with the doors open for a short while to allow the light breeze to take the worst of the heat from the interior, and then got in, started the engine, put on the air conditioning and a Sibelius CD. Sarah had said she loved Sibelius, too, especially the *Karelia Suite*, and that hadn't surprised him. They were a fit: he knew it from the beginning.

Halfway home he realised that he'd left his sunglasses hidden by the greenery on Madeleine's grave, but he decided he couldn't be bothered going back for them. They could stay there with the leaves and stems in a stolen pot, with the plaque clear and clean above them, with the woman in blue jeans in tearful retreat through the graves, for he planned no return.

———

WHEN SHE CAME BACK to Auckland, Sarah didn't agree to a meeting at the motel, but said she would meet him at the Magnus instead. As Hartley watched her walking to his table, he told himself she was just the same, yet sensed in her a purpose not entirely romantic.

'How was the time at home?' he said after they had briefly kissed. 'It's wonderful to have you back. I miss you, you know. All the time I miss you.'

'We need to talk,' she said. 'Look, all these texts are becoming too much for me. It's getting so I don't like to have the phone with me, and I've run out of excuses when Robert asks who's been in touch. We're sitting there together a lot of the day, you know that, and it's odd if it's turned off all the time. He used to check it for me quite often, and now he probably finds it strange that I'm not keen on that.'

'I like to hear from you, to know that you think of me sometimes, and so you know I miss you.'

'Well, it's more likely to make me worried. It's okay for you. You're alone at home, or at work where it's nobody else's business who's in touch with you. It's different for me.'

'So you could set me a ration then, a limit. Maybe a text once a day, but only after you've sent an all-clear signal. Maybe on alternate days, or when you're in the loo.' Even as he said it, he regretted the sarcasm, but couldn't stop himself.

Both of them were quiet for a time, looking away, Sarah moving a teaspoon back and forth on the smooth tabletop with an index finger, Hartley leaning back in excessive and counterfeit relaxation. The noise of others around them seemed to swell to fill the silence created.

'Let's not be like this,' said Sarah finally. 'Even if it's not working, let's not be this way with each other.'

'It's not working because we're not together. You know that. In your heart you know that. It's a hell of a situation, I know, but nothing will change until you make up your mind whether you want to be with me or not.'

What did he expect of her? That she was going to leave her

husband while he was ill and go off with a man she'd known for three months? That because they loved each other, all the other people she loved became irrelevant, all other ties negligible? That the occasional peaks of pleasure in a motel room outweighed loyalties and shared experience over more than thirty years?

'I can't start on it all today,' she said. 'You're right that we have to sort things out, but not now and not here. I'm just not up to it. Going home was good, but also unsettling, and Robert starts more treatment tomorrow. Can we just leave it?'

'But that doesn't solve anything, and you said you wanted to talk.'

'That was the texting, and anyway, the whole thing's too important to talk about sitting here. We need to have time privately together, and before that have a chance to get everything clear in our own minds. I know I can't go on like this. It's different now somehow.'

'How's it different?'

'It just is.'

'Do you love me at all?' he said. He was looking at her again, wanting her to meet his gaze. He had never thought it necessary to ask before. Abandoning his previous pose, he was all forward intensity once more.

'I do,' Sarah said. 'That's what makes it so difficult. I love you and other people as well. There's life with you and other lives, too. We're not Romeo and Juliet you know, not at our age.'

'Sure, okay, but there's a choice you—'

'No, I won't talk about it now. I said that. Not here and not before you think it over,' and having interrupted him, Sarah stood up and briefly touched his wrist. 'But you're right, we do need to talk. Soon we will, I promise. Now I've got to go.' As she walked from the café, turning her hips a little in the confined space between tables, Hartley felt that something between them had been stretched farther and farther, and then snapped with an almost physical impact.

He stayed sitting there, aware now that Sarah had gone of things around him: the marshmallows left on a saucer at the next table, one white, one pink, the bald man laughing close by, the Chinese waitress with an appealing smile and slightly bowed legs, sunlight a-glitter on the glass fronts of the food trays. All that and more came flooding into the emotional space created by Sarah's absence. And as well there began in the left periphery of vision the drifting dislocations that presaged a migraine. The lettering on the menu board began a vibratory deconstruction, sounds seemed at a greater remove. Bugger, he thought. He needed to leave straight away, get home before the light became unbearable, before the pain above his left eye and the vomiting began. Bugger. Soon the world would begin a dancing dissolution.

'Not your bloody headaches again,' his father used to say. 'Take a bowl to bed with you for Christ's sake, then, so you're not sick on the blankets or the floor. It's time you grew out of them, isn't it? The others don't seem to have any trouble.' As he drove home, Hartley deliberately thought about his father, not at all from affection, but in a futile effort to delay the onset of the migraine.

His father in gumboots hosing down the concrete floor of the milking shed, or feeding out, turned back in the tractor seat to watch the trailer. His father's constant, indiscriminate swearing at both stock and inanimate objects on the farm, his father eating as he read the paper, with the unexamined food just a form of necessary refuelling, his father's complex expression of embarrassment and derision at any display of finer feelings. His father dressed for the races in a suit long become too small for him. His father strangling a Friesian cow by ineptly dragging it from the bog with a rope tied to the tractor. His father's patent disregard of his mother's feelings. His father's dismissive impatience when Hartley didn't measure up to any job at hand. 'For Christ's sake, boy, give it here.'

His father's greatest pleasure seemed to be in the misfortunes of his fellows. Despite himself, a slight, hard smile would crease his mouth when he heard that the bank had foreclosed on Alistair Prue, that old Mrs Patchett had driven off Coal Pit Road, that lightning had struck the newly renovated war memorial, or that the youngest Hargest girl was pregnant to a rabbiter from Omakau.

Hartley couldn't recall his father ever touching him with affection, or asking much of him except to perform a duty. It'll all be the same in a hundred years, his father used to say to curb any enthusiasm. Whatever else Hartley had to endure in life, he hoped not to become like his father.

Chapter Twelve

The next day was a Wednesday, one of the two weekdays on which he still went in to Hastings Hull Legal Associates, but Hartley rang and said he wasn't up to it, told Gillian that his appointments would have to be rescheduled. He lay in bed with the curtains drawn until after nine, then got up, had a cup of packet chicken soup, sat on the leather sofa and worried about Sarah and himself. After the migraine attack he was washed out and knew he needed to just sit with a clear mind, but whatever train of thought he started on always led back to Sarah. Sarah at the exhibition of Samoan art, walking with him in the city parks and streets, beneath him in the white motel, talking and laughing with him in the café, making a trio with the white dog on Omaha Beach, sitting with him and looking over the varied green bush to central Auckland that one afternoon, just as he was doing now. A mere turn of his head and he could see the photo he'd taken of her at Magnus, despite her reluctance.

It would be over, unless he did something to ensure the best outcome for them both. If he weren't man enough to take command of the situation then all the forces of inertia, anxiety, irresolution, would bear down and suffocate their love. You had to fight for the most important things even if you lost, otherwise you never knew if they were possible.

Hartley understood that it was a more difficult and exacting decision for Sarah than for him. She had a sick husband, a daughter and grandchildren, a comfortable, long-established life of activities, friends and prospects, while he was single, dissatisfied even with the memory of the woman he'd married, though only recently had he admitted that to himself. Yes, he must be insistent, make the things happen that would allow the two of them to be together. If he failed to do so, the random drift of life would separate them.

It occurred to him that what he imagined would be so fulfilling with Sarah, he had never met in the marriages of others, or his own, but that increased its value rather than proving attainment impossible. What he was determined to avoid was the barely suppressed impatience that his father showed towards his mother, and the meek, but resolute, disappointment she bore in response. What did his own son think of his parents? Would that show whether Hartley had learnt anything from the example of his father and mother? He would ring Kevin, talk to the only family who shared in his life at all now. What time would it be in the great grey expanse of London in winter?

Kevin was there, on the point of going to bed, but happy to talk.

'You got the money for your birthday?' Hartley asked him.

'I did. Thank you. I've been meaning to get in touch, but it's been pretty hectic here. My best driver left all of a sudden and I've been in the vans as well as keeping up with the paperwork. They go on about all these guys unemployed, but it's still so hard to get good people. So many are fucked up one way or another, or they just want to make a few pounds and piss off over the Channel.'

'How's Anna?'

'Good, thanks. She's still doing community social work with the elderly. In time I hope she can come into the office for me full-time. She sees some real characters. You have to laugh or cry, she says.'

'So when do I get an invitation to the wedding?' Hartley's tone was light, and his son laughed.

'Well, it'll happen. No doubt about that. It'll happen when we're not so damn busy, and her mother's not good at the moment. Some respiratory thing they don't seem to be able to get to the bottom of. When she's come right we're definitely thinking about it.'

'Still, you're happy together and that's the main thing.' Hartley wandered onto the deck with the phone to his ear. In a puriri tree a tui flicked from branch to branch, the tuft of white throat feathers glinting in sunlight. The Sky Tower and the centre of Auckland were clear, but subdued at that remove. The fragrance of the bush moved up the slope. He could imagine the dark cityscape about his son's flat as they talked, but didn't ask about it. London in winter wasn't unknown to him.

'Anyway, Dad, you don't have to wait for a wedding invitation to come over to see us. Get on a plane. Get yourself over here and use us as a base to have a decent holiday.'

'I might just do that,' said Hartley, and after a brief pause, 'I've met someone here recently. A really nice woman.'

'Good on you.' Kevin didn't sound surprised, or especially curious.

'I'm hoping it will work out. We get on well together.'

'Bring her over,' said Kevin. 'You're both welcome.' It was typical of his open, uncomplicated way. The inhibitions and anxieties that marked both Madeleine and Hartley seemed to have passed him by.

Hartley wanted to ask him personal things, but it was too late in their relationship for that, too great a distance both physically and emotionally.

'Anyway, it's nice to have someone to share things with. Her name's Sarah.' Kevin didn't say anything, but it wasn't a hostile silence. 'So the business is ticking over okay?' Hartley asked, after the pause. 'Aren't things supposed to be pretty tough there?'

'Actually we're getting by not too badly. As I said, keeping good staff is the main bugbear. There's plenty of business if you're prepared to get stuck in. I've got four vans now.'

'That's really good.'

He knew Kevin was a grown man and was talking to him as such, but the image he had was of a boy: a quiet boy of modest accomplishment who had never demanded, or received, special attention. Hartley would have liked an assurance that he'd been a good father, better than his own, but you don't ask that of your children. He took comfort that Kevin had never accused him in any way, though that was no guarantee grievance didn't exist. He talked of mundane things with his son on the other side of the world. No more was said of Sarah. He kept the image of his son as a schoolboy, and was somehow rendered both sad and happy. He remembered the Christmas they had bought Kevin a new bike. He was thirteen, but he came into their bed and hugged them both fiercely. Hartley could see him still: smiling, his hair roughed up, his thin wrists well beyond the cuffs of the red pyjamas he was outgrowing.

'I'm really pleased things are going well for you,' Hartley said as the phone call ended. It was his way of telling his son he loved him. Love for their son was the most significant bond that Hartley and Madeleine had shared: something endorsed and understood, when so much else of each other's character was difficult to access.

Hartley had wanted to protect his son, give more than his own father had offered, but from an early age Kevin had wanted to be with other kids, and usually at their homes rather than his own. Hartley had always supposed that was natural enough, but it had disappointed him all the same. He wished he had a recollection of any particular occasion on which he'd accomplished something at least mildly heroic in his son's eyes.

Often when he was recovering from a migraine, Hartley found a walk helped. So after the phone call, he took a cap bearing the name of a golf club he didn't belong to, put on the yellow and white sneakers that unbeknown to him Sarah disliked, and walked into Titirangi. Trees and ponga grew close to the road, and shaded him as he went, and when he looked into them the spaces were dark and soft like cows' eyes. Two or three steps into that bush and you vanished from the world. He didn't hurry. He still felt shaky after bouts of puking in the night, his stomach muscles tender from the spasms, but his head was clear and he was starting to think about food without total repugnance. Few cars passed, and when they did, he kept well to the side, walked resolutely with eyes ahead so drivers understood he wasn't looking for a lift. Most of the time it was so quiet he could hear bird calls and the sound of his own footfall.

In the weekends Titirangi was a favourite spot for city people to have lunch, or a coffee, but on other days it had only the natural pulse of local trade and people. Hartley chose an outside table at his usual place, which was set back somewhat from the traffic noise of the main road. The table had a wobble, so he shifted to the next, and explained the reason when the waitress came with his hot chocolate. They knew each other by sight and chatted briefly. 'We have to take them in after closing,' she said of the tables and chairs, 'otherwise we'd fix them down permanently. People steal them, you know. People steal anything, don't they. It's the council won't let us fix them down for good.'

Most of the tables were unoccupied, and so Hartley was mildly surprised when a tall, young guy came and sat down opposite to him. At first he thought it could be a client from Hastings Hull, although most he dealt with there were older, at an age to require his realm of expertise in conveyancing and business practice, and with sufficient resources to afford it.

'Another beaut day,' the man said. He wore shorts and sandals, and stretched out his brown legs until they reached beneath the table and out again. His shorts and T-shirt were of good quality, but slightly soiled at the neck and the pocket openings. He carried no number to show he was waiting for an order.

'It is,' said Hartley, and he waited for an explanation.

'Tim,' said Tim. He stretched out his arm to shake hands.

'Hartley,' said Hartley. He accepted the offer without enthusiasm.

'Most days I take up a challenge to come to a place like this,' Tim said. Hartley just smiled. He knew the guy would come round to talking of God, or asking for money. Probably both.

'The Almighty tells me to go out and bear witness to Him,' said Tim. 'He inspires me to make Christianity relevant in the modern world. It's a form of declaration. An urban pilgrimage if you will.'

'Actually I'm having a bit of quiet time. Recovering after a stinking headache.'

'I know the feeling,' said Tim. 'So many pressures today, aren't there. Is there anything that you'd like to share? Anything you'd like to talk about?' Hartley noticed that he had a small, closely tended goatee beard, so reduced and fair that it blended with the mild suntan of his face.

'I'm in love with a married woman,' said Hartley. 'That's my problem. I'm in love with a woman who loves me, but can't be with me. That's my problem.'

'Well, we can share in a meaningful discussion about that. God knows a lot about love. Jesus is all about love.'

Tim leant back in the sun, put his hands behind his head as if he expected to be a listener for some time. He withdrew one long, bare leg from beneath the table and crossed it on the knee of the other. But Hartley didn't want to give any detail. He wanted for once to state the truth aloud to someone, not receive any advice, or opinions. If he wasn't able to talk about it with his son, he wasn't going to tell a wandering pseudo-Christian evangelist what was on his mind. He'd just wanted to say it aloud, establish it as fact by having someone hear of it.

'I'll tell you what,' he said, taking out his wallet, 'I give you twenty dollars for a drink and bus fare back to the city, and you go and convert somebody else. How's that?' His tone was not vindictive.

Tim started to speak, but Hartley held up one hand with palm towards him, and the other with the twenty-dollar note. 'Now or never,' he said gently, and Tim stood up, plucked the note, mouthed 'Good luck' and walked to his vehicle in the small parking area only a few steps away. He looked more like a surfie than a missionary, and perhaps he was. It was difficult to imagine him in theological conversation with the Almighty. Tim's car was a battle-weary Mazda MX-5 with the wipers daubed with green house paint to delay the rust, but the seat covers were new, resplendent with rococo roses entwined with dragons. At least he didn't need a bus fare, and he lifted a casual hand to Hartley, equal to equal, as he drove away.

What had he said? Is there anything you'd like to share?

Hartley was reminded of Rory Menzies, the counsellor, who had asked him the same thing when he went with Madeleine to seek advice. Menzies hadn't understood that for Hartley the lack was not of things to share, but of people he felt he could confide in. He was an amiable enough man, but Hartley's sharpest memory of him wasn't of insightful counsel, but of his ginger eyebrows and hair, the consequence of a gene said to be prevalent among the Scots. Menzies had talked a good deal about sharing, especially within marriage, but Hartley and Madeleine had long before established frontiers for their intimacy, and were uneasy with any negotiation for change.

Hartley thought of having a second drink and perhaps even a sandwich, but decided against both. He would make something light for himself at home. As yet he didn't feel fully recovered. He was pleased that he'd talked to Kevin and been invited to visit. And Kevin seemed sincere in his response to the news his father had found a companion. There were so few people Hartley could tell about Sarah, and yet he felt a longing to do so. He took his cell phone and sent a text to her, asking when they could meet, saying how much he loved her, that he'd spent a lot of time thinking about things. His need to be in touch was greater than his awareness the message might create difficulty for her. His hand was trembling on the table. Maybe he wouldn't walk home, but take a taxi back. Maybe he wasn't right yet. The full sun was lulling, and he closed his eyes and consciously relaxed. Without images as competition, the sounds around him became more distinct and individual: cars at a distance, the soft flap of the umbrella in a puff of wind, the murmur of voices from the service area of the café. Even with his eyes closed he would know if Sarah replied — the unobtrusive ring accentuated by the phone's vibration on the wooden tabletop.

With his eyes still closed he counted slowly to twenty,

hoping that he would hear the phone before he'd finished. He was feeling not too bad, but would still take a taxi home. There was no reply from Sarah. He remembered Menzies suggesting some sessions with him alone, no doubt to explain aspects of Madeleine's behaviour without her presence, but she had died suddenly and so Hartley had seen no need to go again. He'd thought about it later when he found he could no longer work a full week at Hastings Hull, but decided that these things were best left to remedy themselves. After all, there had been only the two subsequent episodes and then no recurrence. He'd found Menzies' ginger hair a distraction at their meetings, and didn't want to talk about a lot of stuff that could never be changed. Simon Drummond in his tactful way suggested there may have been deeper emotional issues involved with the occasions of temporary amnesia and volatility, but Hartley was convinced that any troubles were the outcome of overwork and the loss of his wife. The business with the Mercedes driver, and later the complaint concerning his presence on enclosed premises, were just minor blips in an unexceptional and law-abiding life.

The legally styled premises were in fact the backyard of Hartley's neighbours, the Stanfords, where he had gone at twilight in pursuit of Zeus, their mongrel dog. The Stanfords' place wasn't visible from Hartley's house, separated by a gully and tall trees, but Zeus, as befitted his name, considered all within roaming distance as his domain. The dog had a habit of shitting at the base of Hartley's deck, which had led to an altercation between the neighbours, and finally a visit from a senior constable, who officially warned Hartley not to enter the Stanford property without an invitation. He obeyed reluctantly, but kept a store of stones on the deck, which he used to hurl at Zeus whenever the dog was trespassing.

Chapter Thirteen

As a consequence of Robert's obsessive winnowing, different photographs came briefly to the surface of the piles on the table, and then vanished beneath others in their turn. Generally Sarah paid little attention to them, and even that casual interest was often merely an obligatory response to her husband's enthusiasm. The photos were a reminder of how much of value and emotional intensity she'd risked by loving Hartley; she preferred not to be confronted by them.

One evening, however, when Robert had already gone to bed, and she was making a cursory attack on his bits and pieces encroaching on the table space, she saw the photo of Jean, her mother, taken in the room by the sea where she had been placed to await death. Robert had written nothing on the back: maybe he'd wanted Sarah's advice, maybe he realised the picture was one entirely beyond the power of words to encompass. Sarah didn't pick up the photo, but sat down and hunched herself over it, glasses settled firmly, her face brought close to allow recognition of detail. She remembered the place well: a secure dementia unit in the large facility close to the ocean. When her mother could no longer look after herself, and was recognising less and less of the life around her, Sarah and her brother had arranged for her to be admitted. The speed of Jean's decline was a surprise to both of them, and that was a great sorrow and also, towards the end, a great relief.

During the last weeks, Sarah had stayed with her brother and visited most days, sometimes twice, ringing the bell to have the door opened, and then locked behind her, walking through the bright, modern corridors to her mother's room. There was a living room for the dementia residents, with a television, sofas, a piano and a life-sized pony made of felt stuffed with newspaper. The pony's teeth were made from yoghurt pottles and its hooves from black irrigation sprayers. It had been created by those residents who still enjoyed freedom, and staff encouraged those in their care to pat it as a therapy. But Jean refused to spend time watching television, or to show affection to a stuffed horse, and sat in her room close to the large window with a view of a strip of green lawn, then the untamed marram grass, the dunes and the sea.

In the picture Jean was sad and diminished, just as Sarah recalled her being in the last weeks, and in painful contrast to the person she had been for most of her life. Jean hadn't been able to remember Sarah, and rarely spoke, rarely ate, occasionally swore fiercely in a way quite foreign to her. In the picture her mouth was closed and she sat stiffly in the chair with the slightly affronted look that was typical of her during the final days. What was missing, Sarah realised as she bent closer, was the noise of the sea. Hour after hour she had sat with the woman who used to be her mother, that wonderful, caring, intelligent person who had gone away and left a simulacrum in her place. There was only so much Sarah could think of to mention when her mother made no contribution that would enable conversation. The last thing that Sarah could recall her saying was, 'I'm afraid there's no accommodation for you here, lady. Some people have taken over my house. I tell them they have to leave, but nobody takes any notice. I expect my sister any minute. She's coming to visit me, and if you don't mind I'd like to be alone with her. No offence.'

Despite all the time Sarah spent in the secure unit, she wasn't with Jean when she died. Sarah had been having lunch when the home phoned, and she had to spit out a mouthful of quiche onto her side plate before she could answer. The news added little to her grief, because her mother had left them months ago. She had done nothing to deserve such an end, and had feared the very thing that was imposed on her. There had been no justice in it.

Sarah made a final scrutiny of the photograph, placed a finger below Jean's face in both affection and acknowledgement. Yes, all that was missing was the sound of the sea. Hour upon hour they had sat together, mother and daughter, sometimes with the shore visible outside, sometimes with it cloaked in darkness, but always with the sad, incessant, sucking sound of the sea.

It had been a small funeral. Jean had outlived her husband and most of her acquaintances. Sarah found it hard to recognise in the few rather doddery mourners the hearty and assertive friends who were often about her parents' home when she was young. None of them cried at the funeral: their mien was rather that of detached resignation, and their subdued conversation centred on ailments and medication rather than memories of Jean.

'Life's a parabola,' Bronwen Hughes told Sarah, 'but

you're never aware of the high point when you're living it.' They had been at the funeral parlour after the ceremony and Bronwen had been smiling up at Sarah, an egg sandwich in one hand, the service sheet in the other, conscious that she was being philosophical. She had once been Jean's bridge partner, but it had led to a falling out. She'd shrunk, and her sparse hair was the colour of candy floss. 'Poor Jean,' she'd said, with the faintest implication that poor bidding had played a part in the tragedy.

THEY KISSED WHEN THEY MET again, when the door of unit seventeen had closed behind them. They kissed with intensity enough, especially on Hartley's part, but also with a shared sense that the kissing was not a prelude to the pleasure that usually followed in that room.

'I'm not getting undressed,' Sarah said. 'I don't want to get on the bed.' Yet she kissed him again before he could reply.

'So we're not going to fuck?' It was unlike him to say that, but it came quickly and before subconscious censorship, perhaps because he wanted to shake her composure.

'I don't think so. Not until we've talked anyway, as we promised. And it's not just fucking, is it.' Did he imagine that she would blush like a girl, that she wasn't practised enough to equate the vulgarity of the word with the vulgarity of the physical act; the noises, the close smell of breath, the secretions, the contest at times awkward and selfish and at other moments an almost other-worldly release. 'Let's sit,' she said, 'and talk.'

'And lie down afterwards, I hope,' he said.

'First things first. We could make love all day and it wouldn't solve the problem, would it?'

In that small, impersonal room there was only one comfortable chair. Hartley insisted she take that, and he sat on a hard-backed seat by the table. It could be a turning point, he told himself, a time that they would look back on when they had been long together, and recognise its importance. That was the moment, they would say complacently: that was crunch time.

'Are we in session now, then?' he asked lightly, but she didn't smile as he'd hoped.

'It's becoming too much for me,' she said. 'All that's happening between us and all that's going on with Robert. It's as if I'm living in two bubbles that can't join and sooner or later one will burst, and I can't make a choice. I'm talking with Robert about the photos that he's got so keen on and suddenly I think of you, and wish I was here, right here, and when I'm here I worry about him, I think of how hurt he and Donna would be if they found out. And the texts you keep sending make it difficult to keep the lives apart.'

'I want to know you're okay, that we're in touch even if apart.'

'How would it look, though? It all seems so natural, so separate from responsibility when we're together. Harmless even. But think how it looks from the outside — a grand-mother with a husband fighting serious illness, and she's having it off with someone she met during his treatment.'

'Who gives a bugger what people think? It's no crime to be in love, or to leave a marriage. Half the world does it. Everyone's entitled to be happy, and there's no little kids involved.'

She knew, however, that not everyone who leaves a marriage finds what they hope for, that a second love faces perils and regrets just the same. She had friends who had made the choice and not all had found happiness. Sarah watched him as he was talking, responded to his intensity and enthusiasm. She had no doubt that he was sincere, but what did they know of each other after a few months of sporadic meetings that could justify cutting loose from all she had been gifted and had earned in a long marriage? And it wasn't just what she might find in his character that was a disappointment, but what deficiencies he might discover in her.

'I don't think I can do it,' she said. 'I'd be lying to you if I let you think I can just walk out. I love the time we have together, the talking and laughing as well as the sex. Until I met you I didn't realise how much my life was narrowing down, everything focused on illness and treatment and tests and reports and bottling feelings up. A sort of sub-surface life. You become the back-up person who's lucky to be okay. Your partner has the significance that comes with serious illness.'

'Well, that's all you'll have forever unless you make a break. It'll just go on and on.' Until he dies, was what Hartley wanted to say, but she understood without the words. Hartley was moving slightly on the chair, his hands restless also, as if words alone were inadequate to express his feelings.

'I shouldn't have started it,' she said, 'but we're good for each other, aren't we. We're easy and natural together. We could've met years and years ago. Maybe then — who knows.'

'But we've met now. That's what matters.'

'Would you feel the same if Madeleine were still alive?'

'Yes.'

'You don't know that,' she said. 'It's easy to say, but you don't know. You don't have to leave anyone, hurt anyone, and I have to give up on a marriage. It's not the same. It's not your fault, I know, but it's not the same. I don't think I can cope any more.'

'I'll do anything you ask,' he said, 'any bloody thing at all. I'll shift to Hamilton when you go, and come round and mow the lawns for you. Anything.'

'I don't think I can do it, and that's the truth, and if I can't do it then I can't carry on either, because there's even less honesty in that.'

'We'd be happy. You know that, and we'd be unhappy any other way.'

'But actually we don't know that. We're hurting each other already.'

'No.'

'Yes we are,' Sarah said.

'Hurting is a sign of being alive,' he said, changing tack. 'Only kids think love is all about happiness.'

They were quiet for a time, watching each other, searching in their minds like debaters for persuasive argument, or rebuttal.

'If we stopped the sex,' she said, 'we could still have everything else, just like we did before. We could be friends and see a lot of each other. You could come round as often as you liked. You'd actually like Robert, I think, when you got to know him.' She didn't believe it, and what relevance did it have anyway?

None at all, conveyed Hartley's slight and bitter smile. 'So I would call round and sit with a hard-on while we all talked about politics, or gardening. Yeah, right.'

'I'm just saying that a lot of what we enjoy sharing isn't about sex. We're not just two people on heat. I don't think that's even what brought us together — not for me anyway.'

'Love's all or nothing, though,' said Hartley in exasperation. 'And if it isn't everything then it's not love. Jesus, Sarah, you know that.'

'Love, love, it means anything you like, doesn't it. It's hopeless talking about it. If you have to talk about it then you've already lost it.' She said it with a flare of vehemence that matched his own, and left them for the moment at the end of words.

Then he stood up and came beside her, cupped his hands over her hair and laid his head on his hands. 'Ah, Jesus,' he said brokenly. 'I can't bear it. Let's leave it for now and go to bed.'

So they did. It was the first time with Hartley that she would rather not have made love, though the feeling wasn't unfamiliar to her. It had happened many times with Robert during their marriage. There was physical pleasure enough, and the understanding of Hartley's need to have that acceptance of him, but she acknowledged to herself without dispute that she wouldn't leave Robert, that she wouldn't go off in search of a different life, or a different self. And with that realisation came a subtle change to the way she must think of what they did with their bodies. Even as Hartley tongued her breast, and felt between her thighs, as she saw tears on his eyelashes, and heard the urgency with which he repeated her name, she knew that, with the decision not to leave Robert, this became just an affair, with the furtiveness and blind-alley conclusion that affairs have, and not some once-in-a-lifetime meeting of souls for which all else should be sacrificed.

She couldn't tell him, though, not lying enclosed within his arms while he talked excitedly of how they would find a way to be together, and how essential that was. 'We just need more time,' he said. 'There's an answer to everything.' He smoothed the hair back from her forehead, then relaxed on the pillow, and using both hands in a synchronised action wiped sweat and tears from beneath his eyes with his fingers. 'Ah, Christ, but we'll work through it,' he said. 'We'll work through it because we love each other.'

'No one must be hurt,' she said, yet knowing it was

already too late for that. She'd never been in such a situation before, and felt a sense of constriction, a sense of unavoidable advance towards pain and confusion. As he talked of new beginnings she grew fearful of an approaching end. She looked at the brightly coloured fishing boats clustered in frames on the walls, and through the frosted glass of the motel's sliding door was the golden blur of the pot that stood beside it. Hartley kissed her, laughed, shook her bare shoulder tenderly, even as she experienced the appalling sadness that can accompany authentic love.

'I'll never let you go,' he said.

LATER, WHEN BACK IN the apartment, and sitting with Robert to watch the news on television, Sarah felt an almost overwhelming sense of isolation. Who could she turn to? Hartley and Robert were her confidants, yet both were denied to her, one because she must break with him, the other because he would be injured by disclosure. A threesome — in which she was on her own.

There had been no previous affairs, not because she hadn't been the target for such intentions, but that her life had been full, her career challenging, her marriage and family as happy as those she saw about her. When she knew Robert was carrying on with a woman in his dental practice, she'd been tempted to respond to Malcolm Fryer, a scientist from the United States Fish and Wildlife Service. Malcolm had been seconded to DOC for six months to observe the New Zealand success in establishing predator-free environments for endangered species. Sarah was his principal liaison in the department and he made it plain to her that he hoped there would be a relationship in more than just professional matters.

'We've gotten quite close, haven't we, Sarah?' he'd said to her on the way back from one of their trips to Kapiti Island. They were standing side by side on the launch, hands on the rail because of the choppy sea, and watching the coast of the North Island come closer. 'We could have a bit of fun together without anything serious,' he said. 'What do you think?' He was completely at ease and appeared to consider it a quite normal proposition, even though he'd been several times for meals with Sarah and Robert, during which he talked of his wife and young family in Vancouver. He'd accepted Robert's offer to take him to a rugby game.

Malcolm had been attractive enough in a gangly, boyish way, and good company, but Sarah thought that to fuck with him just because she knew her husband was doing that with someone else wasn't a sensible reaction.

'That's fine, absolutely fine, Sarah,' Malcolm had said when she told him she wasn't interested. 'I just had to ask. A man has needs, you know, and I really like you a lot.' They had continued to enjoy working together, he had come again to her home, and after his return to America they had emailed occasionally before the exchange lapsed. Neither of them made mention again of the proposition on the lurching launch with grey sky and gulls overhead, but there was no awkwardness.

Thinking back on Malcolm, and several other similar situations, she had the rather odd feeling that they should provide moral capital if she confessed to Robert her affair with Hartley. All those times I was loyal, she could say, and he couldn't argue the same. All those times to put on the scales against this one lapse in special circumstances. But she knew it didn't work that way.

Earthquakes were on the news, and Robert had a coughing

fit. It worried her. The coughing seemed to come at his low points during the treatment. 'We need to get something for that,' she said. 'I'll go in tomorrow.'

'I'm okay,' said Robert. 'It comes and goes. You know, one of the things I've learnt is that it's bloody boring to be sick. I'm bloody sick of being sick. Tomorrow we'll get out and do something together. I want you to choose a special place. I want us to be happy.'

Chapter Fourteen

'Here's a great one,' said Robert. He was at the table again with his photographs and albums. He wasn't feeling so good and was still in his dressing gown, although the sun was high in the sky. Sarah sat down with him, aware of her own slight disassociation. Until his illness, he'd never been much concerned with records and mementoes of the past, but retrospection had gained on him. He was unshaven, unwashed, and the grey bristles lay in the creases of his face and neck, the skin pouched beneath his eyes, the pores of his nose were accentuated. He was sixty-five years old. He was a sick, ageing man and it showed. Sarah couldn't help but make a comparison with Hartley: younger, healthier, eager, slim and agile despite his grey hair.

'So where's this great one, then?' Sarah said, and put her hand on Robert's shoulder. He hadn't always been that way, and there was more to him than appearance.

It was a photograph of the three of them on the wharf

at Queenstown before they had taken a boat ride on the lake. Donna, only seven or eight, stood grinning, with her arms open as if to embrace the world. Some passer-by must have kindly snapped the picture, because the three of them had travelled there alone. Robert had almost forgotten how skinny his daughter had been then, and her smile was gap-toothed. His younger self and Sarah's looked out quite unselfconsciously — a tall, athletic man in short sleeves, and the woman relaxed, also smiling, and surely too young to be the mother.

He remembered the trip. Donna had just recovered from chicken pox, and he'd recently bought his way into the dental practice in Wellington. Their whole life then seemed an assumption of happiness and increasing achievement. What car did he have then he wondered, and decided it was the white Ford Cortina. They had spent time in Wanaka and Arrowtown, too, following their fellow tourists from one activity and restaurant to the next. On the third night they spent in the Queenstown motel there had been a thunderstorm at dawn, and Donna had come running and climbed into their bed for comfort. The three had sat snuggled together watching the lightning, the rapid, barrelling dark clouds and first light rising behind.

'Remember the thunder that night?' he said, and Sarah did so, immediately.

'She'd just had chicken pox,' she said. 'We bought her those sandals in Wanaka because it was so hot.'

'There's others here of the same trip.'

'Well we used to get more developed then. Now most of them just get left on the computer.'

'I'll get everything sorted and identified in time,' he said. It was as if a completed jigsaw of his past might provide security for the future. Robert wasn't a vain man, but looking at the photo he saw that he'd been good-looking enough, and married to an attractive woman. The thought pleased him. 'You look damn good,' he said.

'A long time ago,' she said. 'Anyway, you need to get cleaned up and dressed. It's about lunchtime.'

'I will soon. I feel a bit queasy. I'll take it easy for a bit.' He took it easy all the time now, but neither of them chose to point that out.

'We can have a later lunch,' Sarah said.

'Here's another goodie.' He had a more recent group picture of six of them dressed up for the hospice charity ball. Professional people, slightly complacent in the nature of their relaxation, their dress, their support of a worthy cause. 'Wallace always goes up on his toes a bit for photos so he looks taller,' said Robert. 'See.' He held it up. 'It's the same in every one he's in. That was a great night.'

Sarah felt a sudden return of impatience. Robert so often engrossed with the past now as an evasion of existing reality, indulging in sentimentality that hadn't been part of his personality. 'I don't really care,' she said.

'Why not?' He was taken aback.

'All this concern about the albums. Nothing's more boring than other people's photos. I wish you'd remember that when visitors come. Don't you think there's more important stuff to deal with?'

'What stuff? Jesus, Sarah, I don't want to sit around talking about radiation and chemo all day.'

Sarah regretted what she'd said, knowing that her reaction had more to do with Hartley and herself than Robert, or his photos. 'No, I suppose I mean we should try to make the most of now. Look ahead even,' she said.

'It's all one life, isn't it?'

'You're right. I'm sorry. It *is* a good one of the group,' and she took the photograph as a form of apology, talked about their friends who looked out of it, while still not caring about them. They were no help to her in what she faced. 'Those charity balls were great fun,' she said.

'Wallace isn't so good now himself, he says.' There was no satisfaction in Robert's voice.

When in the kitchen to prepare lunch, she checked her cell phone and found three texts from Hartley pressing for a meeting, or a reply at least. In the first weeks his messages had given her a frisson of excitement and pleasure, the feeling that she had a depth to her life apart from the dutiful surface presented, but now the intimacy threatened to become constriction. 'Bsy txt latr', she sent, but she didn't, despite knowing that silence was no solution, and when she and Robert were having cold ham and salad Hartley rang.

'I've been waiting to hear from you,' he said. 'Is anything the matter?' Never before had he phoned, except when he was sure she was by herself. Robert continued his slow chewing, but raised his eyebrows in mild enquiry. He hoped it was Donna. Again Sarah noticed his slumped posture, even as she felt a sudden flash of fear and anger at Hartley's voice.

'I don't think we're interested,' she said. 'We're only renting. We're not permanent residents here.'

'Call when you can then,' he said. 'I love you.'

'Thank you, though.'

'I'll be waiting, as always,' he said.

'Goodbye.'

Robert didn't ask, but she felt she had to say something. 'Some insulation people. They always call at mealtimes, don't they.' She could feel a tremor in her hands, and wondered if her face was flushed.

'I'm glad we got all that over and done with at home. Double-glazing is something we should perhaps consider, though.'

'Are you feeling any better? You haven't eaten much.'

'I might lie down for a bit,' he said.

He took off his slippers, stood meekly while she peeled off the white and blue striped bed cover, and then he lay down with a small, wordless noise of relief. Sarah was saddened by his vulnerability. They held each other's gaze for a moment as he lay quietly.

'Don't worry, I'm going to be okay. It's just one of the down days,' he said.

'Sleep if you can,' she said. 'I'm going to have a walk. Not far. Later I'm going to get a new battery for my watch.'

At the apartment gates she looked for Hartley's car, and was relieved not to see it. She went far enough from the entrance to be out of view even if Robert happened to go into the living room, then walked down an alley that led to a loading bay and a row of trash bins with a neat stack of orange traffic cones at one end. As she waited, cell phone in hand, for Hartley to answer her call, she thought how distasteful it was at her age to be in such a place and making a surreptitious call to someone she was screwing on the side. She forced herself to think of it that way for once, rather than as another price for love.

'Don't ever do that again,' she told him, her voice quiet, yet taut with anger. 'God, we were sitting side by side and you ring. Didn't you think how it might be for me? I've told you how awkward even texts can be, and you just call, at lunchtime, too. For God's sake.'

'Well, you hadn't answered my texts. I thought something must be wrong, that's all. I worry about you. Can we meet later?'

'No, I have to go out. I answer texts when I can. You know that. All this hassle, it's starting to get to me. I make what time I can for us, but you keep pushing. It's getting to me. It's spoiling everything.'

'What's more important than us?' he said. 'You said we come first.'

'I never said that. You can't say I said that.' She noticed for the first time that there was a large Polynesian man sitting on a stool in the shadow of the loading bay doors. He was smoking, watching her with calm curiosity.

'We've got to be first. There's no other way.'

'Please don't ring again like that,' Sarah said, stooping, turning away from the smoking man.

'I'll text then,' Hartley said, 'but you need to reply. I think of you all the time, so surely you owe me that much.'

'Don't ring again. I've got to go. Bye,' and she finished before he could reply, made her way back to the street. Careful, she told herself: she had to be careful now or things could go wrong. She felt herself oddly distanced from the people about her, and those passing seemed to make a point of looking away, as if aware of her distress and not wishing to share it. Everything of the visible world seemed to be hollowed out, fragile as blown glass, as if one clumsy move would shatter everything.

Hartley had taken the call at the supermarket. He sat in his car in the parking area, with his purchases in three plastic bags on the back seat. He didn't regret calling Sarah, even though it had upset her. Decisions had to be made, otherwise when Robert's treatment ended he and Sarah would go back to Hamilton, and Hartley would be finished. Even if things were meant to be, they didn't happen without full commitment to achievement. It came to him that he needed to talk to Robert, see what he was up against. He'd glimpsed him briefly twice before, but everything he knew, apart from those brief physical sightings, had come from Sarah, and all in her husband's favour and from concern for his infirmity. Of overt criticism there was none, but she couldn't really love him. No. If she still loved him she wouldn't be coming to the white Spanish motel, taking off her clothes with such freedom.

So he drove until he was close to the apartments, then walked to the real-estate office from which he could see the entrance of her building without being obvious. He was about to give up when he saw her come out to meet the taxi just drawn up. She would've been at the big third-floor window watching for it. To see her was enough to cause a rush of possessiveness and tenderness within him, an inclination to call out to her before the car door closed, to tell her that she was not just another solitary woman past turning heads, but someone watched over and loved. Someone known intimately and cherished by another.

Instead, Hartley walked past the lawn plot and seats, into the apartment block, checked the names on the letterboxes, took the stairs rather than the lift and rang at the door of number 3B. Maybe Robert would be asleep, maybe watching television and unable to hear the bell, or ignoring it. He'd always been keen on sport, and as his participation had lessened the viewing had increased. He did hear, and chose to come to the door. Hartley was surprised by the physical vigour Robert summoned to meet him. A big man, but starting to cave in on himself, shoulders and head trending to a centre, a face, once more substantial, slipping a little from the features. Hartley knew his age, but had it not been for the cancer, Robert would have retained considerable presence.

'Robert?' Hartley said. Robert nodded, still holding the door with one hand. 'I'm Colin Olders from the outpatients service unit of the hospital. I'm calling to see if there's anything we can do to help. I understand you're up here only during the period of your treatment. We have information services, and some activity and transport resources. I don't know if you would find these things helpful, but I could run over some of them if you have time.'

'I think my wife would have covered most of it, but

she's not in at the moment. We're pretty much settled into a routine. Come in if you like, though. I'm lucky to have someone with me while I'm up here so I don't suppose I need a lot of extra help.'

Hartley followed him in to the living room, neat and modern apart from the clutter of photographs and albums on one end of the table. Robert had been watching the television, but as they sat down in leather chairs close to the large window he put it on mute — not switched off, however, as a sign to Hartley that he didn't expect the interruption to be long. As merely a temporary home, the apartment had little reflection of Sarah. Hartley knew that, but was disappointed nevertheless not to have a greater feeling of her presence there. She would sit in the same chair, have the same elevated view of the busy street and the city buildings, watch the clouds tow shadows across the asphalt, or outlines blur as rain spat and ran on the window, or at night the winking, jostling flow of vehicle lights, a listless moon perhaps above it all. There was one sign of their love, however: the small, blue jug from Matakana, his gift, and he had to resist the urge to touch it, acknowledge it in some way.

'I won't hold you up,' he said. 'It's routine really. One of us from the unit tries to make contact during the first few weeks. We've been a bit lax, I'm sorry. Sometimes we phone, but I find I get a better sense of the circumstances by making a visit.'

'We're about okay, I think,' said Robert. 'We could bring a car up from home, but my wife doesn't like to drive in this traffic, and, quite frankly, neither do I now. I suppose the only situation I can think of when help would be useful would be if Sarah weren't well, or needed to be away for a few days.'

Hartley made the expected reply and laid out various adjunct services he said were available, though he agreed in Robert's case it was unlikely they would be required.

As they talked, Robert's attention switched sometimes to the flickering television screen — medieval treasure troves unearthed with the aid of metal detectors — and Hartley assessed the man who stood between Sarah and himself. What would happen if she came back and found them together, seated companionably, discussing her husband's needs? He had no idea how long she would be away, but the thought gave him a charge that was as much excitement and anticipation as fear. Everything would surely come out then, once and for all.

'Nothing more then?' asked Robert to indicate an end. How much more there was, and all of it of vital importance to him, but Hartley knew the time would come for that, and he just smiled and accepted his dismissal.

They didn't shake hands as they parted. Hartley favoured that brief meeting of flesh, but maybe if it had occurred he would have found it difficult to let go, would have used his free hand to give Robert such a thrust that he would stumble head first into the door frame. Robert was bigger, but he was older, he was sick and he was unsuspecting. Hartley was in no hurry to leave the apartments, even standing at the entrance to the building for a while looking across the lawn strip to the street. There was time for Sarah to meet him as she returned, but he saw only a young mother in tight jeans, and her small daughter, who turned towards him after passing with solemn scrutiny.

Robert went back to the television after Hartley left, but the golden amulets and roughly cut emeralds and rubies of turbulent times had vanished into history again, and he was faced with another gaggle of competing and emotional amateur chefs. He turned it off and went to the table to be with his albums and memories. In a soiled envelope addressed to 'The Householder' he found a photo of himself and Ashley Dicks on a motorbike outside the flat in Moss

Street they had shared with two others when they were at the dental school. A Norton 500, a brute of a thing that threatened their lives with every outing. Ashley had one ungainly leg on the road surface to maintain the stability difficult to achieve even when stationary, and Robert, without a helmet, grinned from the pillion. He'd lived for two years with Ashley as one lived with a brother, intimate yet with a casual disregard, combining in both the escapades and drudgery of student life, but with essential privacy preserved. Ashley had made a U-turn in his studies, and without explanation left Dunedin to study art at Canterbury. He bequeathed lecture notes that were superior to Robert's own, and also a small mural of St Kilda Beach on his bedroom wall, with copulating dogs in the background as a Brueghelistic touch.

Robert saw him only once again: more than thirty years later in the crowded foyer of a theatre in Wellington, during the interval of a Roger Hall play. He knew him immediately from the long, equine face and forelock. They'd been pleased to meet, but the call of nature prevented them from sharing anything of their lives. Ashley had put a hand briefly on Robert's shoulder after their greeting, and leant in to be heard above the hubbub. 'I'm sorry,' he said. 'Great to see you, but I'm busting for a pee. Fair busting,' and he went off with his hand held up briefly in apology, half a head taller than most others he pushed through.

After the performance, Robert had hung around the entrance for a while, hoping to see him coming out. No luck, and so whether Ashley had made it as an artist, or given up the dream and turned to some mundane competency, remained a mystery. But there he was on the bike when they were young, and Robert remembered how morose he was at exam time, his generosity with the baking his mother sent him, the well-upholstered girl studying biology who would leave his room with demure repletion. 'Ashley Dicks,' said Robert to himself softly. He looked up hoping to share his nostalgia. 'Ashley Dicks,' he called, but Sarah didn't respond. He opened his mouth to call the name more loudly, but stopped himself. Of course, she'd gone out, and anyway she'd never met Ashley; he was nothing to her. So Robert, mouth still agape, just looked at himself with Ashley on the Norton and wondered where so much time had gone. Maybe in Moss Street the wooden house still stood, and beneath several subsequent coats of paint was Ashley's mural of St Kilda Beach waiting to be discovered and made special by his fame.

'Some outpatients services guy from the hospital came,' said Robert when Sarah was back.

'What did he want?'

'Nothing really. He went on about the help that's available if you need it. I said probably the only thing would be if you were away for a few days.'

'Which I never am,' she said. 'Did he leave a card to get in touch?'

'No. He was a skinny, jittery sort of chap. What about you?'

'I got the watch battery put in and a couple of DVDs. Are you feeling okay now?'

'Just tired,' he said, 'I'll be glad when I'm not always tired. You never think about it when you're young and fit, just take energy as being inexhaustible. I never thought that I could look forward so much to going to bed alone.' She had to smile at that. 'I've had enough of the television,' he said. 'I've spent a bit of time with the photos, but think I'll rest for a while now.'

Sarah went with him into the bedroom, and they talked as he took off his shoes and trousers, then lay on the bed. When he was comfortable she half pulled the curtains to keep the sun from his eyes. 'I'm going to think of something special for tea,' she said.

'I look forward to it,' he said. 'I'm quite peckish.'

HARTLEY FELT ENCOURAGED BY his meeting with Robert; what could someone like that offer Sarah for the future in competition with himself? Robert was a large, intelligent, self-centred man who had run down into needy dependence. Even if he came through the treatment he would never be an equal partner again. When he returned home, Hartley rang Avignon Furnishings and asked for someone to bring their range of blue curtain material to the house the next day. He remembered Sarah saying that was her favourite colour — a powder blue like a clear winter sky.

That was what he chose for the master bedroom. A lightish fabric that would allow a suffusion of the sun as he and Sarah lay there in the afternoons just as they had when she was meant to be arranging flowers in the Titirangi hall, and instead they had first made love.

'My partner's away at present,' Hartley said as the young guy took the window measurements. 'It'll be a surprise when she comes back.'

'Nice,' the salesman said. 'Jesus, some view you get here.'

'Blue is her favourite colour.'

'Right.' He wondered how you got to live in such a place, which must be worth over a million easily. This old guy must be a doctor, or a lawyer. One of those people who can charge hundreds of dollars an hour even if they're just yacking on the phone.

'I don't want those cheap plastic runners,' said Hartley.

'Right,' the guy said. It was okay for some. He still flatted with two girls in Otahuhu, both of whom kept him out of their bedrooms because they wanted a boyfriend with better prospects.

'If there's any over, perhaps you could make up a couple

of cushions,' said Hartley. He was pleased with the idea, showing surely the sort of sensitivity to décor a woman would appreciate. 'In fact I'll have them anyway,' he said.

When the van had gone, Hartley walked through all of the rooms, endeavouring to see them as Sarah would. He'd heard that women had difficulty in feeling fully settled in a home that bore a strong imprint of a predecessor. The obvious personal belongings had gone — the clothes and shoes, toiletries, the worn toys speaking of family togetherness and the favourite knick-knacks — but what of the choice of towels, the unusual multi-coloured glass whorl Madeleine had bought at a charity auction, the travel souvenirs? Whatever went, the photographs of Kevin would stay, even those that included all three of the family. Hartley was sure Sarah would have no trouble with that, would bring in elements of her own former life. They wouldn't try to deny any of their past, just celebrate the new beginning.

He was proud of his home, although he knew that he had done nothing to earn it except marry Madeleine. And Sarah admired it, which made it even more attractive to him. When he'd first come to Auckland, not much more than a boy, he'd boarded with the Ironside family in Mangere. His bedroom had no wardrobe and a view of the clothesline. It was next to the only lavatory in the house, and elderly Reg Ironside came down the passage at least once every night, to appease his prostate, with a friendly fart or two in passing.

Mrs Ironside always cooked fish on Fridays, and only years later did Hartley twig that they must have been Catholics, for he wasn't aware of them attending church. Mrs Ironside smoked while she stood over the fry pan and watched television, rejoicing in any sexual innuendo. Reg grew Super Toms, and winter and summer wore thick socks and sandals. He had a strange crab-like walk on the stairs so as to avoid the worn middle of the carpet. Hartley had come to be fond of them both, but also was now pleasurably aware of the improvement in his accommodation.

Once Mrs Ironside went away for three days to look after her sick brother in Wanganui, and Reg and Hartley had bached inexpertly. They spent more time together than ever before, or afterwards, sitting at the kitchen table and talking, Reg picking idly at the yellow contact over the wooden surface, and telling him about being in the navy during the war. He served in the Pacific, but never shot at anyone, or was shot at himself. Reg said everything then had to do with booze. Any sort of booze: they drank polishes and put kerosene in the beer, even drank ethanol stolen from torpedos. Booze, booze, booze, said Reg. There was bugger-all sex, and booze was king.

The three days had ended badly. Reg ate the last of an ageing takeaway on the third day, and it gave him violent diarrhoea. He didn't even make the lavatory, and Hartley helped to clean up the mess, a rich chowder all down the hall. They did their best, but weren't able to deceive Mrs Ironside, who held both equally responsible. Reg's embarrassment was so great that from then on there was always a slight reserve on his part. He'd lost face, and wouldn't risk such vulnerability again. They still got on well, but Hartley regretted the change for he'd enjoyed Reg's war stories — so much less heroic and more human than most. Guys coping as best they could, and taking any means to forget where they were.

Hartley had spent fifteen months living with the Ironsides, and had gone back once later to visit them. Mrs Ironside was happy to see him, but said Reg had died some months before. She insisted Hartley come in and have a coffee. When he entered the small living room, made even more restricted by the piano that was never used, he got a shock to find Reg seated there in his usual chair by the sash window. But Mrs Ironside introduced him as Winston, Reg's brother, and sure enough there were differences as well as similarities when Hartley had a chance to notice them. He wore brown shoes, not sandals, and had egregious teeth. Mrs Ironside and Winston were quite at ease, and neither felt the need to offer any explanation of his presence. Mrs Ironside told Hartley he would be welcome to come back to board if he wished, and Winston confirmed the offer with equanimity. 'The room's lying idle,' he said, 'and might as well be used.'

'You were never any trouble. Quiet like. Not like some we've had. One had stuff growing under the bed,' said Mrs Ironside. Hartley assumed the stuff was weed.

'Think it over if it takes your fancy,' said Winston. 'Of course the board would have to be more now. Everything domestic's gone up to hell, hasn't it.' Hartley had taken a dislike to him, not from any perceived evil intent, or deficiency, but from loyalty to old Reg who had been so easily supplanted. He never visited again.

One of the things that worried Hartley a bit concerning a future life with Sarah was that he had no significant circle of friends to invite her into when they were together permanently. He wasn't sure how that had come about. Madeleine and he hadn't been without acquaintances, some from his work, some from hers, some gathered by common association as Kevin progressed through his various schools. But no one close, and after Madeleine's death they seemed to drift away. Hartley felt no discomfort, or inadequacy, when with other people, and could be quite talkative, but he felt no pressing need to assemble them on his own account. He had developed a glib conviviality and a carapace of assurance.

His gumboot family in the south were distanced more by lifestyle than geography. He told himself that if you had a soulmate you didn't need anybody else. Yet he didn't want Sarah to think him some sort of loner, a widower without friends to encourage him, or welcome a new partner. Simon

Drummond was a pleasant guy who liked music, and his wife did extramural papers on European history. Hartley had been to their house twice since Madeleine's death, found them good company, but neglected to return hospitality. Sarah had already met Simon, and liked him. Hartley decided he would invite the Drummonds to go with him to some exhibition, or recital, and then take them to a restaurant, or to his home. Naomi Drummond had a calmness and independence of disposition not unlike Sarah's own. She knew something of art, would make an ideal companion for a coffee morning, a festival event, an occasional dinner, without seeking an intimacy and frequency of contact that would hinder Sarah's and his concentration on themselves.

He'd become lonely in the two years after Madeleine's death, yet admitted they had never achieved the closeness he'd hoped for in the marriage. It was his fault as much as hers perhaps, but her deficiencies were clear in his recollection. Her absorption in her work at the airport, and a walled privacy lest the ravening world break through. Madeleine could have turned to alcohol, and Hartley admired her courage in not doing so. They hadn't argued much, though when Kevin was little, she was conspicuously loving towards the child after any dispute, as if to emphasise his attachment to her rather than his father. When there was only the two of them living together, they had done so mainly in companionable disassociation.

He would try harder with Sarah and do better: he would learn from his marriage with Madeleine to be more successful with someone else. Sarah wasn't perfect and neither was he, but they loved each other and knew how to be happy together. They would have something special together that very few people achieved. He was convinced of that, and nothing must stand in the way of it.

Hartley was surprised to find that he was crying, tears

running freely on his cheeks although his thoughts were of love and happiness. It had happened several times recently, and slightly embarrassed him. It was just that he was able to release his feelings more readily since finding Sarah, he told himself, and went out onto the wooden deck, wiped away the tears and took several deep breaths. He was a lucky guy, he told himself. He had the hiccups, and concentrated on more long, even breaths in an attempt to stop them. There was a light wind that caused a slight swaying of the tree branches and an accompanying subdued music of comfort. He was a lucky guy to be living in such a place, and the best of times lay ahead.

Chapter Fifteen

'Wen + wer?' was the message. Sarah received it, as she expected, early on the Friday morning, for the two days before were his work days at Hastings Hull and he had distractions, so didn't send texts until he was settled in his office. She had been cleaning the bathroom, and she didn't reply immediately. Robert was sitting close to the big living-room window so he could see the goings on in the street and look into the city. He liked watching the pedestrian crossing: how at busy times the walkers continued to stream over the road even when the lights had turned against them and the car horns were sounding. How some people took no notice of the red anyhow and just crossed when there was opportunity, some strolling, some swiftly adroit, and not all young, impudent people, but businessmen, too, with a purposeful stride proclaiming that their personal priorities outweighed regulations for the proletariat.

'Somebody's going to get flattened there you know,' he said. 'I can see it coming.'

'If enough do it, though, they get away with it. It's like we saw in European places, where people drove and parked and walked wherever they could and there were just too many for the traffic people to cope. Mass disobedience defeats authority.'

'Somebody will get flattened, and the driver will be blamed because the sympathy is always with the pedestrian,' Robert said. 'People play silly buggers with the lights and expect to get away with it.'

'Well, it's good, then, that you didn't bring the car up.'

Yes, she decided, she would meet Hartley of course, at unit seventeen, but only to tell him that they had to finish, that their friendship, fulfilling though it was, had to give way before the overall context of their lives. She knew it would be painful for them both, that she would lose a part of life still special to her — but not essential. Hartley must be made to understand, and both of them would get over it in time. The loss of sexual excitement wasn't the main thing, more that the comradeship, the community of attitudes, the happy distraction and mutual admiration had to be let go. That was the reality, and there was no other way. She had enjoyed the certainty that she was the most important person in Hartley's world, and she was drawn to his personality without fully understanding it. But even the best of experiences must end.

'Shall we go into town for lunch?' she asked Robert. 'Do you feel like it?'

'Sure. I'd like that. I'm feeling okay. Not doing handstands, but not too bad. I think my system is actually getting used to some of the stuff. I'm sleeping better, for one thing.'

'Good. We'll do that, then. Perhaps that place by the ferry terminal. It's not too noisy and there's always something going on. I think I'll do a bit of shopping later, and you can taxi back here. You'll need to take a jersey with you, though. Sometimes there's that breeze from the sea and you feel it more now. Why don't you ring for a taxi? Give me twenty minutes to get finished here.'

But Robert was in no hurry to prepare to leave. He went to his workplace at the end of the table. 'I found a couple of really good ones of the Aspen Street house,' he said. 'Come and have a look.'

She assumed interest and joined him, taking one of the photos he offered. The Aspen Street house was the first place they owned: brick, two bedrooms, decramastic roof and an open carport rather than a garage. The photograph showed Sarah in gardening clothes standing beside a slim silver birch that she'd just bedded in.

'I was pregnant then,' she said, but there was no sign of that in the picture. She was tall and strong and with an attractiveness that was part genetic disposition and part youth itself.

'You looked sexy even in those clothes,' said Robert.

'I had a waist then — even pregnant.'

'I don't remember taking it.'

'You didn't,' she said. 'Mum was down giving a hand to tidy the place up. You would've been at work. There's one of her somewhere on the same day, standing by the gate, I think. When you come across it keep the three together.'

She didn't need to find the photograph of her mother to have her image in her mind as sharp as if she stood beside her, and all that had been around them that day so many years ago, reformed also. The rough, neglected lawn, the wheelbarrow full of plants, the chill, spring wind that caused her mother to push back her hair with a wrist rather than the damp, soiled gardening glove. The way her mother rustled her hands in the rhododendron bushes to dislodge the brown and shrunken stalks of past flowers. Sarah stood still in a conscious effort to hold the memory in all its exactitude, but it went as suddenly as it had come, and she was left with just the flat photograph of herself. 'Mum did a hell of a lot for us in that place,' she said, 'especially when Donna was a baby.'

'I liked your mother,' said Robert, 'and your dad, too. They were closer to me in many ways than my own parents. Your dad died far too early.'

'I was so lucky, and never realised it at the time. Good people, but so sad for Mum later on. Life's so unfair sometimes, isn't it.'

How angry and upset her mother would be if she were still alive, and knew Sarah was going to lunch with her husband, and then on to a motel to be with her lover. It was exactly the sort of deceit she had most despised. That end point was easy to condemn, but was reached by way of a hundred small decisions each equivocal in itself and so difficult to rescind. Her mother would never know of Hartley, could make no accusation from the grave, yet Sarah felt a strange sadness that she'd let her down, and as distraction went to the kitchen and began emptying the dishwasher. The loss of her mother's good opinion was quite certain, even though it would never be expressed. She loved her mother and felt ashamed to have failed her. Again she saw her in the garden of the Aspen Street place, slight and cold, but willingly giving all she could to help her daughter, as she always did. I won't cry, Sarah told herself, and she drew in a long breath.

'Have you phoned the taxi yet?' she said from the kitchen, knowing he hadn't.

'Just doing it,' said Robert, who wasn't. 'Sarah pregnant in the Aspen Street garden' he was writing on the back of the photograph.

ROBERT ENJOYED LUNCH ON the waterfront, not so much the food, but the view of the harbour, and the parade of men and women from so many levels of city life, most in that protective mode of self-absorption that allowed them to stand on trains and buses close enough to feel the body heat of others, without any recognition of their presence. The less energy he had himself, the more he was absorbed in the activity of people around him, especially those in the careless possession of health. He watched two guys with skateboards flipping on and off a low metal railing, each catcalling derisively at the efforts of the other. They were young men, not adolescents: tall, muscular, with both easy grace and sudden power, and aware of the spectacle they made, although taking no apparent notice of anyone who watched. 'Silly buggers,' said Robert with tolerant envy. 'You wonder how they get the skateboard to jump up like that.'

'A skill born of idleness, I suppose,' said Sarah. 'Guys like that take accomplishment for granted just because they're young.'

'Well, you don't know anything else then,' said Robert. 'When you're older you remember being young for comparison. You've been there. When you're young, old age is just a concept.'

'Hey, we're not old yet.'

'You know what I mean,' he said. 'Anyway, I've got a few years on you.' He was quiet for a time, seeming to watch the skateboarders, then he turned to her. 'I'm not too much of a sad sack, am I?' he said. 'The last year or two have been pretty ordinary, I know, but I'll make it up to you when all this is over. We've got plenty of good times ahead of us still, haven't we? And we'll make the most of them because of the crap we've been through.'

'Of course we will,' she said. He must have considered

death rather than recovery, but she wondered if it had ever occurred to him that she might leave before either eventuated. Well, there would be no need for that now. He would have gone on, though, she was sure of that. He had a stubborn resilience, born of selfishness, or pride. She was for a moment curious about his reaction if she'd told him she had a lover and wished to end the marriage. 'When you're better, we should go down and have a long visit with Donna and the girls,' she said.

After she'd seen Robert to a taxi, Sarah took one herself to the Spanish motel. Hartley was there before her, as she knew he would be, watching at the window, opening the door so she could slip in without being kept waiting, drawing her to him for a first kiss.

'Look at that thundercloud. It's going to piss down soon,' he said. 'It was on the forecast and now it's building up for sure. Anyway I bought some sushi. I bet you haven't had anything to eat.'

'I have, though,' she said. 'I've been at the Viaduct Basin.' But she took a piece, not from hunger, but because it allowed a small delay.

'I'm so glad you're here. It seems ages.' Even though she hadn't finished eating, he stepped close, his body very straight, and with hands on her bum, pressed her to him. Sarah remained passive, still chewing, then she swallowed.

'There's stuff we need to talk about,' she said.

'But afterwards,' he said. 'Talk can come afterwards. I've been waiting for days.' And often in that time he'd imagined her taking off her clothes, or himself removing them which was even more arousing. How familiar yet revelatory were such memories, how closely observed, how much a consolation when he was alone.

'No. It can't wait. It has to be now,' she said.

She drew his arms away, and went and sat on one of the

two upright chairs by the table. The sky was almost absurdly dark, there was one intense shower that slapped and bounced raindrops on the asphalt outside, and then the clouds rolled away without thunder, and sunlight gleamed on the wet surfaces. It had briefly claimed their attention, but then it was over and there was just the diminishing noise of water in the drains from the motel roof. The dramatic cloudburst was entirely indifferent, yet to Sarah the coincidence oddly heightened the significance of her decision.

'I've made up my mind,' she said. 'I can't do it any more. When I thought I might leave Robert because of us, then it seemed okay, but now that I know I won't leave him it changes everything. To go on making love now, even the meetings, is just selfish pleasure and deceit, isn't it. Somehow for me it's an all or nothing thing and I'm not going to leave him. I'm sure now. I'm sorry, but — I'm sorry.' She tried to look at him as she spoke, but it was too painful to keep her gaze direct, and she found her glance flicking away, and back again. She was aware of her own voice, and it seemed to have a tone of prim imposture quite foreign to her intention.

Hartley closed his eyes as she spoke, gave a small grimace as denial. He pulled the other chair close and sat leaning towards her. He took her hand in his. 'You're frightened,' he said. 'I can understand that. Jesus, what we're deciding is the rest of our lives. Of course it's a huge ask, especially for you, but we're in love now and everything else has to be measured against that. Okay?'

'I'm sorry. I've spent hours going over and over it, driving myself half crazy. I can't toss away everything — not now. I can't even say that we should continue as friends, because that's probably too difficult, and dangerous as well. We got carried away. I suppose because we had so much in common. Also I was looking for support maybe. These things happen — you slide downhill into them somehow. I know a lot of it's been my fault. It's just that . . .' Her voice wavered, and she had to stop, but then forced herself on. 'I don't regret it, none of it, but it's got to end now.'

'You don't mean it,' he said. 'It's just all too much at the moment. That's it. What you have to remember is that there's two of us, not just you by yourself: two of us to work through it all so that we can be together in the end. Okay, there's issues for sure — of course there's stuff that's bloody hard. That's life. We're together, though, that's the big thing.'

His hand tightened around hers; he leant even closer as if proximity could ensure an emotional bond. Sarah had the unpleasant and abrupt understanding that he wasn't open to reason, that his devotion was unswerving. Only the most plain, almost brutal, declaration had any chance of penetration, and she made herself meet his gaze.

'I'm finishing it. Right now, right here,' she said. 'I'm sorry for hurting you, but I can't do anything about that. It hurts me as well. There's too much against us and I should've seen that at the start, but you don't, and one thing leads to another. Anyway, I'm sorry, but I'm going now and I can't see you again.'

'You can't walk off just like that and pretend something so important is over.' His voice was almost gentle, as if improbability in what she said was self-evident. 'Everything will work out if we stick together. Love finds a way. We can make it work. We can come through it.'

'Going on about everything only draws it out,' she said. 'I don't think I made any promises, and if I did then I'm sorry, but I can't carry on now. It's driving me silly so I can't think straight. All of it has to stop.'

'We're meant to be together,' Hartley said, but she didn't reply. To talk about it was painful and called for futile explanation. How could love become so sad? Why couldn't he shut up and let her go before it was all too much?

She pulled her hand slowly from his grip, stood up and moved to the door. Hartley followed her closely. He wanted to drive her home: it could rain again, he said, but she wished to walk, to arrive back to Robert with an interval between the two men. Already the asphalt of the motel was drying, faint vapour drifting from the surface, the sky almost completely blue. A man was taking cases from a white car not far away. His little daughter was standing watching and he said, 'We'll ask Mum if she wants the stuff on hangers,' and they went inside. How could the rest of the world be imperturbable when Hartley and Sarah were in the firestorm?

'Goodbye,' she said, and gave him such a rapid hug that he wasn't quick enough to clasp her. She wanted to thank him for all they'd had together, but it would seem so out of place, when she was refusing the things most important to him. She wanted to say have a good life and be happy. And even in that most difficult farewell she wanted to say — don't forget me. That they had to give up all they had formed together, didn't negate the value of it. Love is special, whatever the circumstances, but sometimes it comes at the wrong time and won't fit with the rest of life's jigsaw.

'I'll text. We'll work everything out, you'll see,' said Hartley loudly as she walked towards the street, but she didn't trust herself to reply, or to turn to see him. 'I love you, Sarah, we'll make it work,' he called, as a young man might do. Maybe she'd never see him again, and one part of her hoped for that, while another suffered a pang that almost caused her to stumble. It's for the best. It's for the best, she kept saying to herself, and made herself walk on, conscious of the physical effort of moving her legs and the awkwardness in her arms. She felt taken apart in both body and spirit. The glances of people passing seemed to have a quality of both pity and complacency, the sounds of the city around her were strangely muted.

How reduced and ordinary the motel seemed once Sarah had gone. Hartley wanted to be away from it, but stood inside for a few minutes in case she came back, as he was willing her to do. He had an odd and passing inclination to rough up the bed so that it would appear they had made love as usual, but knew that no one cared, or kept a tally, that the cleaner would register just brief satisfaction for one less chore. He felt pummelled emotionally, weakened by Sarah's withdrawal of love.

He went to the office and gave the key to the guy with the tartan slippers and hair as stiff as that of a dead dog. 'How was that for a dump of rain? Jeez,' the man said.

'Came down all right,' replied Hartley woodenly. He was thinking of Sarah walking steadily away, going back to Robert and a life accumulated over many years. He could see Robert as he'd been when they met in the apartment — a big, capable man depleted and bemused by illness, and trying to come to terms with that. Someone no longer capable of being the partner that Sarah deserved.

When he was home, Hartley began to prepare a rather complicated stir-fry meal from a cook book with a bright cover showing assorted cupcakes. He wasn't hungry, but he needed to be doing something as he thought about what had happened and what his response would be. A restless urgency wouldn't allow him to sit still, or even stand on the deck and look over the bush towards the city. He rattled about in the kitchen, but the ingredients he prepared meant nothing to him. He noticed his hands were shaking, and he observed that with a detached curiosity.

Of course Sarah had become frightened: she'd realised that the greatest price of their love was pain for others close to her. Maybe even her daughter wouldn't understand. She had to be supported, encouraged to make the right choice, convinced that he'd stick by her and that it was worth all they would go through to be together. Sarah's misgivings had to be overcome by redoubled love and commitment on his part.

He would write a letter, Hartley decided. It came to him suddenly and with such impact that he paused in the slicing of mushrooms. He'd never written to her before. Surely there was a permanence and open declaration about a letter that other communications lacked. He began again on the vegetables, sorting phrases as he did so. It would be their first love letter, and he imagined they would read it and smile years later when all the present difficulty and agitation were over. Yes, he would write a letter and it would be a path for Sarah to follow back to him. The more she wavered, the stronger he had to be for both of them.

'My darling Sarah', he would begin, and he would describe for her the sky blue curtains and pillows of the bedroom bought for her, and the trips they would have together in warm, dry places where gumboots were unknown and language unintelligible, yet wonderful to listen to for musicality alone. He would put up a fight for her to prove his love, and that the future lay with him, not Robert. Yes — 'My darling Sarah, Now or never they say, and it must be now and ever for you and me' — that's how he would begin.

He left the littered bench of the kitchen and went to his desk to write, but almost at once the shivering distortions of migraine began their drift across his vision, and he stood up in search of his pills. He would write in the morning if he were up to it. He turned away from the evening sun and prepared to lie down in the bedroom with the blue curtains drawn, his half-prepared meal forgotten. I can persuade her, he reassured himself. I can do it.

How he wished that Sarah was already with him. Robert wasn't the only one in her life who needed comfort. The familiar ache in his left temple began, but he tried to keep his focus on Sarah. When he was walking with her, even their gaits were synchronised and they moved naturally together, talking at a Magnus table, always with close attention between them, lying on the motel bed, close enough to see individual eyelashes, and the depth of folded green-grey in the iris of her eye that reminded him of the favourite glass marbles he possessed in boyhood. Within the glass were fixed sweeps and veils of multi-coloured aurora. Tors they were called then. Yes, tors, and you played keepers, but never gave up the tors if you lost, proffering only lesser substitutes. It was the recollection of boyhood marbles and Sarah's eyes that comforted him before the pain became the single awareness.

Chapter Sixteen

T he letter was in the box when Sarah and Robert came back from an afternoon chamber music performance at a former lodge hall in Ponsonby. Both the performance and attendance were poor, though as Robert slept during most of the selections he had little to criticise. The envelope bore the insignia of Hastings Hull Legal, which unsettled Sarah even before she knew the contents. Was it meant as a challenge to anonymity, or a hint not to open it in Robert's presence? Was it just that Hartley had no other envelope to hand? She kept it beneath the other mail as they went up to the apartment, but Robert showed no interest. He had for some time resigned himself to the belief that good news from any source was unlikely.

She read it that night, when Robert was in bed, and she sitting close to the large window with the changing city kaleidoscope of external colour and movement. 'My darling Sarah, Now or never they say' it began, and continued for several closely written pages. Nothing was held back, and through it all was a fixed, incontrovertible sincerity. Much of what he wrote was on their future, and regarding that he was as specific and confident as on their past. 'Don't be afraid,' he wrote, 'don't be afraid to rely on me. We have the chance to live in a way few people ever do.' She couldn't doubt his devotion, but rather than being warmed, or exalted, by that, she felt a sense of almost threatening constriction. He wasn't going to let her go. He wasn't going to accept her decision that it was over between them. She had welcomed love, believing it enriching, and now found its grip increasingly a threat. 'I don't care about anything else,' he wrote. 'Nothing matters to me at all except you, except us. If you're honest you know you feel the same.'

When she finished reading, she crushed the pages in her hands as a brief release. She still felt affection for him, attraction even, but also an increasing sense that his love was unreasonable. Maybe the greater love is, the more unreasonable it becomes. Love is an emotion resistant to management and common sense, but she must find a way through that had the least pain for all. Lovers everywhere survived break-ups without enduring despair, and sailed on through life. There were options, she told herself, and she was experienced enough surely to ensure the best outcome. She would be sensible, though Hartley was unable to be. She would impose conditions rather than be subject to them.

Yet her hands gripping his letter were clenched, and she remembered his close imploring face when they were last together in the motel. Can love be ended without being lost?

'It'll be all right. I know it will,' she murmured as she watched the lights of the city — pulsing reds and whites of the passing cars, the ripple of advertising, the abrupt change of traffic lights, the blank, yellow windows of the office blocks within which a nameless population of cleaners removed the routine daily stains of official residence.

Robert was asleep when she looked in on him, on his back, his mouth open and the flesh of his face fallen away a little so that he looked thinner. His nose and forehead had a red flush that spread high on his cheeks, and the lower part of his face was creased and bore a grey stubble. He was an old man battling sickness, and he looked like it, yet how readily she could see him as he'd once been, and recall laughter and kindness, confidence and strength.

She took her cell phone, went to the lavatory, closed the door behind her and rang Hartley. 'Don't write again,' she said. 'It only makes it difficult for me. Don't write, don't ring, don't text, don't come, don't anything. I've told you. I don't want to have to tell Robert, or the police, but I will if I have to. I'll do it. Don't ruin what we had by trying to hang on when it's over. I mean it . . . No, I'm not going to talk about it with you. I mean it. It's over. Don't push me into something that blows up in our faces. You know in your heart, don't you . . . No, it's not . . . No, it doesn't. It's bloody over.'

———

OVER? HOW COULD IT be over? Everything that he wanted, everything that he planned, centred on continuation. She would come to see that what he offered was greater than anything she'd experienced before they met. She was just faint-hearted because of her feeling of responsibility towards Robert, and even that was a sign of her decency and sense of obligation. He would love her all the more for it.

In truth Robert was a pain in the arse. 'A pain in the

arse,' Hartley said aloud to himself after the thought came to him. He was sitting with his legs up on the leather couch, the phone still in his hand after her abrupt ultimatum. The lights were on, but the curtains still open, and the yellow glow spilled weakly towards the bush, beyond which the far, compressed and multi-coloured lights of the city glittered. Sarah was there, too — in the photograph so much closer. 'Robert is a pain in the arse,' he said again, looking directly at the photograph.

Hartley had no doubt of Sarah's love: no woman could give so generously and not mean more. It was just that she needed his resolve to help her make the break with the old life, and he wouldn't fail her. He would text in the morning, despite what she'd said. He wondered if Robert were still able to fuck her, and hoped that he was too weak and growing more so. Even the thought of them sharing the same bed was almost unbearable.

It came to him suddenly that he needed to see Robert again, not so much to witness the hoped for decline, but to gauge his adversary. On his first visit to the apartment he'd relished the sense of greater knowledge; Robert accepting him at face value as a hospital agency visitor and having no idea of the contest being waged. What name had he used when they met, Hartley wondered. Olders, that's what it was, and Martin the first name? Or Colin? Yes, Colin. Surely it didn't matter much because he'd left no card, and Robert had shown little interest. But he would write that down before going to bed — Colin Olders from out-patients services.

He sent texts each morning and afternoon over the next two days while at Hastings Hull, but received no reply. On the Friday afternoon he drove into the city and parked by the real-estate agency where he couldn't be seen from the window of Sarah's apartment, but had a clear view of the entrance to the building, even the small lawn and the seat there. A little after two, Sarah and Robert came out together and went away in a taxi, so Hartley drove to his work, although it wasn't one of his office days, and caught up with things there. On Saturday morning he returned to his watching post and settled to wait. He didn't read because he might become absorbed and miss Sarah coming out. Instead he watched the passers-by for a time, and the observation of a dark-haired power-walker with green shorts became the segue to thoughts of the sessions he'd had with Rory Menzies.

He had gone to counselling expecting to dislike Menzies. Even the name, for some reason, predisposed him to antipathy, although he had no particular dislike of the Scots. Maybe he'd been too much swayed by the portrayal of psychologists and psychiatrists in films and books of fiction. Menzies was young and didn't look at all Viennese. He was something of an athlete and jogged to work some mornings. Hartley had seen him once, in green shorts and a loose tracksuit top, maintaining a clockwork rhythm. In the office he provided no couch, and no ink shapes for Hartley to morph into representations of his life. He and Madeleine both had issues with their parents, Menzies had said, issues of communication, expectation, but mainly love. Disappointment and loneliness within a family were like tidal surges, he said. At one session ginger-haired Menzies had placed one leg on the knee of the other, and Hartley had noticed on the sole of his shoe a round paper sticker promoting a charity for the sufferers of autism. As the counsellor discussed the need for commitment in therapy, Hartley had pondered possible explanations for the small blue and red advertisement beneath his foot.

Hartley was shaken from his reverie by the sight of Sarah coming unaccompanied from the apartments. He felt the familiar surge of emotion at recognition, and for a moment thought he might follow and approach her, rather than go up to 3B and meet her husband again. But as intended he waited until Sarah was out of sight, then went up to her apartment.

Robert, dressed but unshaven, came to the door. 'Colin Olders, outpatients services,' said Hartley, as Robert at first showed no signs of recalling his last visit. 'I'm making a second check to see that all's going well.'

'Fine, thanks. Did my wife get in touch with you about something?'

'No. It's just a follow-up policy that we have.' He remained, expectantly, in the doorway.

'Do you want to come in?' said Robert finally.

'Maybe a moment or two. I don't want to be a bother,' said Hartley. 'Just a couple of quick things.' He watched Robert closely as he turned and led the way into the main room. He looked no worse than on Hartley's last visit: better perhaps. Probably that was because of the stage in the present round of treatment, Hartley thought, rather than any lasting improvement. At his age he could hardly expect to pull through such a serious illness. 'How have you been feeling?' Hartley asked.

'Not so bad.' Robert didn't sit down, but stood by the window and looked rather quizzically at his visitor.

'We have a new programme of volunteer visitors,' said Hartley. 'People who are happy to spend a few hours with out-of-towners, or people who lack support. Often a bit of company can be a lift to people during treatment.'

Robert said he was okay, didn't feel any need for more support than he was already getting from Mr Goosen and the team at oncology. In fact, he said, one of the nurses there came from Hamilton.

Hartley asked him about his career as a dentist, just to delay departure, and enjoyed again the feeling of being in the place where Sarah lived, of having links with Robert's world and wife of which Robert had no knowledge. How easily he could step into Sarah's life, whether she wished it or not. And he felt entitlement.

The familiar red case of Sarah's reading glasses was on the leather armrest of the sofa, a magazine was folded open at pages depicting summer salads, a green and yellow silk scarf was a soft heap on the end of the table farthest from Robert's photographs. There, too, was the Matakana blue jug, the Quisling among the ornaments, loyal surely to its purchaser. Hartley should be the incumbent, the one in possession of the room and all it signified. He wanted to tell Robert to bugger off, that he was unwanted and unnecessary, that it was best he give up on the treatment and die quickly. Hartley felt exasperation rather than hatred, the sort of impatience morphing into anger that arises when some knucklehead is holding you up in the queue and time is running out. He wanted to encourage Robert to the balcony, have it no barrier, and propel him from the third-floor height so that his bulk finished on the concrete below.

Instead, Hartley agreed that those who complained of the charges for dental care didn't realise the level of overheads. 'The hidden costs of running a professional practice are much greater than people realise,' said Robert. 'Office staff, insurances, accountants, KiwiSaver contributions, ACC, rates. It goes on and on. And the price of specialist equipment and materials has sky-rocketed: all sourced overseas, you see.'

'I can imagine,' said Hartley.

'And the years of training without an income. That's conveniently forgotten.'

'Good point.' Hartley was well aware of all the arguments, and the defensiveness they disguised, but he adopted the tone of the converted.

And when Robert turned to lead him out, Hartley adroitly whisked the silk scarf from the table and put it in his pocket. 'It's good of you to come again,' said Robert, 'but no need. We're okay here and I don't require anything. We've got things pretty well sorted, I think.'

'Great. That's fine, then. Good luck with it all.'

As on his first visit, he had no apprehension that he might meet Sarah returning. Almost he wished it, and stood for a time by the gateway as people flowed by, and beyond them the traffic, faster, noisier, and tainting the warm air. In the car he took Sarah's scarf and laid it on his shoulders. Its weight was barely discernible. He expected it to have Sarah's fragrance, but there was only the faintest hint of face powder, and the original, exotic smell of the silk. He gave no thought to how he looked, seated in his car with a woman's green and yellow scarf at his throat. No one paid any attention; few even glanced at him as they passed. How very ordinary the people were, all purposeful on errands of trivial significance, and lacking the sustaining love that he had found.

At home, he spread the scarf on the pillow of his bed. The sunlight gave a shimmer to the silk, and the glint from the green reminded him of the bright bodies of the large flies of his boyhood: iridescent blues and greens that were quite beautiful, although borne by insects inhabiting a morass of shit and mud. That ambivalence was clear in almost every memory he had of childhood, and as Hartley sat on the deck of the fine house that had become his through family deaths, as he enjoyed a glass of Marlborough wine in the late-afternoon warmth and listened to the tui and native pigeons in the bush that surrounded him, it wasn't at first Sarah and Robert whom he thought of, despite his visit to the apartment, but the far Southland dairy farm where he'd grown up.

It doesn't matter at all what the star signs were on the day you were born, who came with small, home-made gifts to see you, or that much earlier some great-grandmother with a reputation for bad temper left an Irish bog to come to the south seas. Life starts with your first memories and ends with the last of them. Whatever the nature of a family, it is accepted as normal by the children within it until there is opportunity for comparison.

Hartley had left home before he understood that his father's failings had warped the relationships of them all. He wasn't an alcoholic, or a wife-beater, just a sour and selfish man who had no time for those who didn't share his own views and interests. He showed little affection for his children, and gave greatest attention to those who proved most like himself. Hartley was the youngest and bore the brunt of his father's impatience. A son either wishes to imitate, even surpass, his father, or by a process of negative charge is driven to the opposite in everything. They had almost stopped talking by the time Hartley moved north: not as the result of any specific confrontation, just the tacit acknowledgement that they had nothing in common beyond a kinship that was biological rather than emotional. He'd gone back occasionally, briefly, to see his mother, and when his father died he had felt no grief, not even the inclination to attend the funeral. And he received nothing in the will.

His father did a great deal of hard, physical slog and considered any other activity of lesser value, even an evasion of effort. He derided any occupation, or recreation, that didn't bring on a sweat. There must have been an inner life, but Hartley caught no glimpse of it. 'Getting stuck in' seemed his father's response to everything. He was once persuaded to attend a theatrical performance to raise funds for the local primary school, and reacted dismissively; laughed in the wrong places, scoffed at the sentiment, and rapidly stacked all the chairs at the conclusion of the show as a physical release. Hartley had done well at high school. Most subjects came easily to him, especially maths. He received awards at senior prize-giving, but his father was more impressed by his brothers' sporting achievements.

Only many years after he'd left home did Hartley understand the significance of the apparently trivial preferences that distinguished his parents. His mother always drank tea, his father always asked for coffee: his mother loved egg sandwiches, his father said they stank of farts. His mother left the television on whether watching it or not, his father said it drove him crazy. His mother always put an orange cushion on the chair by the phone, and his father always took it off. All such divergences were subtle instances of psychological recoil, although the marriage carried on with dogged resignation. They were a Jack Sprat couple without the benefits.

Oddly enough his father kept a diary. Hartley came across it on the sideboard on one of the last visits he made to the farm, and flicked through the entries. Each day's weather was noted, tasks accomplished, or intended, prices and purchases, stock tallies, but nothing of his family, or his feelings, nothing of his hopes and fears. The single sustained reference to his community was the record of the deaths of those around him. Old Reg Trumpeter snuffed it today, Will Nicholl's oldest boy crushed by a stock truck in the yards, Adele Brownlie hung herself Thursday. His father had no close friends, and even his dogs didn't love him, although they'd learnt to obey. Hartley had only one reason to wish his father still alive, and that was to have him witness his youngest son's material success, and be forced to acknowledge it.

Hartley had no nostalgia for childhood, and when he did return, it was to re-enter a memory of separateness tempered only by passing affection from his busy and fragile mother that was never enough for his needs. She had been especially protective of the one daughter in the family. A man needs a woman's love all to himself. He'd hoped for that in marriage to Madeleine and been disappointed: with Sarah he was convinced it would be different.

Hartley could feel the heat of the low sun on his shirt. He leant back in the deckchair, closed his eyes so that the bright light became just a reddish-gold glow through the lids. He thought of sitting beneath a table umbrella at Magnus, with Sarah laughing at some shared absurdity. He thought of strolling with her in the city, among people less fortunate and less happy. He thought of the coloured silk on his bed and imagined Sarah lying with it, and he there with her. There was nothing he wouldn't risk for that.

There was time for a different and better life: a decade before he reached the biblical span of three score years and ten, which modern living and medical science had pushed out much farther. He and Sarah could have twenty years of close companionship, and with the resources to make the most of it. Hartley kept his eyes closed and paraded in his mind scene after scene of imagined pleasure.

––––––––

'THAT CHAP OLDERS CAME again when you were away,' said Robert when Sarah returned. He was back sitting at the table with his photographs.

'Who?'

'From the outpatients back-up service, or whatever. I thought you must have asked them to call again. Odd sort of a bloke.'

'I know nothing about them. What did he want this time?'

'Same as before. Just any ways they can make it easier. I suppose it's a good service for some people who aren't able to cope, or are going through it without any support, but I'd already told him things were okay for us.'

'Obviously he hasn't got enough to do.'

'Maybe. He wasn't in any hurry — just gawped about, and asked about dentistry and Hamilton. I guess they have quite a file on everybody.'

Sarah didn't answer. She had been to see an exhibition of architectural drawings, and been disappointed that the impact hadn't been sufficient to take her mind from Hartley and what he might do. Almost certainly there would already be texts on her phone, and God knows what follow-up if she didn't reply. She wasn't going to, though; she would be strong, day after day, until he got the message and let go.

Robert was concentrating on the photos again, sorting little piles that stood by the albums like packs of cards. Among them he came across occasional newspaper photographs, clippings that were faded, and wrinkled from competition with the firmer backed images. The more recent ones were of Donna's school achievements, or her fortuitous background presence in a gala shot, maybe a Santa Claus procession. One of the oldest, on jaundiced, seamed paper, showed Sarah and Robert among the finalists for the provincial sports person of the year award. Forty years ago, and there they were among their peers, proud yet self-conscious, scrubbed up for a special night. Robert had known he had little chance of winning, but at the dinner he'd met Sarah for the first time and so the night was in retrospect a victory greater than he could have envisaged. He was partly obscured in the photo, but they all looked into the camera with the bravado of youth and optimism.

Apart from themselves, Robert recognised only one

person: Marie Sellers, who had gone on to win a national tennis title and maintained a sporting profile. The others, like Robert and Sarah themselves, having reached the limit of their moderate sporting talent, had moved on to everyday careers that merited no special publicity. Perhaps they, too, had cut the photograph from the paper and would come across it some day, look at the forgotten faces and wonder where time had led them. A pissed guy had set off the fire alarm, Robert suddenly remembered, and the night had ended in some confusion. That and meeting Sarah were his only enduring memories of the occasion. He'd forgotten even the night's main speaker, who must have been someone of note at the time.

Robert flourished the newspaper cutting, and told his wife he hadn't realised they still had it. 'All sorts of stuff is turning up,' he said, but Sarah remained standing at the glass doors to the balcony, looking out without attention, wishing she was at some happier point in her life.

Robert fossicked some more, found another photograph of interest. 'Here's one I know you'll like,' he said, and she made herself come to him and lean down to see. It was the beach at St Clair, and the two of them ankle deep in the sea with Donna between them, a hand in each of theirs. All of them in togs. Sarah's mother stood a little farther up the sand, fully clothed and with a smile towards them, knowing she was not the focus. It was a picture that flattered Robert.

'She loved the water,' said Sarah brightly as a deflection.

'She became a good swimmer. Won prizes at school for it.' Recognition was important for Robert. Most of his life had been reckoned in terms of measurable achievement. Staying alive had become the most recent goal.

'Here's another one.' He held up one of Sarah and a friend in ballgowns, lifting fluted glasses as if to toast the camera. 'Lydia and you at the festival ball. Remember the damn car wouldn't start afterwards.' The photograph was black and white, but Sarah saw the dress in its true lilac. The strap on the left shoulder kept working off and she hadn't worn it much afterwards; maybe not at all. She had no recollection of the problem with the car that Robert had found so annoying.

'You must be about finished sorting all these,' said Sarah. 'It would be good to clear up the mess on the table. It seems to be getting worse all the time.'

'Here's another,' said Robert, paying no attention. 'You and that crazy woman who was in the DOC office with you.'

Her name was Pam. In the photograph she had her arms around Sarah from behind and was grinning theatrically over her shoulder. On the wall beyond them was a poster soliciting money for pest-free island habitats. It was a glimpse of a time in their lives when everything seemed so much simpler, and difficulties were laughed away. Pam wasn't crazy: she was just a woman friend in a way that men found hard to comprehend. She wasn't a lesbian, but women were more important in her life than men, not because she was unable to gather male attention, but because she preferred the company of her own sex. Pam was fun, both open and intense. She was also supportive and confiding. Robert had been quite attracted to her initially, but came to resent his sense of exclusion when the three of them were together. 'Why is she always laughing?' he used to say, and Sarah in reply had to avoid the truth that she was laughing at him. Sarah could do with Pam's comfort now, someone close, to whom she could tell the story of Hartley and herself, and the predicament to which it had led.

'Dear old Pam,' she said. 'All we do now is exchange Christmas cards. I miss her.'

'She was always laughing, though. See, she's laughing here.' He put his finger to the photo.

'Why not?' said Sarah sharply. 'Good on her. I hope she's still laughing. I wish to God I was.'

Robert took that as an expression of concern for himself. 'Don't worry,' he said. 'We'll come through this okay. You'll see.'

Chapter Seventeen

There was no set lunch hour at Hastings Hull, but Hartley and Simon Drummond occasionally went out together to a nearby café, and if they had no appointments they would sit for an hour or more and in their talk make no distinction between professional and private life. Without conscious acknowledgement, they felt greater freedom to pass judgement on both their colleagues and their clients when they were out of the office. Simon was more than an acquaintance, almost a friend, but, at the café only days after the phone call in which Sarah had dumped him so decisively, Hartley found little in the conversation to hold attention.

Simon was mocking the senior partner of the firm by recounting the strenuous efforts he made each half-year to gain nominations for a gong in the honours list. Simon and Hartley had both been obliquely approached, and indicated they would give support, without any intention of doing so. 'I know he gave a sizeable donation to the Nats, and Gillian found a draft of a letter in which he complained that the judiciary were over-represented in the honours lists at the expense of those in private legal practice. No individuals mentioned of course!' said Simon, his large head nodding on his shoulders, a smile on his pale face.

'Pompous old prick,' said Hartley. 'I can never work out what he does in that office hour after hour. When he does write a letter it's so stuffed with obsolete legalese that it's unreadable. He never remembers what days I'm in, and moans that I'm never there when he needs me.'

'Who else bothers with a waistcoat, for Christ's sake?'

'You're right.'

'And who else has a bottle of port in the office cabinet?'

'Yes.'

'He got lost in the carpark at the club.'

'Lost?'

'You know he's just bought the Audi, and he came out late and a bit pissed, and wandered around in the dark looking for the car he had before: the red Beamer. They found him almost in tears.'

The man deserved ridicule, and Hartley would normally have enjoyed joining in, but only Sarah was of real interest to him, and the nagging ache of his abandonment distanced all else. Why was he sitting there with pleasant, smiling Simon Drummond when his happiness was at stake? Sitting on his arse instead of fighting for his life, for without Sarah the world had no lustre. He felt his throat constrict, and Simon's voice and those of people seated further away had an echoing inconsequence.

'I've got to get back,' he said. 'I have to go out soon,' and he was impatient with his colleague's staid progress as they walked back to Hastings Hull. Once there he hunted out a black permanent marker pen, told Gillian he'd be away for an hour or so, and drove to Sarah's apartment. He couldn't get a park close by, and had to leave the car on yellow lines and walk several blocks. It was Murphy's Law, he told himself. One thing goes to Hell and everything starts to crumble. A lanky kid in a Disney T-shirt swerved past him on a skateboard, shouldering him and sweeping on without apology. Little prick. Hartley felt like ramming him, at least shouting after him, but just pulled a face and hurried on.

When he reached the apartment building he stood for a time looking up at the balcony and window of Sarah's rooms. He was in plain view, and deliberately so, but there was no indication that he'd been noticed. He went up to 3B, waited briefly, regarding the light wooden expanse of the door, then he took the marker pen and wrote in extravagant printing 'LOVE ME I AM DYING'.

He could feel himself shaking slightly, but had a sense of exhilaration in making such a public declaration. He knocked on the door and went quickly to the stairwell, where he wasn't easily seen. No one came to the door so he went back and knocked again, retreated again. No one came. It was an anti-climax, and for a time he remained standing, several steps down, rather foolishly staring at the closed door. 'So you're out,' he said softly. But the message was there, wasn't it, waiting for Sarah and Robert when they returned.

Hartley felt relief in having done something positive to show Sarah the depth of his love, and encourage her to acknowledge openly that she felt the same way. He felt free for a time from uncertainty and the inability to make life conform to his expectation. He went back to the office, sat awaiting a three-thirty appointment that Gillian came through to confirm. 'Do you ever wish for a different life?' he asked her.

'Not really,' she answered. Why would she reveal her dreams to him when he had shown so little interest in her everyday existence?

'Most people settle for too little.'

'Right,' said Gillian.

'I don't intend to give up so easily.'

'Okay. Anyhow, so you're set for Mr Friedland, then?' said Gillian. She knew that Hartley was really talking to himself. She'd grown accustomed to having words bounced on her without her replies being given value.

Maurice Friedland came to discuss the purchase of the building in which he'd operated a fish-and-chip shop for twenty-six years. His name was pronounced 'Freedland', but when written made a visual pun connected with his trade that normally Hartley would have appreciated. Now he wasn't in the mood. The day was one of the most significant in Friedland's life, and he was aware of it. Finally he would own the premises in which he'd laboured for so long. He wore a tie, and was both uneasy and borne up with the unaccustomed formality. He carried a cardboard box containing his papers, and talked with great enthusiasm of his intended purchase.

Hartley nodded his head, and offered the occasional phatic comment, but his own life was his concern. He would provide the necessary legal service, which was more rudimentary than Friedland imagined, with professional competence, while his real self was elsewhere. He was thinking of Sarah, the message on the door, the life that was possible if she returned to him — the emptiness if she didn't.

He had never smoked, but had on his desk a ceramic ashtray with a reddish glaze in which he kept paper clips, rubber bands, parking meter coins and a couple of memory sticks. He picked up a stubby pin with a plastic top and pushed the point into his thumb. When he withdrew it a small, dark orb of blood followed, didn't run, and remained glinting in the round. Hartley's hands were below desk level and Friedland noticed nothing, continued talking of the scale of mortgage payments he could sustain. As his client went on, Hartley replaced the pin in the bowl, and took up one of the memory sticks. The orange plastic cover was clear enough for him to see the intricate circuitry beneath, like the innards within the translucent body of an insect. With his index finger he made a small smear from the blood on his thumb. Despite the sun slanting into the office, despite the peerless, blue sky of summer, despite the rising fortunes of Maurice Friedland, who leant smiling towards him, he felt cold. What was the value of anything if you weren't loved?

'I wish my father was alive to see the day I take possession of the building,' Friedland was saying, easing his tie slightly. 'Even in his eighties he'd come in well before six o'clock to do the chipping, and he had gout and rheumatism so bad that sometimes he'd shout out despite himself. Right out loud no matter who was there, the pain was so bad. He slogged all his life for us kids and for bugger-all. Owning the premises was his dream, and he'll never know it. Mind you, I had to create a different sort of business model to the old man's.'

'Where would we be without a good father?' said Hartley, savouring the irony.

ROBERT AND SARAH HAD been close at hand during Hartley's visit to the apartment, but unaware of it. They had been one floor down, at the Ellisons. The rooms were much the same, but the outlook was not of the street, but a carpark and offices. Robert was feeling better than he had for some time. He'd enjoyed the lunch, especially the apple crumble, and even more the discussion with Tony Ellison on the bureaucratic encroachment of government on private business enterprise. Tony was a retired importer of veterinary equipment and medications. In Auckland Robert had little opportunity to talk with other men about business and politics. He appreciated his wife's intelligence and knowledge, but there were times in his new setting when he missed his male friends and colleagues. His one reservation about Tony was the beard; the colour of cigarette ash and untrimmed down his neck. Robert considered beards an affectation, like cravats, or kissing women on both cheeks.

Rather than take the lift when they left, Robert walked up the stairs in a minor display of fitness, but even so Sarah reached the apartment ahead of him, and there was her lover's unmistakable message. Love me, I am dying. Sarah knew what it meant. Hartley's challenge to her decision, his demonstration of how easily he could reach into her world. The flaunted expression of unrelenting devotion.

'What the fuck is this?' exclaimed Robert, half in astonishment, half in annoyance. He took his handkerchief, wet it with his tongue, and rubbed at the L of love. It smudged only slightly, and was otherwise unchanged. 'And it's permanent too. Someone's playing silly buggers.'

Where was he? Was he watching? She glanced at the stairs behind them and at the closed doors of the lift farther down the hall. She knew it was one of Hartley's office days and he must have been agitated to leave work and come to the apartment to make his graphic plea. Sarah felt angry with Hartley, but also concerned for him. He was changing, mutating in some disturbing way from the man she loved.

She didn't wish to consider what responsibility she bore for that.

She had the illogical and unpleasant thought that he was standing on the other side of the door, waiting for her to open it. It was an appeal, of course, she could recognise that, but it was also a violation of sorts, an intrusion into a part of her life he had no right to enter.

'I'll get the maintenance guy up,' said Robert. 'I wouldn't have expected this sort of thing here.'

'Just ring him,' said Sarah. 'Just ring him when we get inside.'

'Yeah. It'll come off all right I suppose. There'll be some cleaning stuff for it. But "Love me I am dying", what sort of nonsense is that?'

'Kids probably.' She remembered the grave beneath the trees, spangled with sunlight, and the story of Emily and Edward as Hartley had later told it, and the sympathy they had expressed from the safety of their own happiness. 'It doesn't mean anything,' she said. 'Just kids' rubbish.'

While Robert busied himself with arrangements to have the words removed, Sarah went out onto the small balcony and stood there in the sun, her face raised to its reassuring warmth. No, she wouldn't ring, she thought, suppressing her desire to hit back. That's what he wanted — to force her to get in touch again so he could persuade her to see him. But if she didn't contact him then next he would come round, wouldn't he? Knocking on the door he'd defaced, telling Robert all that had happened between them, standing in love-stricken vulnerability to demand she admit their affair.

In her confusion and anger there was love and sadness, too. Behind Hartley's increasingly erratic gestures, she could still recognise the man she'd been so attracted to, still glimpse the ideal future he imagined for them together, despite the circumstances that must prevent it.

Chapter Eighteen

Hartley saw that Sarah was pulling away, more and more retreating to the safety of her old life, and away from the venture and commitment required by love. Maybe he should let her see that he, too, had alternatives, an existence apart from concern with her. He decided to go away for a few days, regain a sense of individual balance. He would drive south for distraction and not keep in touch with her. Maybe distance would give him perspective: at times he was shaken by the intensity of his love. Perhaps she would value his affection more when she saw it wasn't guaranteed.

So on Friday he drove south, and didn't examine his decision to stop in Hamilton for lunch. He would go on later, maybe all the way to Wellington even, and have the weekend there. Sarah was right. Hamilton was a town that had grown large without growing up, still without the sophistication of a city. After sandwiches in a café with loud background music, but no customers except himself, Hartley found the location of Sarah's house from the phone book, told himself that it was merely idle curiosity that drew him there.

A broad, low, modern place that gave little to the street view other than an expanse of metal garage doors and an entrance protected by walls of glass blocks. Because the section was flat, there was no panorama such as his own home possessed, and it seemed strange to him to see houses stacked one behind another in that way.

He walked to the front door, saw through the frosted glass beside him the colourful blur of the garden, rang the bell, and although he expected no one to respond, imagined Sarah coming in answer, happy to see him. He then went around the side of the house, opening a wrought-iron gate so low he could as easily have stepped over it. A glasshouse without plants, a tin shed, a brick barbecue area and a well-kept lawn with silver birch trees at its end. Nothing distinctive, yet the woman he loved lived here, and so it should possess a special gloss, a shimmering montage of Sarah about her day. No shadow, or outline, of Robert, however. Hartley went to a window close to the back door. He could see into the kitchen, which had the total neatness of absence. There were the touches of her favourite colour just as he expected: on tiles above the hot-plates, and blue ceramic containers in diminishing size at the end of the granite bench surface. 'Blue, blue,' he murmured to himself, and craned his neck in an effort to see the far end of the room where there were a table and chairs.

'Can I help you?' It was a neighbour to his right; her head and half-torso showing above the wooden fence. A tall woman, well made-up with pendant ear rings and bright lipstick, as if she were about to go out, or had recently returned.

'Hi. I'm a friend of Robert's and Sarah's. I'm passing

through and thought I'd call in.' He moved towards the fence and smiled to show his good intentions.

'They're in Auckland,' the woman said. 'Robert's having treatment there so they're staying for a while.' She was pleased to have personal information to pass on and saw him as no threat. 'He hasn't been feeling great for a while, but he's in the best place he could be now.'

'They did tell me he had cancer,' Hartley said, 'but I've been overseas for a few months and haven't caught up on things. I didn't know they had to stay up there.'

'All that coming and going, so they thought they may as well rent a comfortable place for a few months and be done with it. It's going as well as can be expected. I think it's marvellous what they can do these days. You read in the paper almost every day of some breakthrough, and not just in cancer. Keyhole surgery, growing whole livers and hearts in a test tube. Where will it all end, I wonder?'

'You'll be missing them,' said Hartley. He imagined Sarah coming into the section and this neighbour scuttling out to share her magazine wisdom.

'We keep an eye on the place,' the woman said with conscious modesty. Close up she was older than his first impression suggested. Her face was thin and subject to a slight but continuous vibration that made the jewelled earrings shake and catch the sunlight.

He was about to say what a well-matched couple Sarah and Robert were, in the hope of drawing out personal information to the contrary, but the odds were that the answer would be discouraging, so he thanked her and went back to his car. He checked his phone, found nothing from Sarah, resisted the urge to ring, or text, and say he was outside her Hamilton home, yet he felt a secret advantage to be there, holding her place in view — the flowers she nurtured, the windows she washed, the letter box she visited to collect written evidence of her existence.

How much would the place be worth, if Robert didn't come through the treatment, or met with misfortune, and Sarah came to live with him in Titirangi? A lawyer naturally has such practical thoughts. House prices were much higher in Auckland, but this place was large, contemporary and well kept. There were those financial advisers who were sceptical of investment in real estate, and the politicians moaned about the obsession with home ownership, but Hartley believed in concrete assets, had a rental property himself in Mount Roskill. He'd witnessed too many company collapses to be happy handing his money to others to manage.

There was nothing else in Hamilton that he wanted to see: its only existence for him was as the location of Sarah's home, yet he decided to stay the night there rather than go on to Wellington. The farther he moved from Sarah, the less interest he felt in his surroundings if they shared no connection with her. He found a motel nearby, and the sparse, utilitarian order of the unit reminded him of number seventeen in the Spanish motel, the time with Sarah there, and also of his present isolation. He placed her silk scarf on the hard, white pillow, her photograph on the table, spent time by the bench checking the varieties of coffee and tea sachets in the neatly divided wooden tray, hung his jacket in a wardrobe like an upright coffin, flicked through the brochures that offered him pony rides, group discounts at ethnic restaurants and local minibus tours, skimmed the cellophane-enclosed sheet that gave instructions for the telephone and the television.

The motel complex had one living thing that distinguished and ennobled it — a spreading magnolia tree by the office with a wooden seat round all of its circumference. Hartley could see it from the window of his unit, and imagined how wonderful it would be in spring with the creamy flowers set like candles among the glossy leaves. He went out and sat there in the dappled light from the low afternoon sun, and thought how pleasant it would be there if Sarah were with him: how they would talk and laugh and feel that nothing was lacking in the world.

A woman came out of the office with a tray of milk pottles and sachets. 'How are things?' he asked idly.

'Travelling for business or pleasure?' she replied with a smile. She wore jeans, and shoes that looked like sandals, but had quite high heels. She was so blonde that she appeared to have no eyebrows. Her attractive face had no flush of blood, or sun, or cosmetic, could have been carved from chalk, and even the colour of her irises was indistinguishable.

'Business,' said Hartley. Was there real pleasure to be had alone?

'Enjoy your stay, then.'

'This tree,' he said before she could move away. 'I've never seen a magnolia as big. It must be marvellous in flower.'

'They say it's been on the site almost forever. Evidently, long before the motels there was an estate here, and the magnolia was outside the stables. Everything's gone now except the tree — it's got a protection order from the council. The boss moans that it pushes up the paving. The flowers are beautiful, but they bruise so easily we don't pick a lot for vases.' She smiled once more and, before he could speak again, clattered away on the shoes surely unsuitable for work. No doubt she was used to single guests wanting to while away the time with talk.

Hartley stayed beneath the magnolia for some time. It was a living thing of comfort among the cloned motel units and oil-stained asphalt surfaces. Maybe, too, he hoped the white woman would come by again after completing her duties, but he didn't see her again. He returned to his unit and had a shower, from habit placing the provided shampoo and conditioner sachets in his bag and using his own. Then he sat and chose a restaurant from those recommended by the motel. No hurry: there was a whole night to be got through without company. Sarah would be talking with her husband as she prepared a meal. Maybe they would have friends to stay. Hartley knew his name wouldn't be mentioned, but hoped she would think of him. She was so central to his life that it was unimaginable he wasn't vital to hers.

He went to a Chinese place with red and golden dragons above the door, not because it served his favourite food, but because as a single diner he would be less conspicuous there. Unlike his experience at lunch, the room was well filled with people rather than irritating music, and he had his wontons, sweet and sour pork and a dark ale. He was accustomed to being alone, but not reconciled to it, especially since meeting Sarah. He had a second dark ale. Two years a widower, and even in Madeleine's company before that he had often felt solitary. She had possessed barely enough emotional capital to sustain herself, let alone bridge strongly to a partner. 'I'm just not up to it somehow,' she would say of so many things. She feared life too much to enjoy it. 'I'm just so pushed at work,' she would say. A third dark ale, which was unusual for Hartley.

During their married life, Madeleine had many short-lived hobbies and activities that seemed to offer enrichment, or escape, but all fell by the wayside in disenchantment. Pilates, quilting, hospice visiting, estuarine habitat recovery, reflexology, tarot reading, soap making and stained glass. She even fostered a Labrador pup that was to become a guide dog for the blind, but sent it back in dismay when she discovered little Kevin with one of its turds in his hand. Hartley had learnt to make no comment as each enthusiasm failed to provide fulfilment and was cast aside. Madeleine came ill suited to life, as if programmed for a more generous existence.

He hadn't planned to return to Sarah's home, but when

he passed under the golden dragons and walked back to his car, summer's dusk had barely begun and he wasn't ready to go back to the motel and watch the small television screen on the wall bracket. He walked up one side of a street of shops and down another, looking at the window displays, sometimes even stopping, but with no genuine interest whatsoever. People passed their lives that way and he had no wish to be one of them. A selfie, he decided. It came to him as a small inspiration. He'd take a selfie in front of Sarah's house and send it to her as a lark, saying he'd been passing through.

When he got there, dusk was merging the outlines of trees and buildings, colour was leaching from the day. He parked the car at some distance so as not to attract the attention of Sarah's neighbour. The houses seemed lower, settling down for the night in the fading light. No people walking, but the sound of birds disputing in a roosting tree somewhere close at hand. He paused at the gate briefly, and then went up the path and stood close to the door, shielded from view by the alcove formed by the walls of glass blocks.

He found it hard to accept that he'd been unaware of Sarah until recently; that she had been coming and going from this house for years, living a full life that had nothing at all to do with his own. He couldn't remember how to take a flash photograph with his phone, and gave up on the idea. Instead he had an urge to break into the house somehow, as he had broken into her life, walk through the rooms as a form of possession, open drawers and cupboards that would display aspects of herself, touch things that she was accustomed to use, recognise in her ornaments of choice the personality he had come to know and love. The most he allowed himself was to test that the door was locked, and feel unavailingly for a key beneath the raised wooden plant holder. He would ring though, and surely the novelty of his being at her home would overcome any inconvenience she felt at being disturbed while with Robert.

'It's me,' he said. 'Can you talk?'

'No.' She had picked up the phone from the broad arm of the sofa. Robert, in a chair close by, was watching a film about adultery.

'But you won't guess where I'm calling from. Guess where?'

'I don't care,' said Sarah. 'I'm not interested. Don't call again.'

'I'm at your place in Hamilton,' said Hartley. 'I'm right at the front door and—' but she'd rung off, and told Robert that she was sick of being bothered in the evenings by people who wanted donations, or to sell you something.

She tried to calm herself by rearranging the magazines on the coffee table and plumping a velvet cushion, when what she wanted was the release of crying out at Hartley's persistence. What the hell was he doing at their place in Hamilton — assuming he was really there? If she went to the window, would she see him at the street entrance in the gathering darkness, staring up to claim her attention? 'Fuck, fuck, fuck,' she said under her breath while still stroking the cushion. Robert sat placidly before the television. His flings were well past and expiated, at least to his own satisfaction. He was in a lottery with death, but watched the drama on the screen with a clear conscience. Sarah turned her face away and screwed up her eyes. She was caught, trapped, and could think of no way out. To see Hartley was to prolong the affair and fuel his obsession; to refuse was to lose all influence over his actions.

Sarah made a sudden sound — half-sob, half-hiccup — and it startled both of them. Robert heaved himself from his seat and came to her, putting a hand on her shoulder. 'You're crying. What's the matter?'

'I don't know. I just feel sad all of a sudden. It'll pass,

though. I'm okay.' Her tears caught on her jaw line, and he smoothed them away.

'I don't want you to worry about me,' he said. 'Things will come right. We'll be okay, you'll see.'

'I don't know how much longer I can cope,' Sarah said. 'Life seems to have turned sour on us, don't you think? Everything seems to be turning out wrong.'

'We all live in degrees of failure.' It wasn't something that Robert would have said before his illness, not something that he would have believed then. He sat down on the sofa with her and wondered how to give comfort without shallow optimism. 'We've got each other, haven't we? We've got family,' he said. 'I'm coming right. I feel it, really. Whatever happens, nothing can take away the good times we've all had together.'

He misunderstood the reason for her unhappiness, but Sarah still found comfort and reassurance in his concern. She loved him. She loved him in the settled, clear-sighted way that people in successful marriages love each other.

HARTLEY WAS ANGRY, MORE he was despondent, cut off by the woman he loved and left standing on the step of her empty house in the darkness. He had eaten and drunk too much at the restaurant. Was he going mad? Not berserk in some tumultuous outrage at misfortune, but losing touch with reality, drifting into a realm of echoes, cyphers, self-deceiving mirrors and unattainable expectation. But what was it they had if it wasn't love? Surely it was love? It must be.

As a consequence of Sarah's rebuff, the house seemed

less receptive to him. Its emptiness became sterility, its modernity a lack of character. Robert would have made most of the choices regarding it, Hartley decided. Before he went, however, he felt an atavistic impulse to mark the place somehow, as a dog marks a post in passing, and he took his car keys and worked scratches into the dark wood of the door, close to the lock.

He was ashamed of the action even before he completed it, and rubbed hurriedly at the marks with his finger. 'Jesus, what's this about?' he admonished himself. 'Jesus, come on.' A man nearly sixty, a lawyer and a father, defacing property as a thirteen-year-old kid might do. He was gripped by a sudden sense of the absurdity to which he had been reduced by infatuation. A fool, that's what he'd become, and he was fixed in the role. He walked through the garden fragrances of the summer darkness to his car, and drove back to the motel. What he'd done was such a trivial indiscretion, yet he felt demeaned by it.

People in the adjoining unit were making a lot of noise: loud talking and frequent, careless laughter. Children's voices, too, which he found jarring in pitch and frequency. And all reminding him that he was alone. He made a coffee and took it through the night to the large magnolia tree, sat on the wooden seat with his back supported by the massive trunk. It wasn't comforting, and he began to feel cold. Why was he alone in the world when he had found someone to love? And surely she would be thinking of him just as he was of her?

He remembered a visit he'd made to the zoo when he first came to Auckland, and the otter alone in a netted compound. It had a scuttling, almost manic routine of movement, and patches of raw skin on its feet. The keeper who was observing it told Hartley that the otter was injuring itself, overgrooming because of loneliness and imprisonment. Sitting under the magnolia, alone in Sarah's city, Hartley felt his predicament was much the same, the futile restlessness, the isolation, the self-harm that was in his case internal rather than displayed.

He decided he would go home the next day and see Sarah again somehow. Nothing else mattered much in his life. He could feel tears on his face, and made no effort to check them or wipe them away. He felt sorry for himself, and considered he had justification for indulging in such commiseration. He was sitting alone in the night under a magnolia tree within the precinct of a motel in a strange town, and the woman he loved, and who surely loved him, would no longer talk to him, walk with him, or lie down with him. He tipped his head back and looked into the mass of branches overhead, through which he could see the hard glitter of a single star. 'Ah, Jesus,' he said softly. 'What to do, eh?'

When he returned to his unit, the noise was worse, unrestrained and convivial, laughter and overriding inter-ruptions, all an unwitting mockery of his own silence and isolation. Hartley thumped on the wall. The racket dwindled for a brief time, then recovered. He thumped again and longer, and someone began banging back, someone called 'Shut the fuck up' and people hollered. Hartley said nothing, but beat on the wall again, a rhythm of defiance more against life than temporary neighbours. It was answered with laughter and calls of derision, and he heard a door slam and almost immediately there was a pounding on his own locked door. He turned off the light and lay on his bed in the small, dark room. He heard someone return next door and be cheered in, and the noise continued, as if he had no existence. Hartley gave no further resistance. He wished he had remained in his own home, where he could feel that he was of some significance, and could control the immediate surroundings as he wished.

Chapter Nineteen

Simon Drummond came to the open door of Hartley's office, and as a courtesy made a knocking gesture without contact with the surface, then carried on to one of the chairs before the desk. 'Christ, it's hot,' he said. His large, pleasant face had a sheen and his glasses were misted slightly. Despite the heat he wore a tie close around his short neck so that it seemed to tongue from his chin. But his sleeves were folded neatly partway up his forearms. 'Busy?' he enquired.

'Not particularly, although I'm getting brassed off with family trusts. I've two on the go at the moment.'

'So?' said Simon. Trusts were a routine task in the firm. He took off his glasses, and Hartley noticed the small, pink indentations, one on each side of his nose, where they had rested.

'I'm wondering whether in fact trusts are safe from clawback if people have to go into care. The advice we've been giving for years seems a bit shaky now.'

'True.'

'Well, people trust us, but the department's starting to shift ground.'

'We can't be held accountable for changes in official policy. All we can do is give the best opinion for the time.'

'I suppose so,' said Hartley. Simon must have come with a specific purpose, so he sat back in his chair to show he was ready to give attention. From the ceramic ashtray he took a paper clip and began to straighten it out as a way to keep his hands busy. The bird-shit stain on his window drew his eye, still there although he'd twice asked office staff to get something done about it.

'The thing is,' said Simon, 'I'm worried about you. All of us are, in fact. I don't want to poke my nose in. I wasn't going to say anything, and then I decided that as a friend I should.' He paused, smiled, giving time for a response, but Hartley said nothing. 'It's just the business with the McWhinney crowd, and those missed appointments. No big deal, but I want you to know if you need to talk to someone I'm here. I don't want to push in on anything, but I'm here if it helps. Okay?'

'McWhinney's just peeved because he didn't get special treatment. I'm not putting myself and the firm at risk to suit him.'

'The letter you sent, though. A bit off, wasn't it? Some of the things you said would have been better not put on paper. Pretty hard to defend some of them.'

'All true, all justified,' said Hartley. Maybe he had got too personal, but McWhinney's assumption of privilege annoyed him, and at the time he'd been especially down about Sarah's refusal to see him. And despite his wealth McWhinney was an inferior person of no genuine achievement. Money disguises failure, but never compensates for it.

'Anyway,' said Simon, 'I felt I should let you know there's a bit of a groundswell. We're just concerned and wondering how to help. Nothing major. You seem a bit closed off lately. If you need to talk, you know I'm happy to listen.' In the silence that followed he glanced around the small room as if in search of a change of topic.

'I'm okay, but thanks,' said Hartley.

'Right, then I'll let you get on with it.' Simon sat long enough to give Hartley the chance to say more if he wished, and then stood up. 'Better go. There's always work to do. The heat's a real killer today,' he said, marking his withdrawal with the same neutral topic as his arrival.

Hartley knew Simon's comments were well intentioned, and normally he would have been responsive to that, if not to the others' view of him. But what was mere friendship, collegiality or professional responsibility when love was at stake: a love that equated with life itself? For a lover, there are only ever two people in the world. He folded the paper clip back to shape and replaced it. He needed to get out, to do something, bring himself again into Sarah's life.

He went into the outer office, not bothering with his jacket. Gillian wasn't there, but Rachel was at the next desk. Hartley tapped the face of his watch, lifted a finger and mouthed 'Back in an hour,' although he imposed no such limit on himself. It was the time of the afternoon when Sarah and Robert often took a walk. If he went to the real-estate office he would be able to watch the entrance to the apartments, see if they were going out into the bright sun of the city. Simon's door was closed and Hartley went quickly and quietly past it and into the street. Even to be heading in the direction of Sarah's apartment was better than nothing: moving towards her rather than away.

WHEN THEY REACHED THE Magnus café, Robert didn't even bother to suggest they stop there; Sarah had made it plain recently that she'd gone off the place. They walked slowly on down the street that sloped slightly towards the central city, their pace more a response to the heat than any debility on Robert's part.

Since his illness Robert seemed to have recovered a simple pleasure in observing the people and the scene about him, instead of restricting himself to the narrowed focus of a busy professional. At times he would stop walking to inspect a gutter that was unaccountably gushing water, stand smiling at the lights to watch a bare-chested Maori boy break-dancing for coins, peer up a flight of narrow stairs, his mouth opening as his head rose, to see what was the cause of sudden, joyous laughter there.

They went into a mall, seeking coolness as much as anything, and found a large snack place on the second floor. It was full of exuberant young people, but Sarah had decided that because of the heat she wanted a smoothie instead of coffee, and Robert was happy to agree to the novelty. 'I can't think when I last had one of those,' he said, and stood deliberating before the wall board that listed the flavours, as if the distinction between a berry banana and a tropical island was of more than passing significance.

Though they found a table in a corner, the noise was such that they had to lean towards each other across the table to talk. It wasn't only voices, although they were babble enough, but an underlying pulsation of air-conditioning, multitudinous pieces of commercial apparatus, the human herd on the move, and the snickering of invisible urban gremlins that inhabit such places.

The smoothie was thick and cool, and it brought back for Sarah memories of the milkshakes she'd enjoyed as a teenager. The close girl group to which she had belonged, the Formica table tops of the milk-bar booths, the pop music buoying up their chatter while their real interest was in the quick glances they gave the boys who were watching them.

'These places make me feel old,' said Robert.

'What?'

'We must be the oldest people here,' he said more loudly. He was looking ruefully at the throng, as if he too had experienced a vision of his youth.

'Well at least we're getting out and about instead of sitting inside watching television.'

'I suppose the people our age are probably in wine bars anyway, aren't they, not places like this? How come all these kids can roam around town spending money?'

'Things are more flexible now, the working hours and everything, and Auckland's full of students.'

'Beats me how they do it,' said Robert.

He leant back from the table to give a pause in their conversation, and Sarah saw, through the clear glass behind him, Hartley watching them from the mall walkway. Many people were passing, but he stood quite still, a pace or two from the glass, looking directly at her. He wore a white shirt and a dark, striped tie, but no jacket. His hands were clasped low in front of him. His expression wasn't at all threatening. It was more that he was hoping for recognition from her, and he had the beginnings of a smile prepared for that.

Sarah burst into tears — the shock, the sadness, the loss, perhaps even the betrayal of love.

Robert was taken by surprise and in clumsily getting up to comfort her, he knocked over his chair. No one paid much attention, or to Sarah's tears, which she quickly suppressed. Noise and movement continued to swirl around them as he stood beside her, a hand on her shoulder, his head bent towards her in concern.

'What is it?' he said. 'What's the matter?'

'It was all too much for a moment. Sometimes I just have to let it out. You know? You keep stuff bottled up and then it just blows. I'm okay now.' She sniffed slightly, dabbed her eyes with her handkerchief, blinked deliberately, straightened in the plastic chair. Hartley was no longer there. People walked by beyond the glass, but there was no one standing and looking in.

'We'll go home. I'll get a taxi,' said Robert.

'No. It's fine.'

Hartley had gone, and she couldn't see him when she glanced around the tables. He hadn't come in and must have gone on through the mall. Anger began to replace her other feelings. It wasn't fair to follow her like that, to follow Robert and her, and suddenly appear. If he cared about her, he wouldn't do that, would know how startling it was, how threatening.

'I think we should go home. It's that bloody hot you won't want to walk any more anyway.' Sarah rarely cried, and Robert took it seriously.

'I'd like to go to the park and sit for a while,' Sarah said. 'It's good for us to be out. It's exercise, and even more important it takes our mind off things.' She wasn't going to be intimidated by Hartley, driven indoors because he chose to manifest himself. He'd followed her, as he must have done at other times. 'Yes,' she said. 'Let's get away from the worst of the bustle and go to the park.'

At each crossing on the way, Sarah looked for Hartley among the people massing before the lights, but she didn't see him. Twice she felt a small shock when for an instant she thought some slim, white-shirted businessman might be him, and once, having turned a corner, she stepped back deliberately to see if he was following, but Hartley wasn't there.

Had she imagined him standing in the mall? Had it been an apparition born of guilt and suppressed affection? But she knew it had been him, tried not to think of the longing and desperation that drove him to leave his work and seek her out as she went through the streets with her husband.

The park was quite full. The benches were occupied and people sat and lay on the grass, most where there was shade, but some in full sun. Robert and Sarah sat rather awkwardly on the concrete kerb of a rose garden, close by a young shirtless guy lying on his back with a handkerchief over his face and a small tattoo of an eagle on his shoulder.

The kerb wasn't high and Robert's knees were forced up towards his face. 'Do you want to just go on?' she asked him.

'I'm fine for a bit. Even the concrete's hot on your bum, though, isn't it.'

'Just say when you want to go on,' she said. She supposed they looked odd there: an older man and woman squatting uncomfortably on the rim of a rose garden, Robert with a hand to his forehead as a shield from the sun, she holding her dress close to her raised legs.

'Keep an eye out for anyone quitting a bench and we'll nab it,' said Robert.

It was the same park in which she and Hartley had been approached by the foster mother and the little girl who said 'shit'. Sarah could see the bench on which she and Hartley had sat with the gift of slippers, experience a brief reprise of the exalted mood they'd shared. How was it that when a place of powerful memory is revisited time's divisions are not dissolved? She almost expected the elderly woman to come forward again, the blonde, small-eyed girl urged gently before her as an introduction.

Hartley was the one who appeared, walking in from the

street onto the gravelled path, standing at a distance without drawing attention to himself, his hands held low in front of his body just as they had when she saw him behind the glass wall at the mall. This time he was farther away, and his expression unclear, but he was looking at her. This time she wasn't surprised and she gave no sign of recognising him. She put a hand on her husband's shoulder and began a conversation with him about their granddaughters, whether they were too young to come up by themselves in the school holidays. Talk of family was always easy between them.

'My backside's getting numb,' Robert said. 'I need a proper seat.'

'We'll go home now,' Sarah said.

'I'm okay if you want to go further.'

'It's too hot. We'll get a taxi if you like.'

For a moment she thought she might walk right past Hartley as a challenge, as a sign she wasn't frightened of anything he could do, but he might take that as flaunting her repudiation of his love. She didn't want to hurt him; she just wanted him to let go.

She and Robert went off in the other direction, and she glanced back only once as they turned onto the street. Hartley hadn't moved. He was still watching, still in the same posture, but diminished in perspective. Still alone. She had a brief, inappropriate inclination to wave, but knew she had no right to that. She'd made her decision, but could still be overtaken by a confusion of feeling, by the wish to hold onto things that she was forcing away for greater good. She didn't know her own mind, and was filled with sadness.

'You know, it's a funny thing, but back there I thought I saw that hospital services fellow,' said Robert.

'What fellow?'

'I can't remember his name, but you know who I mean. I told you about him coming to the apartment and asking if we needed any help with anything. It looked a lot like him, but maybe it wasn't.'

'Who was he again?'

'No. I can't remember the name at all,' said Robert. What did it matter anyway? He was of no significance in their lives, and Robert started to talk of the heat again, and the possible purchase of Greg's bach at Manaia, which he wasn't really serious about, but found pleasant to discuss partly because he had the money to do it. Quite often he found himself totalling his assets: he knew the answer, but found satisfaction in arriving at it. Whatever losses he was being forced to accept in other ways, he knew he was still financially secure.

SARAH WOULDN'T SEE HIM, wouldn't answer texts, cut him off whenever she recognised his voice on the phone, never left the apartment alone on any of the occasions he was watching it. Hartley told himself it was merely loyalty to a sick partner rather than any lessening of love for himself. He convinced himself that her scruples were a sign of decency and self-denial that made her even more admirable.

There was only one answer. It had been there all along, but he'd hoped for some alternative. Since Robert wouldn't die conveniently from his cancer, then he must die from some other cause, and equally conveniently.

Hartley was in the office at Hastings Hull when he made the decision. He had been talking with a client about the repudiation of a fire insurance claim, and the man was still clumping down the stairs when Hartley resolved to do what was necessary for Sarah and him to be together. There was no sense of the momentous: the whispering hum of the desk computer continued the same, the pale bird-shit stain on the right-hand corner of the window remained, Gillian in the outer office answered the phone with rote response as always. Robert had to die. Hadn't that always been the only way, no matter what?

Hartley considered the means as he drove home, and later as he sat in his quiet room with the view to the city heart. The subtleties of crime drama were no benefit to him. What did he know of poisons, choke-holds that left no bruises, hired assassins, or the illegal purchase of pistols with silencers? Life is not a television programme. He sought simple and direct means, and took no pleasure in the planning. He didn't hate Robert, and if things went wrong he might lose his own life, or spend the rest of it imprisoned. It was a desperate and terrible thing to kill someone, but there was no other way now that Sarah and he could be together.

By the time he went to bed the simple plan was made. He would have Robert come onto the balcony of the apartment, and push him over to his death. If for some reason that was impossible then he would stab him unawares. Hartley thought he might dream that night of carrying out the act, but although he lay awake for several hours in turmoil before he could sleep, sometimes talking aloud to comfort himself, sometimes in tears, in the morning he had no recollection of dreams. And, rather to his surprise, the emotional stress hadn't brought on a migraine.

He felt a strange release that a decision had been made. He assembled all the knives he had on the kitchen bench to gauge their suitability. The largest would be unwieldy and difficult to conceal, the smallest might not penetrate deeply enough to cause death. So he chose a medium one with a serrated blade and a black handle secured by slightly raised stainless steel studs. It was made by Standfast of Ohio, and he laid it on the windowsill before replacing the others.

He would have a coffee. He would take it onto the deck and listen to the birds in the native bush around the house. He would place Sarah's green and yellow silk scarf around his neck and think of the happiness they had shared at the Magnus café, on their walks in the city, at Omaha, and in their Spanish motel. He understood that the future is determined by resolute action in the present.

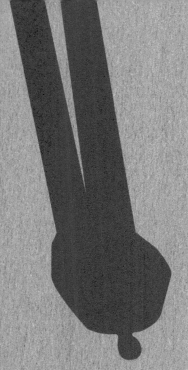

Chapter Twenty

Robert had a dream that he was dying, and woke to find with relief that it wasn't necessarily true. He said nothing to Sarah, gazed at the recessed lights in the ceiling as the image faded. Most dreams were like that — insistent and bright in the instant of experience, but then dissolving before fixed by memory. All he could recall was a green-robed doctor bending over him, repeating, 'He's gone, he's gone,' in the sonorous voice of his old headmaster, and his own desperate inability to express any denial, despite the entreaty in the faces of his granddaughters.

He lay until the unpleasantness passed, saying nothing of it to his wife although he knew she was awake. When they were getting dressed soon afterwards he told Sarah with apparent cheerfulness that he needed to get more regular exercise: the varicose veins on his right leg were getting worse. He put his foot up on the bed to display his calf.

'Maybe it's all that rugby you played years ago,' she said.

'You used to knock yourself about.'

'Nah, it's the treatment,' he said. 'It seems to have an effect on everything. I reckon it's put ten years on me at least. But I need to keep moving more. There's not even a lawn to mow here.'

'Mr Goosen said when the treatment's over, your whole system will right itself again. You know that.'

'I'm hanging out for it,' Robert said. 'Thank God there's not much longer.'

She said he could walk down with her to get some milk, but he thought he'd rather go out later, and when she'd gone, he turned again for reassurance to the photographs on the big table, chose one of his favourites. A photograph taken of Donna after her graduation ceremony, with other happy people in the background, but his daughter as the focus, holding her academic regalia to her body against the stiff wind, but smiling, smiling, delighted not so much for her achievement, but for the pleasure she knew it gave her parents. And it had. Watching her in the capping procession he thought how much more defined she seemed than all those around her, so that she was the gem amid the massed and moving setting that carried her along. Watching as she came upon the stage for her moment of acknowledgement. Watching as in the evening she held a glass of Moët in her small hand and told him of her plans, and as he listened, and as the restaurant thrummed with colour, noise and movement around him, he had known it was a flag day in their family life. He wrote her name and the date on the back of the photo. The information was unnecessary for him, but in time, when perhaps even Donna was long dead, someone could well be thankful for the identification, would look closely enough at the photograph to sense the gratification and love it recorded.

Most of the photographs were of their immediate family,

although Sarah had a good many inherited from her parents, even formally grouped bearded and bonneted forebears of two and three generations before, who struck a conscious pose before the novelty of a camera. Robert had none of those, and few even of his parents, or himself as a boy with them. They were both dead, and his sisters must have taken possession of the family photographs, knowing his own lack of interest then. His parents had seemed preoccupied with their own lives, and so Robert had learnt to concentrate on his own. There was one family shot of them all on a tartan picnic rug with willows behind them and dry hills farther back. His mother sitting, his father half lying, propped on his elbow, his two sisters close by, and he a little apart, cheerful and squinting into the sun. Robert found it incongruous, for they had been a family who never picnicked, or so it was in his recollection, yet the anomaly was almost the sole remaining pictorial record of his childhood.

Largely obscured by other photographs there was an image that roused very different recollections and feelings. An informal shot of a Christmas party for his dental practice colleagues. Sarah, of course, and his partner Bill and his wife, the receptionists and nurses, the part-time hygienist, even their accountant, though both Robert and Bill said at the time they couldn't recall inviting him. It had been taken late in the evening, and they were all in slight disarray, a sheen to their smiling faces, and arms around shoulders. In such cheerful inclusiveness there was no sign of the trivial feuds, offences and grievances that had run through the working year. However he would write nothing on the back of this snap: maybe he should tear it up and dispose of it privately.

Polly was in it, whom, over some months, he had fucked happily in the locked surgery after-hours. In the party photo she is towards the end of the table, leaning forward, eyebrows lifted comically, looking directly into the camera.

Polly was a hard-case and knew what she was doing. He had greater guilt concerning Natalie, the hygienist, whom he never even kissed. She had come to him, knowing what was going on, and said she couldn't remain working there if it continued. There was no threat to expose him, no self-righteous lecture. Everyone in the practice must have known about Polly, if Natalie did, but she was the only one to do anything about it. And Robert had taken her resignation rather than her advice, although she was a solo mother with two young children.

No, that picture wasn't one that Robert wished to keep. Months afterwards, when Polly was long gone, he'd rung Natalie and asked if she wanted to come back. She said she would think about it, but he never heard from her. Occasionally he saw her shopping, or at events. Once there was a picture in the paper of her elder son receiving a regional youth art award. In their brief conversations no mention was ever made of the circumstances of Natalie's resignation, or her decision not to return. Not all of the photographs in the albums, or loose, or on the computer, were ones that he wished to linger on.

All of them seemed to have gained in significance, though, since he became sick, reassurance to balance present uncertainty. He was forced to accustom himself to having no role in life that assured him of deference and respect from other people. No longer was he the senior partner in a professional practice with staff and patients attentive to his opinions and whims: he had become just another ageing man undergoing cancer treatment, dependent on his wife, deferential to Mr Goosen the specialist, grateful to hear of his daughter's life and family when she had the time. He sat back and spread his hands on the table. 'Jesus,' he said to himself softly. 'Jesus.' He rarely indulged in self-pity, and was pleased that Sarah wasn't with him, though what he felt was closer to dissatisfaction. He wished the photographs, even more the memories, showed greater love, valour and fair dealing on his part than he could discern. Maybe he was dying; maybe the cautious but encouraging reports he received from Mr Goosen were merely emotional palliatives to hide the truth. Death was a big thing, an enormity that made the humdrum achievements of his life seem even less important.

———

'**WHAT HAVE YOU BEEN** up to?' asked Sarah on her return.

'Just the photos again. I'm almost finished and you'll be able to have that table tidy-up you've been itching for.' A deliberate cheerfulness infused his voice.

'I'll believe it when I see it.'

'Well, it's been quite a job, you know.'

'I'm joking.'

'I'd like to go out,' he said. 'I know you've just come back, but I'd really like to go somewhere for a while instead of being stuck here.'

'Oh, okay. It's not great outside at the moment.' They both looked at the low cloud being bundled through the sky by the wind. 'I needed a scarf, but couldn't find my green and yellow one. I must have a proper hunt.'

'It doesn't matter then,' he said.

'No, no. We'll wait awhile to see what it's doing. We could take a bus, go down town and have a wander.'

'There's always the Magnus?'

'Boring,' she said. 'No atmosphere at all.' Hartley might be there, and even if he weren't, the place had associations she wanted to avoid. Ever since his phone call from the house in Hamilton she worried that he would do something stupid to make contact. He just wouldn't let go, and she had a sense of him out there somewhere, intense, determined and with a sort of heart-rending yet threatening devotion. It must be her fault as much as his that they found themselves so unhappy. She tried not to cry. 'It's shitty weather,' she said vehemently to pull herself together. 'On days like this I can't wait to be back in Hamilton.'

'Me, too, and we'll get there.'

For a moment she felt that she could sit down with him, tell him that what had happened with Hartley was no big deal. That she'd met him by accident, come to enjoy his company because she was isolated and worried, been flattered by his attention sufficiently to welcome sex between them for a short while, but ended it all rather than leave her marriage, or continue the deception. She'd been foolish, but not ultimately dishonest, surely? Lots of people had the same story, including Robert himself. Almost, almost, Sarah did sit down beside her husband and tell him everything, wanting release from unrelenting anxiety. If he'd been well she may have done so, but he was sick, and looking at him she decided she couldn't do it. Not then. And things could still turn out okay couldn't they, if she just hung on? Hartley would get over her and veer off on his own life path again. If she held on, it would be all right. Hold tight to ordinary things as protection.

The weather didn't improve, but after lunch they took coats and went out to the bus stop. At home they never used buses, but in Auckland, although they could afford taxis, they had come to enjoy the occasional novelty of a bus if they were together. Now, however, Sarah could take no pleasure in it, her mind turning always with misgiving to Hartley's persistent affection. Despite everything she still cared for him, and felt sympathy. How could love become something you seek to escape from?

They soon tired of the streets and the crowds, for scattered rain began to be flung by the wind at them despite the overhangs, and paper rubbish swirled against them. People abandoned courtesy in an effort to preserve comfort, pushing and crowding towards the more sheltered side of the pavement: reluctant to give way. The shopping malls were unaffected by the weather, maintaining their own artificial and gaudy atmosphere of retail carnival. But Sarah enjoyed little refuge there. The lines of cramped, glass shops with young women assistants imprisoned within like Amsterdam prostitutes, the lights casting jelly colours, the stale fragrances of Asian cooking, the incessant wail of pop music with an underlying throb of the air-conditioning and the escalators, and all with the sense of trivial and ultimately futile activity like the third-deck games room of a cruise liner. Yet she knew of course that she was casting over all about her, a disenchantment from a quite different source. One song seemed to pursue her from shop to shop and level to level — 'Knocking on Heaven's Door.'

They escaped to a first-storey café with a view across to the wet waterfront. Even the one flight of stairs was enough to have Robert breathing heavily, but he wanted to convince Sarah that he was enjoying the outing. He took her coat and put it with his own over a spare chair. 'This is nice,' he said firmly.

'I have to say I've gone off Auckland,' Sarah said. She looked about to make sure Hartley wasn't there.

'Eh?'

'It would be good to be home again, don't you think?'

'Well, yes,' said Robert, 'but the treatment's not over, is it.'

'Maybe we could travel up for it when necessary. It's not all that far after all.'

'We talked about all that. I thought this was the way you wanted it? No need for driving back and forth.'

'But you've stood up to it better than we expected, most of the time, and there aren't many sessions to come, are there. Maybe we could talk to Mr Goosen and see what he thinks?' She would be safer in Hamilton, she thought. Farther away from Hartley, and that would help him to forget, or at least lessen the chances of a meeting.

'I know it's been damn tough,' said Robert. 'Away from home and friends and all that. I don't mind coming back and forth if that's what you want. Okay, let's talk to Goosen if you like and get it sorted.'

'Only if you're happy with it as well. That's what's important.'

'Why not? And it wouldn't be so lonely for you.'

Outside the squalls continued, the wind persistent, but the rain sometimes giving way to interludes of sun that glinted on the wet streets and traffic before the cloud blew in again. Beside her Robert was intent on his hefty carrot cake with soft, pale icing, slowly dividing it with a small fork. Hartley would have been entertaining her, intent on her response and needs, open in admiration, painting emotional colour on the world. Now she was content with the relaxed and accustomed companionship of marriage. 'We'll take a taxi back if it's still raining,' she said.

WHEN THEY WENT TO the oncology department three days later, they asked to talk to Mr Goosen before the radiation therapy. The specialist had Robert's latest results, and was reasonably positive. Not spectacular, but nothing upsetting and that was the main thing, he told them. 'It's quite common', he said, 'in such treatment to have an apparent lull, a sort of marking time. Overall progress is the significant thing and we're doing well enough.' The specialist liked including himself when he could be positive.

'Perhaps, then, this isn't the best time for what we wanted to ask,' said Sarah. 'We were wondering if it would make any difference if we came up from home for the sessions rather than having the apartment. We'd still stay overnight if that was necessary, if Robert didn't feel up to the drive home.'

'Whatever you find works best,' said Mr Goosen. His hands were placed side by side on his desk and aligned with care, as if they were surgical instruments for the moment idle. 'If you're happier at home, I don't see why not. I wouldn't recommend Robert drive, however.' He looked at them in turn. 'And when we're no longer juggling both chemotherapy and radiation you should be able to be treated at Waikato hospital anyway.'

'That's what we'll do then, I think,' said Robert. 'It's less than a two-hour trip after all.'

'It's good to have an option,' Sarah said. She'd already decided. As soon as possible they would move back home. They would go before Hartley could bring anything to a head, and the shift would show him that she was absolutely decided the affair was over. She should have thought of it before, but it was a relief to have action to take rather than just fretting. She was pleased with the outcome of the discussion with Mr Goosen. Things would be better when they were in their own home again. She wouldn't have to pass the Magnus, or the Spanish motel, with their associations both reproachful and oddly treasured. Her accustomed life would close up the gaps left by no longer seeing Hartley.

When all the visits were over she would give Mr Goosen a gift, and also the reception nurse who was so pleasant and understanding while Sarah waited for Robert's sessions to finish. Yes, gifts in appreciation, but also to show the conclusion of a time in her life she wanted to bring to an end. 'We appreciate everything that's being done, don't we, Robert? I think it would be positive for us to be back in Hamilton from now on.'

'We do, yes,' he said, but shifting home again was unlikely to have any effect on the outcome of his treatment, and that was the important thing for him. He felt reduced, distanced, saw Sarah and Mr Goosen as if through a small, high window, and strained to concentrate on what they said. Illness is a form of isolation.

So they ended the interview, each in a different way: Sarah encouraged, Robert inwardly downcast, and Mr Goosen professionally unmoved.

Chapter
Twenty-one

'Hello Robert, it's me again,' said Hartley, while Robert gaped a little at the door. He wasn't feeling well, had a cough and a cold as well as more deep-seated ailments, and was in the midst of a debilitating round of treatment. It took him some time to place his visitor and then, finally, ah, twittery Olders, the outpatients guy.

'Yes,' he said without enthusiasm. A clear drop hung for a moment from his nostril and he wiped it with the back of his index finger. Such a trivial social offence, but unlike him. Niceties fell away in the struggle to preserve essentials.

'You'll be thinking that I'm pestering you, but it's just a routine check that your situation hasn't changed. We've acknowledged you don't require any of the services.'

'Right.' The tone was of endorsement not invitation.

'If I could come in for a moment,' said Hartley.

'Actually, we're moving back home in a day or two. We'll be commuting for the rest of the treatments and so won't need anything. Nothing at all.' Robert continued to block the doorway, not belligerently, more because he had one hand on the frame for support as he coughed.

Hartley felt he'd been struck hard on the chest, and although there was no physical contact he almost stepped back. Had he been alone he might have given in to the urge to cry out at the sudden news that Sarah was leaving. She'd given up on him and lost faith. She was taking off. And she had so little trust, so little honesty, that she was leaving without saying anything to him. He was only just in time, and he took that as a validation of his intention.

'If I could come in, though. There's a couple of standard questions required before clearance,' he said, attempting a smile. As if he had stepped into a dark, chill pool, he felt sadness rising through him. Also conviction that the final decision was close at hand. The knife seemed to throb slightly in his jacket pocket.

Robert heavily led the way into the living room. He looked older and less resolute than on both previous visits Hartley had made. He was breathing audibly through his mouth because of his cold, his lower eyelids hung slightly so that an inner moist red rim was visible, and through what hair remained, brown spots like giant freckles could be seen on his pale scalp. Even in the shock of Robert's news, Hartley, though smaller, was aware of his own health and physical competence. He was slim, upright, with a good head of hair, even if it was grey. He was younger than Robert and had visited a doctor since meeting Sarah only to renew his pills. For an instant he felt like emphasising his fitness and superiority in some way, but instead he kept moving, on to the French doors that led to the small balcony, and beyond. As he went he noticed again Sarah's Matakana jug. For him it had a luminosity that was lacking in all of the other ornaments. It was a talisman that urged him on.

'What a view these apartments have,' he said, his assumed enthusiasm drawing Robert somewhat reluctantly after him. 'I've often looked up and admired the balconies, wondered what it would be like out here, and now I know. Gets the morning sun, I guess, and that's when you really need it, especially in winter. And you've got double-glazing to keep the traffic noise out when you're inside.' It was only a couple of paces to the balcony rail, and Hartley stood there, leant a little to see the drop and the paved area below before the lawn and main gates. He'd given up any pretence to be Olders from outpatients. He would say and do what he liked and Robert could make of it what he would. Sarah was killing their love, and any other harm, any revelation, any other death was rendered insignificant by that.

'Your wife's never been here when I've called,' Hartley said. 'I would've liked to meet her, because you say she's been a great support during your treatment.'

'She's at the shops,' said Robert. He came to the balcony edge and the direct sunlight made him sneeze. As Robert fumbled for his handkerchief, Hartley wondered if a determined shove might send him over and down. He tensed himself for the physical effort, but realised the rail was too high to act as a fulcrum, and Robert too heavy to be lifted quickly.

Hartley could feel the knife in the inner pocket of his jacket. It was light against his chest, and he could easily half-turn and bring it out before Robert was aware. He could take a step towards him and plunge the weapon into Robert's stomach, which was covered only by a maroon striped shirt. How often he'd thought about such a decisive resolution. Robert would go down immediately surely, too ill for a theatrical death. There would be no struggle, just a heavy, incongruous collapse.

It was the very moment for the knife, but standing there

in the sun, with Robert flat-footed and stooped beside him, Hartley knew the truth — he couldn't do it. He could never do it. It had been a delusion of desperation. Robert was too human, too unsuspecting, too innocent. Hartley saw the reality was far from the heated visions and justifications of his sleepless nights. Even if he could do it, killing Robert was no answer: Sarah had to make the choice between them. That was the only way. No one else could put Robert aside.

The decision, the impact of the moment, left Hartley giddy with intensity. The sunlight seemed to flare in his face, and the traffic noise below became a buffeting roar before subsiding again. It was as if for an instant some great winged creature of flashing iridescence had been about to alight, and then soared on. Hartley waited until the swoon had left him, and then made conversation again. 'How do you pass your time here?' he asked. The knife had become inert in his pocket, the slight serrations familiar to his fingers.

'I'm not house-bound, you know. On better days we go out for meals, to galleries, or movies. Twice I've been to the zoo. And I've got a bit of a family project.' Robert told him about the family albums and his ambition to have the photographs sorted and annotated. His uninvited visitor seemed happy to prompt information.

'Will you resume your practice when you go home?' Hartley asked finally. It was as if he had become separate from himself, able to make fatuous conversation, listen to himself, while something vital was dying within him. Spoken words had a derisory, hollow echo. Only Sarah could make things right.

'No,' said Robert. 'I still have a financial interest in it, but I'm past the actual dentistry. I've retired.'

'You'll travel more, I suppose?'

'When I'm stronger. The treatment takes it out of you. Anyway, is there anything else you need for the sign-off you mentioned?' Robert saw no point in the conversation. He had the time and not a lot of company day by day, but he was slightly irritated by Hartley's presumption in heading onto the balcony and asking personal questions. There was something in the way he held himself that suggested he took his presence as of right, something brittle and assertive all at once. Why did this odd chap keep coming when he wasn't required or welcome? And Robert was feeling grotty.

Sarah arrived home as Hartley was prolonging his visit by talking of Auckland life. She put her bags down, came quickly into the living room, drawn by the sound of voices, and with a smile to welcome a visitor. Robert stood somewhat in her view, and she was at the French doors before she recognised Hartley. It was the juxtaposition she most feared: Hartley standing on her balcony, soft, grey hair agitated slightly by the breeze, and talking to her husband.

Both of them turned towards her. For a moment there was neither movement nor speech, and then Robert made a clumsy introduction. 'This is Mr — ah — ah — Mr Olders from the outpatient place,' he said. He couldn't remember the Christian name. 'This is my wife, Sarah,' he added.

For Robert the scene and situation had no particular significance. His wife coming home with groceries, and he introducing a minor functionary of the medical services — a small man rather more inquisitive than his official capacity required him to be. For Sarah and Hartley it was a fracture point in their lives, when clocks stopped and all was fiercely back-lit: when a neural surge gave a momentary aura to commonplace surroundings. When the cock crowed and Satan smiled.

Now she would admit their love, Hartley thought. Everything would come out, and there would be a decision at last. For the first time the three of them were physically together, although they had been bound up with one another for months.

Now it has come, she realised, the confrontation so often evaded. She could feel the world tightening. Within everything there seemed an unbearable pulse.

'I think we may have met,' said Hartley.

'No, I don't think so.' Anger is often the first reaction to shock, and anger was what she felt — and fear. How could he claim to love her and yet plan such a situation? She felt her face flush and a small muscle in her lower lip twitch.

'Maybe some time at oncology when you've been with me,' said Robert. He wasn't aware of any tension. His head throbbed with sinus congestion, and he just wanted this guy to bugger off and leave him with Sarah. 'People are coming and going all the time there.'

'You think that's it?' said Hartley, looking at Sarah, lowering his head so that his eyes were angled upwards like those of a child in mock contrition. 'Of course my work takes me quite often to the unit.' He turned quickly, mounted the balcony railing, and then faced them once more, sitting on the flat metal top with his feet hooked under the bottom rung for stability. Robert gave a snort of laughter at the unexpectedness of it. It seemed an oddly boyish thing to do. 'You think we may have met that way, Sarah?' Hartley continued. He used her name for the first time in Robert's hearing, and to her it sounded like a gong. 'Just a glimpse in passing, eh?'

'I can't think of any other place,' she said softly.

'I'd be careful up there,' said Robert.

'Not a coffee bar, a gallery maybe? Not Omaha Beach maybe?'

'Omaha Beach?' echoed Robert, bewildered.

'No,' she said. It was more an appeal than a denial.

'Perhaps walking in the cemetery?' His hands were spread

one each side on the rail, and he leant forward with that intensity so typical of him.

'No.' It wasn't fair what he was doing. He was bringing everything down to confrontation. She wouldn't choose. She couldn't bear to have it all come out like this. He was spoiling everything they had enjoyed together.

'What are you on about?' said Robert in gruff incomprehension, but Hartley paid no attention to him.

'I hoped I meant something,' he said, 'but now I know better.'

'I'm not sure what you— I'm not sure,' Sarah said. An agony of emotion closed about them.

'If you can't remember,' said Hartley, 'then neither can I.' There wasn't going to be a future with her: she lacked the strength to take what he offered, the confidence to step away from the old life. She was like Madeleine after all. She'd failed him, as everything and everyone had failed him.

Love is dispossession, and Hartley had given more than he could live without. He wasn't aware of a conscious decision. He lifted his feet from the rail and gave a sort of shrug that was enough to start him falling backwards, as he made no effort to hold firm with his hands. Just for an instant he felt the exhilaration of utter release. His hair flopped from his forehead and he gave a strange, broken smile. There was a soughing that could have been a sudden exhalation, or just the air against his fall.

He was gone before Sarah or Robert could move to hold him.

'Christ,' exclaimed Robert, amazed rather than horrified, and when they looked down, Hartley was lying on the concrete with one arm out, and his jacket pushed up by his descent, as if he had just shrugged it on. There was no movement, and from that height no blood, or malformation: just a rumpled and awkward stillness, as if he had tripped and chosen to lie still. He was alone, but people on the street noticed him, and began coming through the imposing gates, at first with shocked timidity and then reassured by their own number.

'Christ,' said Robert, 'why would he do that? An accident, or what? He must be bloody mad.'

'You stay and ring the ambulance. I'll go down,' Sarah said, half-blinded by the sunlight. Her tongue felt grossly enlarged. She could feel bile rising and gagged without being sick. For a moment she persuaded herself that everything was in the grip of grotesque imagination, or dream, and that she could force herself back to a life with reason in it. But all around her was obdurate and would not fade. Something of such strange innocence, value and trust had been lost in horror and despair. She heard herself saying his name as she hurried to the stairs, ignoring the lift in her need for movement.

She wet herself slightly, took her handkerchief and clenched it briefly between her thighs, then continued her descent, adopting a strange trot that she found she couldn't break from. What had they done except love each other? But as she hurried on — down, down, down — the meaning became clear. The past had been contesting with the present for possession of the future.

Acknowledgements

The author wishes to thank the Randell Cottage Writers Trust for the opportunity to be writer in residence at Randell Cottage, Wellington, for the last three months of 2015, during which time this novel was completed. Also acknowledged is the material taken from *Epitaph* by Paul Gittins (Random House New Zealand, 1997).

Previous Works by Owen Marshall

Short Fiction

Supper Waltz Wilson, Pegasus Press, 1979.

The Master of Big Jingles, John McIndoe, 1982.

The Day Hemingway Died, John McIndoe, 1984.

The Lynx Hunter, John McIndoe, 1987.

The Divided World, John McIndoe, 1989.

Tomorrow We Save the Orphans, John McIndoe, 1992.

The Ace of Diamonds Gang, John McIndoe, 1993.

Coming Home in the Dark, Vintage, 1995.

The Best of Owen Marshall's Short Stories, Vintage, 1997.

When Gravity Snaps, Vintage, 2002.

Watch of Gryphons, Vintage, 2005.

Selected Stories, edited by Vincent O'Sullivan, Vintage, 2008.

Living as a Moon, Vintage, 2009.

Novels

A Many Coated Man, Longacre Press, 1995.

Harlequin Rex, Vintage, 1999, published in France as *Les Hommes Fanes* by Payot and Rivages, 2006.

Drybread, Vintage, 2007.

The Larnachs, Vintage, 2011.

Carnival Sky, Vintage, 2014.

Poetry

Occasional: Fifty Poems, Hazard Press, 2004.

Sleepwalking in Antarctica, Canterbury University Press, 2010.

The White Clock, Otago University Press, 2014.

Collaboration

Timeless Land, Longacre Press, 1995. With artist Grahame Sydney and poet Brian Turner.

Edited Anthologies

Burning Boats, anthology of short stories, Longman Paul, 1994.

Letter from Heaven, anthology of poems, Longman Paul, 1995.

Beethoven's Ears, anthology of short stories, Longman Paul, 1996.

Authors' Choice, anthology of New Zealand stories, Penguin, 2001.

Spinning a Line, collection of writings about fishing, Vintage, 2001.

Essential New Zealand Stories, anthology of short stories, Vintage, 2002. New enlarged edition, 2009.

Sunday 22, anthology of short stories, Vintage, 2006.

The Best New Zealand Fiction, vol 5, Vintage, 2008.

The Best New Zealand Fiction, vol 6, Vintage, 2009.

Broadcasting

An Indirect Geography, radio play, Radio NZ, 1991.

'Inside New Zealand' and 'NZ: Sanctuary Seekers' scripts, Natural History NZ Ltd documentaries.

Beautifully written, brilliantly observed and ultimately optimistic, this novel by one of New Zealand's finest writers powerfully captures those times when death puts life on hold.

Sheff is disillusioned with journalism and, with plans to travel overseas, chucks in his job. But first he goes south to Alexandra, where his father is dying. He becomes caught up with his family in the agonising inertia of waiting for death. Slowly he comes to terms with suppressed issues of loss, love, resentment and commitment, and acknowledges he must reach out for new relationships. Sheff's gradual transformation — sometimes darkly humorous, sometimes disconcerting — is handled with insight and subtlety.

'[*Carnival Sky*] is not an eye-catching, attention-seeking novel but one that is distinguished by its wry tone, and an abundance of beautiful observations and memorable descriptions. Marshall's great achievement is to have told a story about the biggest of themes — life, love, death, family — using the most restrained of palettes and on the smallest of canvases.'

— Paul Little, *North & South*

'Owen Marshall's *Carnival Sky* is beautifully written and brilliantly observed . . . *Carnival Sky* is a novel in which, to the unobservant or the skimming reader, little seems to happen, but things are changing all the time. It is a novel that repays close reading, leaving a feeling of optimism despite dealing with loss and resentment, for it also deals with love, compassion and commitment and the necessity for forging new relationships. Like his father's tumbling stones, Sheff's gradual transformation to a better and more colourful life, is complete.'

— Dorothy Alexander, *Manawatu Standard*

'In most respects, *Carnival Sky* is, thus, vintage Marshall. It has all his trademark acuity. Life lifts off the page in tireless vignettes of ordinary existence. Ah yes, you say to yourself, I recognise this. This is how it is. As usual, realism is his mode of transport beneath life's oceans . . . [Sheff's] emergence from emptiness is the book's trajectory — a worthy and true trajectory, albeit so slight that one scarcely notices it until right at the end where one realises he has successfully traversed from awkwardness to easefulness. And that, truly, is a lovely realisation.'

— Margie Thomson, *Dominion Post*

'Big themes are treated delicately — mortality and memory, grief and self-discovery — and, although the book is, at its heart, about a man in the midst of a crisis, *Carnival Sky* also explores the universal pain many adults feel when faced with losing a parent . . . The small cast confront the meaning of life (and death) and learn how, in times of grief, the search for normality is sometimes all that's left to us. It's also about holding tight to the things we hold dear and letting go of the things that hold us back. Owen Marshall earned his reputation as one of our brightest literary stars long ago and *Carnival Sky* reinforces his place in that firmament.'

— Elisabeth Easther, *Weekend Herald*

Based on a real love triangle, this fascinating novel is by one of New Zealand's most respected authors.

William James Mudie Larnach's name resonates in New Zealand history — the politician and self-made man who built the famous 'castle' on Otago Peninsula. In 1891, after the death of his first two wives, he married the much younger Constance de Bathe Brandon. But the marriage that began with such happiness was to end in tragedy.

The story of the growing relationship between Conny and William's younger son, Dougie, lies at the heart of Owen Marshall's subtle and compelling new novel. The socially restrictive world of late nineteenth-century Dunedin and Wellington springs vividly to life as Marshall traces the deepening love between stepmother and stepson, and the slow disintegration of the domineering yet vulnerable figure of Larnach himself.

Can love ever really be its own world, free of morality and judgement and scandal? Moving, thought-provoking and superbly written, *The Larnachs* is a memorable piece of fiction from one of our wisest authors.

'[*The Larnachs* is] a thoughtful, tender love story with . . . an awful lot of lovely, restrained writing by Marshall.'

— Kelly Ana Morey, *The New Zealand Herald*

'*The Larnachs* is an interesting development for Marshall. For many years pigeon-holed as a writer of realist fiction from a masculine perspective, he has proved himself far more than a one-trick pony. He has published two volumes of poetry and *The Larnachs* is his fourth novel. Half of it is written from a woman's point of view.'

— John McCrystal, *New Zealand Listener*

Rich and subtle, this is a compelling novel from one of New Zealand's finest writers. It is a moving study of love and disappointment, of the harm we do to each other, knowingly and unknowingly, of the power and significance of landscape in our lives.

A graveyard is all that's left of the remote Central Otago settlement of Drybread, where miners, often hungry and disappointed, once searched for gold. It is to an old cottage nearby that Penny Maine-King flees with her young son, defying a Californian court order awarding custody of the child to her estranged husband. And seeking her in this austere, burnt country is journalist Theo Esler. He is after a story, but he discovers something far more personal and significant.

'*Drybread*'s success lies in Marshall's dextrous examination of the ambiguities of relationships — between parents and children, spouses, work colleagues and lovers — and how the needs of those on the inside don't often coincide.'

— Kevin Rabalais, *New Zealand Listener*

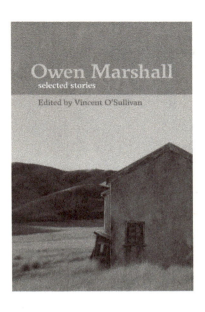

A new and generous selection from New Zealand's foremost writer of short stories. Peter Simpson in reviewing Owen Marshall's stories in the *New Zealand Listener* wrote: 'Marshall is held in uncommon affection by New Zealand readers — generally we admire and respect rather than love our writers.' This love is perhaps evoked not just by the superb quality of Marshall's writing but because his stories so precisely capture his fellow New Zealanders and their country. From the provinces to the cities, the remote landscapes to journeying overseas, Marshall's stories show a deep understanding of who and where we are. Sometimes he skewers the locals with sharp and sly comedy, in other stories there's an elegiac sadness or a grim reality, but always an insightful exploration of human emotions.

From the substantial body of work created over the last thirty years, critic, writer and academic Vincent O'Sullivan has selected sixty stories that give a wide representation of Marshall's range. Marshall once wrote that short stories should aspire to a combination of 'intransigence and poetry', both of which are evident in this fine selection.

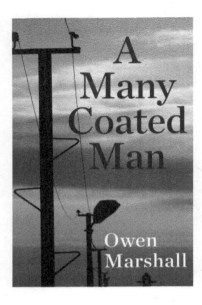

What happens when an ordinary man becomes a messiah? A witty, prescient and eloquent satire by one of New Zealand's finest writers.

Far into the twenty-first century, Albous Slaven's life is spectacularly and irrevocably altered after he hangs for an instant from a power line. While recuperating, he senses a new-found gift; the gift of oratory.

Driven to hold rallies throughout New Zealand, Slaven astounds and alarms the ruling politicians. He, too, is astounded and often bemused by the response of the tens of thousands who flock to hear him. But what is his message? Is he a messiah, a political saviour, or an idealist who conjures up forces he can neither understand nor control?

'[A Many Coated Man] really is a great novel and may well be seen as a landmark in our national literature.'

— Ian Dixon, *The Press*

'In these richly lyrical passages [in A Many Coated Man], Marshall is at his most characteristic and his most brilliant.'

— Elizabeth Caffin, *Quote/Unquote*

'[*A Many Coated Man*] is the work of a master craftsman.'

— W.J. McEldowney, *Otago Daily Times*

'*A Many Coated Man* is a dark, disconcerting novel, a visionary book well worth the wait.'

— Graeme Lay, *North & South*

'[*A Many Coated Man* is] delightfully sardonic, philosophically mischievous.'

— Vincent O'Sullivan

This novel won the Montana NZ Book Awards Deutz Medal.

With the advent of the new millennium comes a new disease — Harlequin Rex — and a variety of reactions to it. The men and women in this intriguing novel find themselves caught up in a terrifying novelty, and all must cope as best they can. Their response is influenced as much by the past as by present events, however, those formative things that lie far back in us all: guilt, loyalty, compromise and love — especially love.

'Redemptive this isn't; but nonetheless it expresses a vision of life which much of the most significant writing of the century to which Marshall is bidding farewell has given expression during its course, a kind of stoical pessimism in which humanity is seen as something that endures rather than something that prevails. By bringing its peculiar plague from the world to New Zealand, by playing out the end of the century at our end of the world, *Harlequin Rex* enlarges the boundaries of our fiction towards the dimensions of those works.'

— Patrick Evans

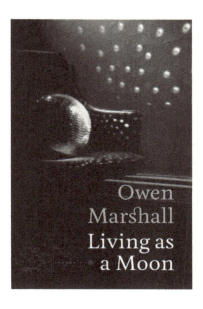

Shortlisted for the NZ Post Book Awards, these twenty-five stories are at once arresting, moving, funny and full of insight into the human condition.

Being a celebrity impersonator, says Aussie Elton John, is like living your life as a moon. 'We give up our identity and become just a reflection of another personality, like the moon having no fire of its own and being just a pale reflection of the sun when it's not there.'

This collection of stories from master short-fiction writer Owen Marshall is rich with people exploring their identities and how they are affected by others. There is Patrick, whose life is radically altered by a random encounter with a killer; widowed Margaret, who faces a new kind of existence alone; David, who experiences the 'spontaneous and passing friendship of strangers'; Ian, whose wife's demands for a better lifestyle lead him to a new career in telephone sex. Set in both Europe and the Antipodes, these stories will be savoured long after reading.

For more information about our titles visit
www.penguinrandomhouse.co.nz